The Circus Comes To Meadowbank

Margaret Alty

Published 2017 by arima publishing

www.arimapublishing.com

ISBN 978 1 84549 701 9
© Margaret Alty 2017

Printed and bound in the United Kingdom

Typeset in Garamond

Swirl is an imprint of arima publishing.

arima publishing
ASK House, Northgate Avenue
Bury St Edmunds, Suffolk IP32 6BB
t: (+44) 01284 700321

www.arimapublishing.com

The Circus Clown

When the circus came to town
We were entertained by a clown
With a big red nose and wearing a frown
He was the star when the circus came to town
His tears were controlled but they could not stop
Falling on the ground of the 'Big Top'
The audience laughed when he fell about
Inside the sawdust ring
Every day he does the same old thing
To make people happy for a while
In his own make-believe style
And when the show has ended
For him there's always a tomorrow
To continue with his sorrow

by Mike Alty

Chapter One

The posters for Beppe Bortoletto's circus were being displayed around the town of Meadowbank for more than a week prior to their arrival, each one of them a colourful reminder to the local residents of the treat in store for them; exaggerated superlatives proclaiming that their circus was the most spectacular, most dangerous, most amazing and the best they will ever witness. To the older generation of Meadowbank it merely acted as a noisy disruption to their daily routine and one they would be grumbling about for the six days they would be installed in the parkland on the other side of the river overlooking the new and controversially high-valued properties in Riverside Gardens. Only Meadowbank's youngsters reacted positively and excitedly to the day when the big top was erected and they would be able to see it from wherever they were in the town.

Predictably, and on cue, the regulars of The Market Inn chose as their main topic of conversation on Saturday morning, the day before the fleet of trucks and caravans were expected, the dire consequences of the council permitting the insurgence of what they described as a band load of foreigners.

'All I can say is,' one of them said as soon as he and two of his cronies had settled themselves on their usual stools from where they had the best vantage point to see each customer as they came in, 'that no good will come of this – of this jamboree.'

'I wouldn't call a circus a jamboree, Fred.'

'What would you call it then, Bert?'

'Well,' momentarily distracted, his interest diverted to the pint of The Market Inn's best bitter Brian Morrison had put down in front of him, 'I suppose it's more of – of an entertainment.' picking up his glass and taking a deep sip.

'Provided you're no more than ten years of age, I'll give you that, but in my opinion,' he continued loftily, 'I call it a jamboree! Do you know the meaning of the word, Bert?'

'Of course I do! I'm not totally ignorant, you know; boy scouts go on jamborees, don't they?'

'There are times when I despair about you. You should do crosswords, Bert; they'll improve your vocabulary. The definition of jamboree is a large gathering or a celebration. And a circus, provided they get enough customers to fill the big top, is an apt description.'

'If you say so, Fred.' Bert answered mildly, taking another sip.

'Fred has a point, you know, Bert;' another of them put in, wiping the beery froth from his white moustache, 'even although the circus will only be here for a week it can still cause trouble.'

'What sort of trouble?'

'Oh,' making an effort to express himself and floundering by the second, 'well – well, what I mean is with the teenagers and I don't just mean the lads. It's called jealousy.'

'What,' Bert grinned, sudden enlightenment appearing on his face, 'with the girls fancying these circus performers and our lads getting into fights with them? Is that what you think?'

'You might think that's funny, but it happened the last time they were here, but perhaps your memory is beginning to fail.'

'There's nothing wrong with my memory, thank you very much.'

'The police have enough to contend with in the town without having to cope with a load of randy young circus chaps.' Fred commented, nodding his head decisively, 'Anyway,' he went on, 'there were at least a couple of them here at the beginning of the week.'

'What makes you say that?'

'Because of the posters, Bert, that's why. Who else would have plastered them all over the place?'

'The council.' George suggested.

'You obviously know nothing about how these travelling circuses are run, do you?'

'I suppose not.'

'They are their own organisers,' Fred pontificated, having by this time drained his glass, 'they bring their own posters, put them up themselves and take them with them when they leave. You can't see the council forking out to pay for them. Just think about it, George; it just wouldn't be practical.'

Brian, resisting the impulse to raise his eyebrows, moved along the bar to serve some more customers. They're at it again, he thought, positive they were getting worse. It would seem that these days it didn't take much to spark and fuel their general pessimistic attitude to practically anything which was happing in the town. He realised only too well that these pensioners were his bread and butter, but he wished at times they would be less emphatic especially when, as today, they were getting well into their stride over something which obviously bugged them. It was only the imminent arrival of a circus, for goodness sake, and he couldn't come up with one good reason why the presence of a traditional circus in their midst shouldn't be welcomed. It wasn't as though they would be in the centre of Market Square. Now that would create major problems, he chuckled to himself.

'What's amusing you so much, Brian?' Melissa asked him coming in from the kitchen.

'Oh,' he smiled at her, 'listening to our band of philosophers. Today's topic, believe it or not, my love, is this circus. How they can find so much to chunter on about it beats me; it really does.'

'It must be strange, mustn't it; never stopping long in any one place. A bit like gypsies, I suppose.'

'I hope not,' he said, pulling a face, 'Meadowbank has had its fair share of them over the years and they haven't exactly endeared themselves to people, especially the farmers.'

'I always thought of them as being a bit scary when I was a kid; I don't know why really because apart from selling clothes pegs and telling fortunes, they kept themselves to themselves.'

'I know what you mean.' he agreed, 'Good,' he added, looking over to the open doorway, 'Simon's here; I wanted to have a word with him about tomorrow.'

'Our baby's christening;' she smiled gently, 'it should be a lovely day.'

Every time she smiled like that he felt a deep love for her. Even now, having been together for six years, the last two of which she had been his wife, he couldn't believe his luck and with the arrival of their daughter three months ago his life was complete. The memories of that earlier, and as it had quickly turned out, disastrous marriage to Stephanie, had receded to the back of his mind and these days, he very rarely thought of that unhappy period in his life.

'Good morning, Simon.'

'Good morning, Brian and to you, Melissa. Are you both all set for tomorrow?'

'I think so,' Melissa laughed, 'I can't speak for Caroline, though; she may loudly object to the trickling of water on her head.'

'Oh, don't worry;' he reassured her, 'Father will cope with her, after all he's christened quite a number of Meadowbank babies. Also,' he grinned, 'Saint Stevens has excellent acoustics.'

'That's exactly what I am worried about!'

'Your usual, Simon?' Brian asked him, taking down a glass tankard from the shelf, his other hand already on the handle of the Heineken pump.

'Please.'

'I should have asked you before,' Brian went on, filling the glass to the top, 'but would you mind taking a few photographs after the ceremony; for the family album.' he added proudly.

'Of course I will; it will be a pleasure; that is,' teasingly to Melissa, 'if baby Caroline can manage a smile.'

***

The christening party emerged from inside Saint Steven's church into brilliant sunshine at exactly the same time as Beppe Bortoletto's circus drove through the square, passing directly in front of the church and turning left into Bridge Street. There was no fanfare to loudly herald their arrival, but anyone who was close enough to the square couldn't fail to miss the long procession of trucks and the dozen or so caravans as they made their way to the parkland.

Derek Frost, the full-time barman at The Market Inn, with assistance that morning from his sister, Joy, was coping well in Brian and Melissa's absence. There had been a steady flow of customers since they'd opened at eleven-thirty; many of them visitors to Meadowbank taking advantage of the good weather and sitting outside, while the local residents had chosen to be less conspicuous by either remaining at the bar or at one of the tables.

Eric Noble was in there as he'd been in the habit of doing every Sunday lunchtime since coming to live in Meadowbank; a relative newcomer who hadn't yet appeared to have made any new friends in the town which to the long-established was hardly considered to be surprising; in their so-called wisdom they viewed him as an outsider and would do for a very long time. To some, this indifferent reception was intimidating and it had been proved that he or she would have to possess more than the normal degree of self-confidence to win their approval and acceptance into their community. For the few who had spoken to Eric since he arrived, none of them had achieved in finding out a great deal about him and this only contributed and strengthened their insular views. They were aware he had taken up the lease of the lodge on the Tilsly estate, that he originated from somewhere 'up north' only because of his accent, and that was about all they did know. It had been obvious from the first evening he had come into the bar that he wasn't the sociable type, showing no particular interest in his surroundings and now, almost eight weeks later, most of the regulars had given up trying to get into conversation with him, but it didn't stop them conjecturing among themselves as to why he had moved to Meadowbank in the first place and the older ones, like Fred and his cronies, had, over the weeks, come up with a wild selection of possibilities, most of which bordered on the extreme and no doubt gleaned from watching too many thrillers on television.

As the colourful line of circus vehicles passed by the windows, Eric's mobile rang, the introduction to John Lennon's "Strawberry Fields Forever" sounding disproportionally loud in the close confines of the bar, resulting in a number of customers to turn round and look at him, a couple of them frowning, making it clear that mobile phones ringing off in their pub was just not permitted. Whether taking any heed of their disapproval or not, Eric, leaving his beer on the bar, walked over to the door, switching on his mobile as he went.

'Hello.' he said once he reached the pavement.

'Hello.'

'My goodness, you're the last person I expected to hear from.'

'No doubt I am, but I think it's time we had a talk, Eric.'

'I don't believe we have anything to talk about.'

'We certainly have. We have to meet – and soon.'

'I have no intention of seeing you; you should realise that. We said all we had to years ago.' he added, curbing the impulse to switch off. This intrusion, he thought bitterly, old memories flooding back, must be nipped in the bud and quickly.

'I don't think so. You left me, Eric, in case you've forgotten, without any explanation.'

'You knew damn well why. There was no need for me to explain then and I'm certainly not going to now nine years later.'

'When you hear what I have to say, you will I'm sure think quite differently.'

'You're talking in riddles.'

'Am I?'

'It wasn't as though we were married,' he reminded her, 'I was a free agent, as you were.'

'I'll ignore that remark. Incidentally,' she said quickly, 'I know where you're living now and if you don't agree to see me I can make life extremely difficult for you, you know.'

Reluctantly, he agreed to meet her, eager to sever the call. He had no idea what she was playing at, but he didn't like the threatening way she had been talking, but then she had always over-dramatised everything, wondering what he had ever seen in her, but it had been such a long time ago, he couldn't remember, not looking forward to what he realised would be an unpleasant confrontation.

***

Jack Corbett had only been working for Beppe Bortoletto's circus for the last twelve months. His career had been a varied one. He had started off by being a stand-up comic in working men's clubs in the Midlands and the north of England, followed by bit parts for one of the film agencies in London, always hoping and half-believing he would be 'spotted' by some discerning director who had recognised his potential as a top actor, albeit still in comedy roles, but as the years slipped by, he began to realise it was never going to happen. He could have continued always waiting for that lucky break and for a while ventured into the more active and infinitely precarious way of earning a living by being a stuntman, again working for the same agency, until the inevitable happened. He didn't remember much about the car chase which, caused by bad timing, resulted in the crash which put an abrupt end to this venture. Apart from a slight limp, there was physically nothing wrong with him, except by this time he was suffering from an acute sense of disillusionment in the way his life had turned out and when he was approached by Beppe Bortoletto, whom he had met a number of years earlier, saying he had a job for him, he didn't hesitate in accepting. He was surprised to find that he actually enjoyed being one of the circus' clowns; it reminded him of his early days as a stand-up comic, recognising with a certain irony that once he was dressed for the part he bore no resemblance to Jack Corbett, finding out also he didn't have to work so hard to make people laugh at his antics in the ring.

He didn't object to doubling up at what was little more than an odd-job man when not performing; fetching and carrying for the engineer and his team when erecting and dismantling the big top and anything else which needed to be done to make the show run smoothly and hadn't taken long to learn how crucial it was to ensure all the safety measures were carried out. Beppe's circus had an excellent track record and it was more than Jack's job was worth to slip up.

That afternoon, immediately they'd all arrived in Meadowbank, each of them with their allotted tasks worked diligently and by six they had finished. He had a free evening ahead of him and decided to take a stroll round the town, hopefully find somewhere to eat in one of the pubs he'd noticed when they had driven through the square. He went first to The Market Inn, had a beer, but was told apologetically by the landlord that they only did food at lunchtimes, but he said that he knew The Bridge Inn did. The Bridge Inn, appropriately in Bridge Street, was not far from the parkland and as he re-traced his steps from the square he looked over to where they would be spending the following week. Immediately across the road from the pub was what appeared to be a new housing development, and he was sure by the size and style of the properties, some of them presumably with mooring rights for that stretch of the river, they would be valued at a price he would never be able to afford. Behind the development, the red and white striped canvas of the big top loomed, creating a surreal appearance.

It was a warm evening and the pub door was wide open and stooping to avoid the low lintel, he went inside. The Bridge Inn was old, possibly he thought at one time it may have been a coaching house; he'd noticed the cobbled courtyard at the rear of the building. Wooden settles lined the walls and looked as though they had been there a long time. In between them, was a stone-built fireplace which no doubt in the winter months would have a blazing log fire, but now, someone had placed a large pot of geraniums, the splash of scarlet brightening up the dark panelling and stone-flagged floor. The bar was also old, well polished over the years, and at the back to the right of the optics, a spiral staircase leading up to what could be the living quarters.

He was half-way through his beer when she came into the bar. Kitty Peters; the girl he had known back in the days when he had been struggling to make a name for himself. Seeing her like this, totally out of context, was weird. She looked different, older naturally, but it was something else and as soon as she came over to him, he realised what it was. She had lost her sparkle; there was an expression in her eyes which had never been there before. She looked as though she didn't smile very much and the Kitty he had known was always smiling, always game for anything new; being with her had been fun.

'Hello, Jack.' she said. 'It's been a long time. What are you doing in Meadowbank; I wouldn't have thought this was your scene?'

'Hello, Kitty; I could ask you the same.'

'Do you actually *live* here?' she asked, 'Because, as I do I'm sure I would

12

have seen you around.'

'I'm with Beppe Bortoletto's circus.'

'The circus!'

'You sound surprised.'

'I am. Very. What on earth do you *do*, though?'

'I'm one of the performers; a clown in fact.'

'Rather a comedown.'

'I've found, Kitty, in life, at least in mine, you have to take the tumbles. Things don't always turn out as you hoped.'

'That's true I suppose.' she said quietly. 'I should know.' recognising the bitterness in her voice.

'Anyway, Kitty, what would you like to drink?'

'Oh, a white wine, please.'

Once her wine had been poured and his own drink replenished, he asked her what she had been doing since he last saw her which he calculated must have been at least fifteen years ago. It wasn't as though she was evasive, but perhaps like himself, she was reluctant to elaborate and he didn't press her.

'So, Jack, there you have it. After I left the agency I was with Guildford Rep for a couple of years until I got married and went to the States with him, but the marriage didn't work out, so I came back to England. I was with the Esther Summers Theatre in Guildford for a while and here I am, divorced, and living in Meadowbank.'

'Any children?'

'No, and probably just as well. I'm not what you would call the maternal type, as I'm sure you would agree.'

She only had the one drink with him saying she was meeting someone. They made no arrangements to see each other again, not that he expected her to. When she had gone it occurred to him that apart from wanting to know why he was in Meadowbank, she had shown no interest in what had been happening during those intervening years. He couldn't remember whether she had always been like that; not particularly interested in other people's lives. It was as if she had wiped that time out of her mind. They had been close, he and Kitty, although in retrospect he didn't think either of them had believed the relationship would last. And it hadn't. He had gone his way and from what she had told him, so had she. Ships that pass in the night. Cynical sod that he was. He didn't stay long, and as soon as he'd eaten the ham salad and chips he'd ordered, he left.

***

The Royal Oak, Meadowbank's country-house hotel, was hosting an antique auction that evening, the event being considered by the residents as something of a unique event. The proprietors, Sandra and Chris Watson, although not particularly liked by many of the residents of the town, it had unanimously been acknowledged that they did run The Royal Oak well. They had made a number of improvements to the property and to the spacious grounds, all of which made it, not only one of the most prestigious hotels in the area, but a perfect setting for an enjoyable evening of wining and dining. David Johnson, the head waiter had been with them for years, long before the Watsons arrived, and perhaps for this reason the people of Meadowbank felt comfortable with the unchanging hospitality he always extended to anyone who visited the restaurant.

Inspector Ian Ash and his fiancée arrived at the hotel shortly before seven-thirty in time for the opening bids. They had already selected a pair of Napoleon the third chairs when they had been along earlier in the day and were looking forward to joining in with the bidding. For Jennifer and him this was the first time either of them had been to an auction and for the first few minutes they studied how the procedure worked. When the chairs were brought to the front and placed beside the auctioneer, Ian with some trepidation picked up on the first bid; immediately followed by a woman sitting in the row behind them and each time he raised his hand, she did the same, right up to the point where regrettably he had to stop. Enough was enough, he muttered under his breath. As the auctioneer's hammer sounded, he turned round to look at her, more out of interest than anything else. He wasn't unduly disappointed at being outbid, although he rather suspected that Jennifer was thinking quite differently.

He knew she had set her heart on those chairs and had even planned where they would position them in their lounge.

'Too bad, darling.'

'Can't be helped;' she shrugged, 'she was very determined to have them, wasn't she?'

'She was, yes. It's odd though,' he said, lowering his voice, 'and I may be somewhat naive, but I wouldn't have thought there would be a great deal of room for extra furniture in a caravan.'

'A caravan?' she frowned, 'Do you know her then?'

'She's Beppe Bortoletto's wife.'

'Oh, I see what you mean.'

'Have you had enough of all this?'

'I think so. Shall we go and have a drink'

'I was just going to suggest that,' he smiled, 'come on, then; the next bidding is about to start.'

'Perhaps the Bortolettos have their own property, Ian;' Jennifer said once they were in the lounge bar, 'surely they're not travelling all the time.'

'More or less all the time, but I suppose it is possible all the same. Not that it matters.'

'Do you know,' she smiled at him, 'we're getting like everyone else in this town.'

'What, you mean speculating about other people? Perhaps eventually it's contagious.'

The auction wasn't due to finish until ten, but already some people, like themselves, were beginning to filter through to the bar.

'She didn't take long to come in here.' he commented.

'Who?'

'The woman who bought your chairs; she's over there, the one in the black dress talking to the guy at the bar.'

'Oh.'

'She's called Cordelia.'

'Very glam and very Italian.'

'Hmmph; I wonder who he is.'

'That's Eric Noble; he took over the tenancy of The Lodge a couple of months ago.'

'You're very knowledgeable, my love; I'm impressed.'

'Don't be,' she laughed, 'it's only because when Jacqueline and I were in The Market Inn having a drink after work, I think it must have been about a week ago, he came in. He came over to say hello to her and she introduced him to me. I must admit I didn't take to him.' she added.

'Good.'

'Silly.' tapping him on the arm.

'What didn't you like about him?'

'I don't really know; I suppose it was just his manner. Not in the least bit friendly. I'm sure he only talked to Jacqueline because she handled the lease for him.'

'Well,' Ian said, watching the two at the bar, 'he seems friendly enough this evening.'

'Must be the Latin charm.'

***

'I've been thinking, Colin.' Rachel said later that evening.

'Yes, dear?' inwardly groaning; when his wife came out with statements like this it usually meant aggro of some kind or another. She had appeared more settled recently and apart from the anticipated grumblings when they had moved into the Old Manor at the beginning of the year, she had become less demanding. Perhaps she finally realised they didn't have a great deal of choice; those bad investment decisions he had made had forced them to take a long hard look at their personal finances and, with prudence in the coming months, it could be possible to recoup the losses he had foolishly incurred and return to their own home in Winchester, but it was early days yet. He had told her when he had first broached the idea of coming to live in Meadowbank she would have more time on her hands, free time to drive into Winchester whenever she wanted to meet up with any of her friends there; it wasn't as if Winchester was a hundred miles away, and this new freedom was all thanks to his father's housekeeper, Mrs Plenderneath. She had been working for his parents for as far back as he could remember and, in spite of her advancing years, appeared to be as energetic as ever. Long may it continue, Colin thought; Rachel wasn't the only one who required some space. He did as well. The relief now of not being constantly concerned about the accelerating debts which had threatened to permanently cripple them, had been enormous. As far as their youngest daughter was concerned, apart from now being a day pupil instead of a weekly boarder didn't appear to have had much impact on her and as his business was in Winchester she travelled with him each day. Also, being a gregarious fifteen year-old, she had adapted well into the slower pace of life in Meadowbank and had even made a number of friends of her same age. So, Rachel, he said under his breath; please don't rock the boat.

'Don't look at me like that, Colin. What I'm going to suggest can only be an improvement.'

'Alright,' he sighed, 'out with it.'

'It's about the lodge –'

'– what about the lodge?' he interrupted sharply.

'There you go, jumping down my throat. Why don't you just listen to what I have to say?'

'Alright, I'm listening.'

'All I was going to ask you was whether it would be possible to make some sort of – of screen, I suppose. I doubt whether you have even noticed it, but all our front windows overlook the back terrace of the lodge which means whenever our tenant is out there we always get a clear view of him and quite frankly, Colin, I find that a trifle off-putting.'

'I hadn't realised.'

'No, I didn't think you would have.'

'I'll give it some thought; perhaps have a word with the gardener. He might have some ideas.'

'Okay,' giving him one of her cat-like smiles, 'but make it soon, won't you? This Eric Noble will no doubt be making use of the terrace over the summer months as he has this evening.'

'Which he is fully entitled to do, Rachel.'

'Oh, I know that.' her voice tinged with exasperation, 'What sort of man is he, by the way?'

'Seems a decent chap; not very talkative, but his credentials were checked out by the estate agency. Jacqueline Wellings told me he was in computers and recently moved from London to set up his own consultancy firm in Winchester.'

'Sounds steady enough.' she commented, immediately losing any interest she may have had about their tenant.

'Perhaps we could invite him in for a drink sometime, Rachel.'

'I don't think so.' she answered promptly and by the tone of her voice he knew it would be pointless to pursue the subject. A pity he thought, it might have been interesting to get to know the man and Rachel, if she put her mind to it, could be a gracious hostess. Eric Noble, in spite of his reticence to 'open up' would, he felt sure, respond to her, but it looked as if their new tenant would remain a virtual stranger to them both.

Chapter Two

At nine-thirty on Monday morning the desk sergeant at Meadowbank's police station took a call from a woman telling him she had seen a dead body among the undergrowth in Riverside Lane. She was close to hysteria and, apart from describing exactly where she was, incapable of saying anything further. Reassuring her that an officer would be there as quickly as possible, and asking her to remain where she was, he replaced the receiver.

Once it had been established the woman hadn't been mistaken, Sergeant Ann Brothers wasted no time in phoning headquarters. While they waited for the pathologist and the forensic team to arrive, the woman had calmed down sufficiently to say she was Mary Reid and had been on her way back home after doing some early morning shopping in the mini-market in Bridge Street, also that it had been the bright red of the victim's dress which had caught her attention. She admitted she hadn't moved any closer, but that she just knew whoever was lying there must be dead.

Within minutes of their arrival, the forensic team had cordoned off the area and after Dave Burrows, the pathologist, had carried out a brief preliminary examination as to time of death, the body was removed and taken to the police mortuary. The forensic team remained for a further thirty minutes, photographing the area, raking the long grass and weeds searching for anything which they considered may have any bearing on what had occurred. Already, as all too often, a small crowd of silent onlookers had appeared. To many of them, what they were witnessing was a disturbing reminder of those sudden and violent deaths over the past couple of years in Meadowbank. Once again, their town would be in the spotlight and no doubt invaded by members of the press eager to glean as much as they could in order to flesh-out their newspaper columns.

Ian Ash had arrived at the site early on in their proceedings and had been in time to have a quick word with Dave Burrows who promised to get his report through to him by the end of the morning. The woman had only been carrying a handbag, a soft leather pouch the same colour as her dress, which Dave, after placing in a labelled plastic bag, gave to him.

Earlier that morning, around eight o'clock, Bob Harris, one of Meadowbank's postmen, had been unable to deliver a registered package to the woman who had bought the cottage half-way along Riverside Lane, the property which had been empty for so long. He was surprised not to get any response when he rang her doorbell. This wasn't the first time he'd had registered mail for her and she had always been in before. He knew from the Meadowbank grapevine, a debatably reliable source for gossip, in particular concerning newcomers, that she didn't have a job, but glancing up to the window of what was likely to be her bedroom noticed that she had drawn open the curtains, deciding as he wrote out the collection slip, that she must have gone out early. By the time he had finished his rounds and had returned to the Post Office, the news that there had been another murder had filtered through to what seemed to be almost everyone, Bob couldn't help feel more than a little peeved to apparently be the last person in the town to hear about it.

Dave Burrows was true to his word; by eleven his report was on Ian's desk. He had by then established from the contents of the dead woman's handbag that she had been called Katherine Peters and had lived at Bramble Cottage in Riverside Lane. There was a small address book with a few names, but only the Christian names, and their telephone numbers. She'd had the book a long time, fifteen years, in fact, reading what she had written inside the front cover: Katherine Peters and the date, 5th April 1992. There was no way of telling when the entries had been made, whether around that time or more recently. Her mobile phone had been in the bag and any calls she had made or received recently would also have to be verified. The only other items were a set of keys, one of them a car key and, presumably, the others for Bramble Cottage; a make-up bag; a wallet containing her driving licence, two credit cards, some sales receipts and fifty-five pounds in notes.

Ian read through Dave's report which re-confirmed the time of death and how she had died which was by strangulation, the force of which had put sufficient pressure on the windpipe to cause death within a matter of seconds. There had been tiny shreds of blue silk caught up beneath her fingernails suggesting a scarf or tie may have been used by her assailant. Dave had added a footnote saying there had been nothing of that nature on or near the body.

'I see you've got the pathologist's report, Ian.' Chief Inspector Graham Ford said walking up to his workstation, 'Quick work on Dave Burrow's part; I'm told the body was only found less than a couple of hours ago.'

'Yes, sir; Dave is certainly good at his job,' Ian agreed, placing the report in the newly prepared folder, 'he's given us something to go on; not a great deal, but it's a start. The first step, however, is to find out as much as we can about the victim.'

'Did you know her?' Graham asked, reminding Ian that he was unfamiliar with Meadowbank and its residents having only recently taken over from Brenda Masters following her transfer to New Scotland Yard in London, although already he had adapted well to what must be an entirely different environment to Winchester. He was a likeable sort of chap, easy to talk to and without Brenda's occasional acerbic manner which Ian had at times found intimidating, but once he had become used to his immediate superior being a woman, he had been more in tune with how she worked and, when she moved on he was genuinely sorry. Like himself, Brenda had been born and brought up in Meadowbank and this fact had been a help when it came to their combined knowledge of those people who had lived in the town for some years as it would have been now if she had still been here; she may even have met this woman, Katherine Peters, while he, to his knowledge, hadn't.

'I knew who she was,' he went on to say, 'and that she had moved into Bramble Cottage at the end of last year. Before then, I believe she had been renting the flat above the dress shop in the square. I was never in her company, but she was often in The Bridge Inn when I was there, but then it is closer to Bramble Cottage. Word got around that she'd been an actress at some time, not in the West End, but in one of the theatres in the provinces, I think. I heard someone mention Guildford. A bit sketchy, I'm afraid.'

'Not to worry, Ian. I expect by the end of today we'll have been able to build up a more detailed profile on her.'

'Perhaps,' Ian suggested, 'we should start from when she bought the cottage and work backwards; where she lived before, when she last worked, whether with a theatre or not, any relationships she may have had, that sort of thing.'

'That sounds alright,' Graham nodded, 'meanwhile as we have the keys, presumably to the cottage, I'll go along there and have a look round.'

'That's fine, sir; I'll get the office to check out her background history while I concentrate on her last movements. Where she had been last evening for instance and whether she was with anyone. The times I saw her she was always with a small group of people, but what sort of relationship she had with any of them, is not at this stage clear, but I'm sure something will turn up, even if it turns out relevant to our enquiry or not.'

'Spadework, eh?' Graham Ford remarked wryly.

***

Rachel was already in the Bridge Café when Letitia Radcliffe, slightly out of breath, arrived. The two women had been in the habit of meeting for coffee most mornings during the week. Rachel had met her not long after Colin and she had moved to Meadowbank and over the months they had built up a friendly rapport. Although she wouldn't give Colin the satisfaction of knowing how much she enjoyed these womanly *tête à têtes*; she found Letitia refreshing, unfairly comparing her with the women she had known for years in Winchester. There was no side to her; she seldom talked about money, that in itself being unique to Rachel. She was obviously comfortably off, enjoyed what seemed to be an enviable single life; no husband to check on her every movement, her son, having recently left home and travelling in the Far East and from what she'd said, enjoying his gap year; in other words, she had no apparent ties. It wasn't that she didn't love Colin because she did; it was just that he wanted to be in control. It was always he who made any major decision, many times not even conferring with her, exactly as he had done over this move to Meadowbank and which wouldn't have been necessary in the first place if he hadn't made such an ill-advised financial decision.

'I'm terribly sorry, Rachel,' Letitia said, sitting down opposite to her, the heady scent of *Jeanne Lanvin* wafting across the table,' I was simply an age getting served in the stationers with everyone talking about the *murder!*' whispering the last word and waiting dramatically, her blonde head tilted to one side, for her reaction.

'Murder? Are you sure, Letitia; you know what the gossips are like here?'

'I'm sure alright; got it more or less from the horse's mouth – oops, sorry, that was rather crass of me. You see,' starting to explain, 'one of my neighbours who lives quite close to me in Riverside Gardens, was in the stationers and although she is a notorious tittle tattler, this time there appears to be no doubt in what she was saying.'

'Go on.' Rachel encouraged her.

'Millicent, that's her name by the way, had been standing at her front window, a position which she takes up quite frequently I might add, when she saw a friend of hers being brought home in a police car. I don't think I know the woman, but Millicent told me she's called Mary Reid and that her house is the first one as you turn in from Riverside Lane. Well, not unsurprisingly, this was too much for her curious nature, so once the police car had driven off, she went along to Mary Reid's house to find out what was wrong'

'Nosy.'

'Very, but that's what she is like. She's a nice woman, except for this unfortunate trait of hers. Anyway,' she went on, 'her friend was only too willing to talk to her; according to Millicent she was still somewhat shaky after what she'd seen.'

'This is beginning to sound a bit grisly.'

'It does, doesn't it?' Letitia agreed, her expression becoming serious, 'Mary Reid had been walking home along Riverside Lane when she saw the body of a woman and although it had been half-hidden among the bushes and long grass and she hadn't felt up to going any closer, she was sure enough to call the police.'

'What a ghastly ordeal for her.'

'It was, Rachel. I honestly don't know how I would have reacted in a similar circumstance. Panicked I suppose.'

'Did Mary Reid recognise who it was?'

'No, she wasn't able to see the head, only the fact she was wearing a red floral dress; she told Millicent it was the colour of the dress which caught her attention, otherwise she may not have noticed it.'

'You know what this means, don't you, Letitia?' Rachel said quietly, wishing this Mary Reid had been mistaken. Meadowbank had had more than enough murders over the last two or three years, recalling what it had been like when Colin's father had been killed, only thankful they had still been living in Winchester at the time.

'Newspaper reporters swarming all over the place.'

'Exactly.'

***

Graham Ford drew up outside Bramble Cottage. He had passed a group of people in front of the blue and white taped barrier which still remained and would be there until forensic were satisfied they had thoroughly covered the area where the body had been found. Why was it, he thought for the hundredth time, looking at them in his rear view mirror that wherever a violent death occurs, people congregated when all they could possibly see was a temporary tarpaulin tent over the patch of ground which now held nothing which could interest them.

Like many of the cottages in Riverside Lane, Bramble Cottage had been substantially renovated and no doubt bore little resemblance to what it had looked like a hundred years earlier. Many of the interior walls had been removed, creating a relatively spacious open-plan living area with, at the end of the room and looking out at a small wood-decking patio, a modern chrome and stripped-pine kitchen and, again pine had been used for the single flight of stairs leading to presumably the bedrooms and a bathroom. Graham closed the door behind him, stopping to pick up that morning's mail. A quick glance told him that among what appeared to be a Lloyds bank statement, telephone and electricity bills, there was nothing of a personal nature, no hand-written envelope which might give him some kind of inkling into the dead woman's life. Taking them into the kitchen, a slip of green paper which must have become tucked in between the bank statement and one of the service bills fell on the floor. He recognised the post office's logo advising Miss K Peters they had been unable to deliver a registered package. Could be interesting he thought, putting it with the rest of the mail on one of the worktops.

He didn't spend long downstairs; after a cursory glance through the bookcase, flicking through the dozen or so books and checking the cupboards and drawers in the kitchen, all of which told him very little, except that Katherine Peters had been an orderly person; everything was in its place, not even a cup or glass beside the sink waiting to be rinsed out, he thought he could be wasting his time.

Before going upstairs, he opened the door leading from the kitchen into the integral garage fully expecting to see her car there, but it wasn't. He stood for a couple of seconds staring at the space where it should have been and wondering whether this was significant. He could only think of two possibilities of where it could be; either the car was in for repair or, if she had used it during Sunday at sometime, and wherever this was met her death there, the killer bringing the body back to where it had been found. It is possible Ian may have managed to discover whether she had been seen by anyone during the evening, beginning to realise that the case was showing every sign of being more complex than they had at first thought. The question now was whether she had been killed somewhere else and not in Riverside Lane after all.

There was one large bedroom, presumably at one time there may have been two or even three, but now transformed in keeping with the ultra-modern style of the twenty-first century, to many it would no doubt be thought as the epitome of luxury. Along the whole length of one wall, a walk-in wardrobe contained an extraordinary amount of clothes and accessories making him wonder how one woman could ever find the time or the occasion to wear them. They would need a closer inspection he decided, but later. At the plate glass window overlooking the patio and in the distance the red roof tiles of Bridge Farm, Katherine Peters had her desk; a long slim-legged piece of furniture in sandalwood, with three drawers on either side and a narrower one at the front. In the centre of the desk, a Toshiba laptop next to her printer. This is more like it, Graham thought, pulling open the top drawer on the left.

Mostly stationery: A4 paper, envelopes, a couple of replacement ink cartridges for the printer and a small box containing business cards which he separated from the rest, but below the paper, whether deliberately to conceal it or not, was a slim packet of the kind used by photographers to hold developed prints but there were no photographs inside, only a single sheet of paper with a number of pencilled jottings. At first glance, Graham thought it was in code until he recognised some of the symbols, remembering back to when his sister had been learning shorthand as part of her business course at college. Eager to demonstrate her new skill she had rapidly written out his name for him and while he couldn't remember the outline of the symbols she had used, what he did remember was that under both names she had put two tiny slanted dashes, explaining that it was to indicate she had used words where the first letter would have been in upper case. He looked again at the piece of paper in his hand and sure enough similar little ticks had been made and regretting he wouldn't be able to translate whatever had been written, he placed it beside the business cards.

There was a file in the next drawer where she had kept the log book and insurance certificate for the car, together with the receipt for its purchase eighteen months earlier from 'Meadowbank Car Sales & Repairs'; the deeds for Bramble Cottage were in there, dated the 7th November 2006, noting she had dealt with 'Town & Country Estate Agents' in Market Square. Everything else in the file related to household bills and appeared to be in order, therefore no surprises there, he thought, replacing the file and closing the drawer.

Katherine Peters' current passport was in a bottom drawer, together with a pile of theatre programmes going back as far as 1997, all for the same theatre in Guildford, and taking out a few at random, he glanced down the cast list, finding she had appeared in each production. In another of the drawers there was a photo album and with the aid of the passport photograph he was able to easily pick her out. Katherine Peters had been an attractive woman; slim, straight dark hair and an elfin face, high cheekbones and slanting cornflower blue eyes and looking at the various photographs he could well believe she had been an actress; the way she was posing in a number of them, coquettishly, hand on hip and a provocative way of looking directly at the camera. There were a number of group photographs and these were the ones he was more interested in. Disappointedly, she had made no mention of people's names, only the dates and where the photographs had been taken. It was like looking for the proverbial needle in a haystack and the fact that often the same man or woman appeared in them wasn't much help to him. She had entered them all in date order and turning towards the end of the album, hoping that if any had been taken in Meadowbank, it would be possible to see whether either Ian or he would recognise either the backgrounds or, more importantly, any of the people she had been with at the time. He kept the album out, adding it to the growing pile of papers and documents he would be taking back to the office.

Finally, he came to the last drawer. There was only a dark red plastic folder inside, the name of a Zurich bank in gothic script acting as an immediate fillip. Was this it? Was this going to provide them with the essential clue to explain, not only how Katherine Peters had conducted her life, but an indication of the motive for her murder? A quick glance told him a great deal. She had not made many withdrawals, but substantial and regular amounts had been deposited over a number of years. Picking up the passport and selecting the last six entries, he saw that she had made visits to Zurich on or about the same date as six of the deposits. Here was the lead they needed and all the more reason to get back to the Station and meet up with Ian, also to see what the office had come up with and, gathering together the items he was taking, let himself out of the cottage. He had already spent longer than he had intended and by the time he drove back into the square, Saint Steven's clock was chiming three and as so often when he became absorbed in an enquiry, especially in the early stages, he was inclined to lose track of time. He had completely forgotten about lunch and would have to ward off the approaching hunger pangs with a sandwich from the mini-market.

***

With very little to go on, Ian, after spending half an hour in the office drawing up a plan of action on how he was going to structure these initial steps in the enquiry, decided to go along to The Bridge Inn, working on the flimsy premise that from what he knew of Katherine Peters' routine, she may have been in there on Sunday.

By this time it was well after midday and, even for a Monday, the pub was busy, many of the customers he noticed not from Meadowbank, but presumably visitors, taking advantage of the warm spell of weather which couldn't exactly be called a heat wave, but was unusual for so early in the summer. There were about half of dozen of them up at the bar waiting to be served, but he didn't mind; he needed a lull where he would be able to talk to either Bob or Matilda Andrews without too many interruptions. It still seemed odd not to see Isobel Gallier behind the bar. She had owned The Bridge Inn for so long, many people in the town, especially her regular customers, had taken it for granted she would be there until she retired as she may very well have been if it hadn't been for Terry Simpson returning to Meadowbank a couple of years earlier. Their growing friendship had therefore come as a surprise, but when he eventually moved in with her, while many of the older generation continued to view Terry with disapproval over the shabby way he treated his wife all those years ago, those who genuinely liked Isobel were happy for her and wished them both well when they heard she would be selling The Bridge Inn and moving with Terry to the West Country.

Bob and Matilda, in their mid-forties, were a likeable and easy-going couple and watching them coping effortlessly with the customers, each vying to be served, Ian thought it would take a lot to upset either of them. It was obvious to him they were used to working together and had quickly settled into the pace of life in a relatively small market town.

'Good morning, Ian,' Bob said, 'sorry about the delay, but this warm spell has made everyone very thirsty.'

'That's alright,' Ian smiled, 'good for business though.'

'Can't grumble. Is this a social visit, Ian or official?' he asked, the intelligent grey/blue eyes looking at him directly.

'Both, actually, but first I'd like half a lager, please.'

'Matilda and I heard about the poor woman they found this morning; we knew something serious must have happened with the police vehicles passing along Bridge Street and, as you can imagine, it didn't take long for the news to filter through.'

'It's always the same,' Ian nodded, taking a sip of his lager, 'human nature I suppose and in a town this size when most people know each other, when something like this occurs, there is always the chance of them knowing who the victim is.'

'I expect by this time, Ian, you'll have her identity. I don't mean to pry.' he added apologetically.

'No, that's alright, Bob. She's been identified as Katherine Peters, although this hasn't been declared officially yet -'

'- Good Lord,' he interrupted, 'how very sad; Katherine used to come in here quite often, you know.'

'I thought she may have done, Bob. What I wanted to ask you is whether she was in on Sunday.'

'Yes, she was; in the evening and to think -' he tailed off, shaking his head in disbelief.

'What time would this have been?'

'I can't be exact, but it was quite early, about quarter to eight, but she didn't stay long; no more than twenty minutes.'

'Was she on her own, Bob?'

'She came in on her own,' he answered, 'and then came over to talk to one of the customers who was standing at the bar.'

'Had you seen him before?'

'No, I hadn't. I can't be certain of course, we haven't lived in Meadowbank long enough, but he didn't give me the impression he'd been in here.'

'What made you think that?' intrigued. Bob Andrews had a keen and agile mind and he must have a good reason, even if it was only something as intangible as an impression.

'Oh,' he said, 'probably because most people who've been in a pub previously are not all that interested in their surroundings; they've seen it all before. If they're on their own, they are only concerned in ordering a drink and if they've arranged to meet someone, they'll only look at those who are already here.'

'Sensible logic, Bob,' impressed, 'and I take it that this customer was taking everything in as you said.'

'That's right. I would say he wasn't used to country pubs, likely more familiar in a city one, like London for instance.'

'Do you think he was a Londoner?'

'Could have been; I think he might have had a London accent, a bit difficult to tell, Ian.'

'Do you think he was expecting to meet Katherine Peters?'

'I don't think so. He looked really surprised when she came in, a bit taken aback as a matter of fact.'

'What about her; do you think she was expecting him to be here?'

'I wouldn't say so; she sort of hesitated when she saw him, only for a couple of seconds, mind you, and then she went over to him.'

'And you say she didn't stay long.'

'That's right; he bought her a drink and after she'd finished it, she left.'

'He didn't go with her?'

'No, he ordered something to eat and had another beer while he waited for Matilda to bring it to him; he'd moved over to one of the tables by the window by then.'

'Did you notice what time he left?'

'I'm afraid not, Ian, we had become fairly busy, but I'm sure he didn't have another drink, so he must have gone as soon as he'd finished his meal.'

'You've been a good help, Bob; given us something to go on. Whether it turns out to be important remains to be seen. Incidentally,' he added, would you recognise him again?'

'I think so,' he said slowly, 'yes, I'm fairly sure I would. He was tall, almost six foot, thin, with one of those bony, haggard-looking faces, if you understand what I mean. Looked as though he'd had a hard life, didn't smile much, with the result he was probably a lot younger than he looked. Could have still been in his thirties, but certainly no more than forty-three or forty-four. Mind you, I could be wrong; it's a bit of a guessing game these days trying to work out people's ages.'

Walking back to the square, Ian thought over what Bob had said. He had given a reasonably good description of the man, but as he'd said, he hadn't been living in Meadowbank long enough to recognise whether the people he saw were residents or not. His theory could have been right about the man never having been in the pub before; it didn't mean he wasn't in the habit of frequenting The Market Inn, deciding he would call in there before going back to the Station. He wasn't altogether unhappy with what he had learned so far, but it was no way near enough going through the times again. Katherine Peters had been murdered between 10.30 and midnight; she had been in The Bridge from, say, 7.45 to no later than 8.30, there remained a gap of at least two hours. He recalled when Bob had described her reactions when she went into the pub; she had hesitated before going over to the man whom she must have known. Did this hesitation mean she was surprised at finding him somewhere she didn't expect? Not just in The Bridge, but in Meadowbank? Katherine Peters had been living in the town for two, perhaps three years and from what he had seen of her had struck him as a gregarious type of woman, confident, enjoying pub life and comfortable visiting them unaccompanied. This would indicate that the man she had been talking to was, as Bob had suggested, new to Meadowbank, otherwise they would have been bound to have bumped into each other at some time and as there were only two pubs in the town, this increased the odds.

As with The Bridge, The Market Inn was busy and as usual when the weather was good customers were sitting outside, beers and wine on the tables in front of them. Both Brian and Derek were serving and, judging by the succulent aromas emerging from the kitchen, Melissa was fully occupied with that day's 'Special' of lamb cutlets, new potatoes, garden peas and gravy which she had written up on the chalkboard. As much as he would have liked to stop long enough to have a lunch, he knew all too well, he couldn't afford the time. At this early stage of the investigation there was no way of telling how complex it may turn out and more crucially, how long it would take to reach a satisfactory conclusion. Each officer was aware of the importance in the need to move as swiftly as possible with the initial enquiries, that period when the incident was fresh in people's minds and memories and would gradually dissipate as each day passed.

'Hello, Ian,' Brian greeted him, 'your usual?' he asked.

'Please, Brian.'

'I expect you're involved in this latest business.'

'I am, yes.'

'As I said when we had those other murders, this is not good for the town and certainly not good for the people of Meadowbank. It's all my customers have been talking about this morning, but what seems to really bug them is the fact that they don't know the victim's name. They're a curious lot.' he added sadly.

'As far as that goes, Brian, her name will soon be common knowledge.'

'She's been identified then?'

'Not officially; by any next of kin, I mean, but we know who she was alright, but we've had no choice but to go ahead with our investigation and the first thing we have to establish is where she was on Sunday evening which has meant we have to mention her name to certain people otherwise we would be stymied until such time as any next of kin can be contacted.'

'I understand; you're going to tell me, aren't you? I'll be discreet, Ian, you know that.'

'I realise that, Brian; she was Katherine Peters -'

'- she used to come in here fairly often.' his voice low, his expression grim.

'I know; I had seen her in here myself a few times, also at The Bridge. She was there on Sunday evening; apparently she didn't stay long and I wondered if she came here afterwards.'

'We didn't see her in the evening, but I don't know about midday. Derek was in charge as Melissa and I were at the christening. Do you want me to ask him?'

'No, leave it for the present,' Ian advised, 'it may be necessary later. It's the evening we're more interested in. When she was in The Bridge, Bob Andrews has told me she was in conversation with someone and I'd like to find out who the man was and you may be able to help us on that.'

'Of course, if I can.'

'It's possible he was a stranger to Meadowbank; Bob didn't recognise having seen him before but at his own admission he says he's still too new to the town to be in a position to know all that many people. Anyway, he has given me a good description which might ring a bell with you.'

'Okay.'

'Tall, about six foot, thin, haggard-looking, appeared considerably older than he looked which could be in his early forties.'

'I think – only think mind you, Ian,' Brian said, 'but he sounds like the chap who came in here quite early on Sunday evening; we'd only been open about fifteen or twenty minutes. He ordered a beer, only had the one. He wanted to know whether he could get a meal here, but as you know we don't do food on a Sunday evening. I suggested he went along to The Bridge.'

'Sounds like the same one. And had you seen him before?'

'No. In fact he told me this was his first visit to Meadowbank.'

'I see; I wonder why he was here.'

'He's with the circus, Ian, that's why. Said he had only been with them for a year, before then he'd been employed as a stuntman. He was quite chatty, gave me the impression he'd been through the mill, sad-looking, but perhaps that's just the way he is. Wouldn't do if we were all alike, would it?'

***

Graham's secretary handed him a copy of the background report on Katherine Peters as soon as she saw him coming into the office.

'The Chief Inspector isn't back yet, Ian,' she told him, 'but I've put another copy on his desk for him.'

'That's fine, Jean,' he thanked her, 'I'll get myself some coffee before I go through it.'

'I'll bring you a cup over if you like,' she offered, 'I don't expect you've eaten.'

'You must be a mind-reader,' he grinned, 'not much escapes you, does it?'

'I don't suppose it does.' returning his smile which instantly transformed her habitual serious expression. Jean Gray had been working for the force for years, long before Ian joined. She was a few years older than the other women in the office and perhaps this was the reason she would now and again reveal the mothering side of her nature. He watched her now as she walked across to the coffee machine: a neat trim figure of a woman, dedicated to her career and always prepared to put in overtime when it became necessary. She must be in her forties now, he thought, wondering why she had never married. Pity. She would have made a good wife, thankful that he hadn't left it too late himself which he very nearly had. He had known Jennifer for a number of years before he had got round to approaching her, the fear of rejection always holding him back, but he had got over that and since she had agreed to marry him earlier in the year his personal life was complete.

The report was not extensive and as he had often found with profiles of this nature there were blanks; periods of time when the office had been unable to find anything. In Katherine Peters' case, there were six years unaccounted for: from 1994 to 1997 and from 2002 until she arrived in Meadowbank in 2005. She had been with the Guildford Repertory Theatre when she married Franklin Bacall on the 8th June 1994 and on the 20th of that month flew to the States with him. No record of any divorce could be traced, but she married Harold Maitland on the 2nd April 1999 and had been with the Esther Summers Theatre in Guildford since her return to England in 1997 up until she left them in 2002. There was a record of their divorce on the 18th May of the same year.

Rather a chequered career path, he thought, pencilling in the dates of the missing years in the margin for easy reference and going back to the beginning of the report, highlighting anything else which could be used to broaden what he had learned so far about her. She had been a Londoner, born in Notting Hill on the 8th September 1969 which would have made her thirty-seven at the time of her death, and had attended Notting Hill & Ealing High School in 1990, leaving there at the age of seventeen in 1991 and studied drama for a year at the School of Drama in Islington before joining Guildford Repertory company.

Ian remembered Bramble Cottage on the market last year and had seriously considered buying the property, but he had felt it would be tempting providence with the relationship with Jennifer being very much still in its infancy. Town & Country Estate Agents had been handling the sale and as Katherine Peters was by then already living in the town, there was every chance she would have gone to them. This train of thought led him to when she first arrived here. If she had leased the flat in Market Square would she, he wondered, have used them. There was only way to find out; call in and speak to Jacqueline.

She was in the outer office of Town & Country when he went in and looked up in surprise when she saw him.

'Ian,' she said, 'it seems ages since I last saw you, but I can tell by your expression it must have something to do with the news which has been buzzing round the town all morning.'

'You're right, of course, Jacqueline. I'm hoping you may be able to help us, that is, if you can spare the time.'

'My next appointment isn't until four, Ian. We'd better use my office; there will be no interruptions in there.' she suggested, leading the way.

'The identity of the woman found this morning has yet to be made official,' he told her, 'but we do know who she was.'

'Oh, dear,' involuntarily putting a hand up to her mouth, 'it's all happening again, isn't it? It is as if there is a jinx in our town; there's been too many murders during these last couple of years.'

'I know,' he agreed, 'there certainly doesn't seem to be much of a let-up.'

'Who was she, Ian?'

'Katherine Peters.' aware of how blunt his reply must sound, but there was no other way of softening the shock she must be feeling.

'Katherine Peters.' she repeated, 'But – but, why?'

'A very good question, Jacqueline, but given hard work and a bit of luck, we'll find the answer.'

'She was such a – such a fun person. Good in a crowd. She'd been an actress, but you probably knew that anyway. Very sad, but how do you think I can help?'

'It's possible you may know a little about her background.' he explained.

'Not much actually. She bought Bramble Cottage from us and she had already been living in the town for about a year and a half by then.'

'Did she rent the flat over the dress shop from you, Jacqueline?'

'Yes, she did.'

'Good,' he smiled, trying to lighten her mood, 'that's what I was hoping to hear.'

'Why?'

'Because the office has been running a check through her background and we've been unable to find out where she had been living prior to coming here in the February of 2005 -'

' – I see what you mean. And you're right; I did ask her for her former address and a reference, income, that sort of thing, all to satisfy the terms of leasing.'

'Right,' hoping what she was about to tell him would kick-start this enquiry, 'could you give me what details you have, Jacqueline and I'll jot them down.'

'I'll do better than that,' she said, swivelling the computer monitor into position and, pressing a few keys, reached the section she wanted, scrolling down the screen. 'Here's the entry, Ian; Monday 7th February 2005. It will be easier for you if I print this out.' leaning over to switch on the printer.

'Thank you, you've been a great help, Jacqueline. I appreciate that.'

'No problem,' she smiled sadly, 'I feel it is the least I can do; if this should assist you in solving poor Katherine's death, well - what more can I say.' she sighed, handing the sheet across the desk to him.

Passing the King's Arms Hotel on the way back to the office, Ian was in time to see the retreating figure of the American woman walking up the steps to the hotel. Right on cue, he sighed, she must have her own personal hotline to Meadowbank. Carol Cliff, the brash, intrepid journalist and definitely the leader of the media pack; regardless of any unwritten law of protocol, she was always the first to lead the questions at their press conferences, also she had an uncanny knack of homing into the crux of an enquiry and, terrier-like wouldn't let it rest until she had answers, most of which she had known or guessed beforehand, her strategy being to be given something which would authenticate her column, the contents of which managed by a thread to avoid being libellous. Her arrival here, within a matter of hours from when the body of Katherine Peters was discovered, implied, unless the woman had extrasensory powers, someone in Meadowbank must have told her. Carol Cliff would now be hell-bent in finding out the name of the victim and he couldn't help speculating on how long that would take her. Over the last couple of years she must have been here at least six times, more than enough for a person of her tenacity to discover how the people of Meadowbank ticked and she would be wasting no time in putting her particular skills into action and no doubt The Market Inn being the nearest, and possibly the best place to tune-in to what everybody would be talking about this evening. He didn't know whether Graham had had the dubious pleasure of meeting her which reminded him of the adept way Brenda had handled her barraging, which to most would have been instantly quelling, but although Carol Cliff remained impervious, she was never successful in extracting from Brenda what she wanted. This was the second time today he had been reminded of Brenda, possibly because this was their first murder case since she left in February and hoping that this one wouldn't turn out to be as convoluted as the others had been, when one murder appeared to have the effect of triggering of another, with the whole town in a state of jitters, worrying and wondering what was going to happen next.

Chapter Three

Town & Country Estate Agents, Market Square, Meadowbank, Hampshire

Lease Application

Name of Applicant: Katherine Peters

Address: King's Hotel, Market Square, Meadowbank

Profession: Actress

Income: £60,000 (sixty thousand pounds sterling) per month

Source: Maitland Holdings
                           (Alimony – divorce settlement dated 18th May 2002)

Bank: Lloyds Bank, 50 Notting Hill Gate, London 3JD
                           (deposit account statement seen confirming savings
                           exceed 3.5 x monthly rent)

Property for rent: Flat One, 20 Market Square, Meadowbank
                           (furnished)

Terms of lease: Six months (renewable)

Monthly rent: £400 (four hundred pounds sterling)

Deposit: £400

Handling fee: £75 exclusive of VAT

Date of entry: 8th February 2005

'Unfortunately, sir,' Ian said, 'we're none the wiser to where she was living prior to coming here.'

'You're right of course,' Graham agreed, glancing again at the form, 'except for the mention of what appears, officially at least, to be her main source of income, we continue to be very much in the dark about that period in her life. Her second husband, Harold Maitland, is obviously a man of considerable substance and presumably this alimony, as it is described, would have continued *ad infinitum*.'

'I wonder where she kept her bank statements; we know she had a deposit account, but she must have had a current account also.'

'She did; that statement which arrived this morning was for a current account.'

'She must have put them somewhere, but obviously not in the same place where she kept the Zurich bank statements. Strange.'

'Strange is the operative word, Ian; it would appear she lived in a very strange way.'

Graham had already been in his office when Ian returned and they spent a while going over, first what Graham had been able to unearth from his visit to Bramble Cottage and then the outcome of his own enquiries at the two pubs, culminating in Jacqueline giving him the print-out of the lease application form, all of which went a long way in formulating a clearer picture of what Katherine Peters had been like, or more importantly as each aspect of her life unfolded, how she had conducted herself. From the moment Graham had shown him the contents of the registered package it had immediately become clear to him there was something undeniably questionable about what she had been up to. The package had contained a thousand pounds in fifty pound notes; nothing else, no covering note, no accompanying slip of paper giving the name of the sender and even the postmark, although relatively local, was no clue. It had been posted from Southampton Head Post Office on Saturday morning at ten-thirty.

'Do you think she was blackmailing someone, sir?' he asked.

'It would be the obvious deduction, also to why she was murdered, but we shouldn't jump to conclusions; that would be too easy.'

'Apart from everything you've told about your findings at Bramble Cottage,' Ian said, at the same time trying to collate everything they had been talking about and to make some sort of sense of it all, 'there is one aspect which strikes me as odd, incongruous even.'

'Yes?'

'Her clothes; from how you described them there appears to be a marked difference in their styles. I'm no fashion expert, but I've always thought that most women will only keep those clothes she would normally wear; or perhaps a couple of items she'd had for years and only kept them for sentimental reasons, but not racks of them.'

'That's a good point, Ian. I must admit I was a bit taken aback when I saw them, but that hadn't occurred to me. It's as if she had led a double life; one set of clothes for the somewhat parochial and more casual life of a town the size of Meadowbank, while the other, which I couldn't envisage any woman wearing around here, more in tune with a cosmopolitan, even international fashion scene.'

'Which could tie-in with those overseas trips.'

'I would say they probably did. I can't help getting the impression that this murder has something to do with her past. We need to find out more about the people she knew before coming here which brings us to those missing years. Her previous passport would have expired in 1999, the year she married Harold Maitland, but apart from the trips she made to Switzerland, and they were only relatively short visits, those were the only times she had used her current passport, which means she must have remained in Britain from 2002 to 2005. She was already divorced by then and the question is where did she go?'

'It might be worthwhile paying a visit to the theatre in Guildford; she did work there for five years, quite a long time for her.' Ian added cynically, 'Or before then, when she was with the repertory company.'

'I think you could be right. We do need to know, apart from the two ex-husbands, who she was associating with; I believe that could be important.'

'So far we only have one person, sir.'

'The chap who's with the circus you mean?'

'Yes,' Ian nodded, 'I don't suppose there is much point going along there at this time of the day; they will all be busy preparing for this evening's show.'

The morning will probably be best.' he agreed, 'Meanwhile, the office have been able to check out Katherine's mobile; there wasn't much on it, only one outgoing call she made yesterday.' looking at the notes Jean had left for him, 'this was made at ten minutes to twelve and it was to a mobile number.'

'Interesting.'

'It was; not what I would describe as a pleasant conversation. Unfortunately she didn't mention the name of the man she was talking to, but the context of what she said bordered on a form of blackmail, forcing him into the position of agreeing to meet her.'

'And where was this to be, sir?'

'Sorry to disappoint you, but it wasn't mentioned, although I would suggest it was at his place as she'd rather threateningly added that she knew where he was living now. However,' Graham went on, 'we'll get back to that later.' pushing the notes to one side, 'Are you able to read shorthand, Ian?' showing him the piece of paper he'd found in one of the desk drawers.

'Afraid I can't, sir.'

'Not to worry,' he smiled, neither can I, but Jean does and although she doesn't get much opportunity these days to put it into practice, I'm sure she'll be able to translate it for us.' pressing the switch on the internal phone.

It took Jean only minutes to decipher.

'Here you are, sir,' she said, handing the note back to him, 'I'll type it out for you, but you will probably want to read what it says now.'

'Thank you, Jean.' and reading what she had pencilled in below each set of symbols and without saying anything, a questioning expression on his rugged features, passed it across the desk to him.

' "Eric's new address," ' he read, ' "The Lodge, The Old Manor, Stockbridge Road." Why scribble it down in this way; why didn't she put it into her address book?'

'Who's to say,' Graham shrugged, 'people do rather odd things at times; perhaps she forgot. It could be she'd been at her desk when she learned where he was living and as she's mentioned this is his new address, indicates perhaps she would have known the old one. I haven't checked through the address book yet, but we can do that now.' picking the book up and turning the pages until he came to the one he wanted, 'This must be it, Ian; she hadn't written his name, or any address, only a mobile phone number.'

'The call she made on Sunday.'

'Yes,' Graham said, checking the number against the one Jean had given him, 'it's the same.'

'I actually saw Eric Noble on Sunday evening at The Royal Oak; he was in the bar when Jennifer and I went in, we'd been to the antique auction there. It was Jennifer who told me his name; Jacqueline Wellings had introduced him to her a few weeks ago.'

'It's times like these when it can be an advantage living in a small town, isn't it?' Graham smiled, shaking his head as he recalled what it had been like in Winchester; really no comparison.

'I know.'

'What time would this have been, Ian?'

'It was around eight-thirty when we went into the bar,' Ian explained, 'Eric Noble was already in there and about ten minutes later he was joined by Beppe Bortoletto's wife, who, incidentally outbid us on a couple of chairs Jennifer had set her heart on -'

' – Beppe Bortoletto's wife,' Graham repeated thoughtfully, 'Where did he meet her, I wonder.'

'I would hardly say he was the type of man she would be attracted to, apart from the fact, of course, that she's married.'

'What's she like, Ian?'

'Attractive, in a flamboyant sort of way and as Jennifer said, very Italian.'

'Hmmph; and this was about quarter to nine. Have you any idea of when they left?'

'No, they were still there when we went half an hour later.'

'Bringing us up to quarter past. Were there many people in the bar?'

'Quite a few; Ted was on duty and I'm fairly sure he would have noticed.'

'Worth checking. I expect you're thinking along the same lines as I am; all a bit too pat, eh?'

'I was, sir. I can't help thinking there is a lot more to this murder. We don't know yet what motive anyone would have had for wanting her out of the way, apart from the rather obvious one of being blackmailed, but

42

then again perhaps it is just a little bit too obvious.'

'I know what you mean,' he agreed, 'best to keep an open mind. Also, I believe it's time for us to publicly reveal her identity before people start jumping to their own conclusions.'

'Especially as we'll soon have the press breathing down our necks and with the speedy arrival of Carol Cliff I would say it won't be long.'

'The formidable Carol Cliff. I've heard about her; fortunately she didn't make her way to Winchester.'

'Too much to occupy herself with here.' Ian caustically commented.

'Quite. Meadowbank has had more than its fair share of crime these last couple of years. I don't know what it is, Ian, but there must be a certain appeal to the sensational seekers to be shown the dark side of what on the surface appears to be a sleepy market town. However,' Graham went on, 'I'll make sure the six o'clock news bulletin will include the name of the dead woman; we don't want the press arriving at that first and accusing us of withholding information from the general public.'

'We appear to have collected rather a lot of odds and ends,' Ian pointed out, 'but so far not a great deal of cohesion to any of them.'

'I agree; large amounts of cash deposited in Zurich over a number of years where no questions would be asked as to their origin; one of the few links with her past suggesting she knew someone with the circus and who arrived on the same day she was murdered; an ambiguously worded telephone conversation with Eric Noble, coincidentally on the same day, a man who gives the impression of being as secretive about his past as the dead woman, and not forgetting, Ian, the missing vehicle.'

'And, like an old jigsaw, there is bound to be pieces missing.'

'True, but let's hope they don't remain that way. I've just had a thought about Katherine Peters' previous address, Ian.'

'Yes?'

'It should have occurred to me when I looked at those Zurich bank statements, but I was more concerned with the deposits and tying them up with her trips to Switzerland. Anyway,' he went on, opening the bank's folder, 'I'll go back to before she came to Meadowbank; when exactly was it?'

'She signed the lease for the flat on the 8th February 2005,' checking on Jacqueline's print-out.

'Right, I notice the cut-off date is on the last day of each month, so the February statement presumably would have been sent here, which it was in fact,' finding the statement, 'Flat One, 20 Market Square and,' turning back to the previous month, '- ah, this may or may not come as a surprise to you, Ian, but she was living in Notting Hill –'

' – where she held her account with Lloyds.'

'Yes, that's right. How well do you know that part of London?'

'Reasonably well and I've been to Notting Hill a few times.'

'It would best then if you went there, Ian; my knowledge of London doesn't extend much further than the West End. Mind you, there is every possibility you may have a wasted trip, but there is always the chance you might be able to locate any friends she might still have had in that area. There's also Harold Maitland; their divorce only went through five years ago, they may have kept in touch. I'm thinking of that divorce settlement. Why so much, I wonder.'

'It shouldn't be too difficult to get the details; even have them sent through later today and then I can make an early start tomorrow morning. Whereabouts in Notting Hill did she live, sir?'

'Number thirteen The Mews, off Lansdowne Crescent.' reading from the statement.

'I know where Lansdowne Crescent is; it's not far from Portobello Road.'

'And while you're in London, I'll pay a visit to the circus and see if I can find whoever it was she met up with on Sunday, also,' he added, 'have a word with Eric Noble. Jean will give Meadowbank Car Sales a ring to find out whether Katherine Peters' car is with them or not.'

'Do you think there's anything to be gained by me trying to have a word with someone at the Esther Summers Theatre?'

'I'm not sure, Ian;' taking another look at the profile on Katherine Peters, 'she left the theatre in 2002 and, as you said, she had been there for five years, which takes us back to 1997, the same year she returned from the States. Two people may be able to help us here;' he said, 'the man she met up with yesterday and Eric Noble. It would appear from that telephone conversation that they hadn't seen each other for over ten years which could mean this had been when she'd been living in the States and before she joined the theatre. I believe we should arrange a search into his background which would be a help when I speak to him tomorrow and, as far as the other man is concerned, everything depends on finding out who he is. You mentioned that Bob Andrews commented on how she hesitated before walking over to him. Had this been because her surprise, if that was what it was, meant it had been a long time since she had seen him? If it is, possibly she had known him prior to her first marriage.'

'We don't know of course,' Ian put in, following Graham's logic, 'what his role is in the circus; he could be employed on the technical side, or he could be one of the performers and if he is, it could signify an acting background.'

'Which would have been either Guildford Rep or when she was with the Stage Agency in Islington.'

'As you were saying, we need to have his name.'

'We will, Ian and hopefully by the end of tomorrow we will be considerably further forward with the enquiry, so,' he concluded, 'in the light of what we've just been saying, I would suggest we leave the theatre alone for the present.'

'I agree, sir and no doubt we'll soon have the media clamouring for a press conference.'

'I'm sure we will, but somehow we must try as far as we can to pre-empt what they are likely to say or do next.'

'Not easy.'

'It won't be and from what has emerged I don't think this investigation will be all that straightforward either. Katherine Peters continues to be something of an enigma; we need to find out more about her. Most people have at least one close friend; it would be unnatural otherwise and not necessarily of the opposite sex.'

'I'll take a quick look through her photo album, shall I?'

'If you would, Ian.' passing the album across the desk to him, 'There was no-one in any of the photographs I recognised, except, in some of them, where they were taken.'

There were a number of spaces where photographs had been removed at some time. Was this another reminder of the woman's secretiveness? Ian was more than half-way through the album before he came to those taken more recently and where he recognised the backgrounds; mainly the bar in The Bridge and some outside The Market Inn, all typical of thousands of photographs of people in a relaxed mood and enjoying a few drinks together. There were some familiar faces he recognised as regular customers, but in each of them Katherine Peters didn't give the impression she favoured anyone in particular; she was never pictured beside the same person twice. Disappointedly, he shook his head and closed the album.

'Not much help to us.'

'A pity she'd removed many of them. Any ideas why she would have done that?'

'Taken at a time in her life which she wanted to forget.'

'Or of someone she wanted to forget.'

'Either of her ex-husbands or a boyfriend?' Ian suggested, but not with any real conviction; there could be a number of explanations for her deliberately taking them out and for them to discover the reason was extremely unlikely.

'Except,' Graham suggested, 'the fact she had dated them may help us as we look into her background. So far, we don't know what her ex-husbands looked like and if they aren't in there, providing the dates tally, could be quite telling.'

'Also,' Ian commented, 'she had none of Eric Noble considering they had known each other for more than ten years.'

'Well, having heard what was said when she phoned him yesterday, it's obvious she didn't like him.'

'Which was reciprocated.'

'Exactly.'

***

Rachel was preparing the evening meal when she heard the television newsreader mention Meadowbank and, moving over to the small set they kept in the kitchen, turned up the volume.

'..... this morning,' the woman was saying, an inappropriate smile on her face, 'disturbing the normal tranquillity of the town. The victim can now be identified as Katherine Peters, a resident of Meadowbank. She had been strangled late last night, her body pushed into the undergrowth by the side of Riverside Lane, a quiet residential area, where it was found by a neighbour. She immediately alerted the police who are now following up on their enquiry into the murder '

Rachel was on the point of turning away when a picture of Katherine Peters flashed up on the screen. She stood in the centre of the kitchen, still holding the tea towel, and stared at the image in disbelief. Katherine Peters was the woman she had seen last night with Eric Noble; she was sure of it. She tried to remember what the time had been; they had just finished their meal and she had gone upstairs for something. She noticed the bedroom window was open and went over to close it when she was distracted by a woman's voice drifting across the garden from the lodge. She had been leaning against the terrace railing with Eric Noble standing a few feet away from her. He hadn't looked happy, Rachel remembered, but then she hardly knew him; perhaps that was the way he usually looked. Colin had mentioned he wasn't the talkative type, but the more she thought about their new tenant, the more disturbed she became. Normally not of a nervous disposition, she wished Colin was home, aware for the first time since they had moved in, of how empty the house could feel. This place, she decided, needed people, not just the three of them. It wasn't too bad during the day when Mrs Plenderneath was here, but once she had gone home, she would be on her own until about this time waiting to hear the car coming up the drive. She felt continually drawn to the library window, looking over towards the lodge, but there was no-one out there. Who had she been, Rachel wondered, the woman they had named as Katherine Peters. And why had she been murdered; the newsreader had said she'd been strangled, the mere thought of it filled her with horror, making her shiver in spite of the warm evening. The gardener had mowed the front lawns earlier in the day and the sweet smell of grass filled the air. This should be a peaceful moment she thought; some hours yet before dusk, very little traffic on the Stockbridge Road beyond the high hedge and at the far end of the garden by the old cedar tree, the chirrup of the blackbird, a regular visitor at this time of the day, but she couldn't appreciate the tranquillity. She was trying to shrug off a feeling of foreboding, but she was finding this impossible, longing to be back in their house in Winchester. No matter how long they stayed in the old manor, Rachel knew she would never recognise it as her home. She had never really taken to the place, thinking back to when Colin first brought her here. It was shortly before they were engaged and Colin, with obvious reluctance, said it was time she met his family. She had already known that he and his father didn't get on, assuming from what he had said, this was due to a clash of personalities. She couldn't deny that Major Tilsly was a formidable character; a no-nonsense type, rigid in his views and quick to express them. The only time he would unbend was when Wendy was there. Colin's younger sister, no doubt unwittingly, brought out a totally different side to him. In his eyes Wendy could do no wrong. Remembering Colin's father and the violent way he had died brought her mind back full circle. She was being fanciful, she knew that, but she couldn't ignore the way she was thinking. It wasn't as if Katherine Peters was murdered here, on the estate, so why on earth was she being like this?

Seeing their car turn in at the gates prevented her becoming immersed in her troubled thoughts.

'Hi, Mum!' Polly called out to her as soon as she was out of the car, dragging her bulging school bag from the back seat.

'Had a good day, dear?' Rachel asked, taking the bag from her, just as she had been doing since Polly's days in junior school.

'So, so;' pursing her lips, her expression an exact replica of Colin's, 'I'll be glad when it's the end of term. I can't wait!'

'Don't wish your life away, Poll.' Colin said, following her up the steps to the front door, 'Alright, Rachel?' he asked, kissing her on the cheek.

'I'm fine.' she said, not wanting to mention anything about the murder in front of Polly who, with a teenager's over-developed sense for the dramatic, would immediately want to hear more, 'I've opened a bottle of red.' she added, following them both inside.

'That's exactly what I need.'

'What time's supper, Mum?'

'In about an hour.'

'Good; I'll be really hungry by then. I've an essay to write for tomorrow; I'm sure that Miss Alison is a witch! Why she sets these projects up after we've spent all this term studying for our exams, I do not know. Believe it or not,' she added, raising her eyes to the ceiling, 'she wants us to write a thousand words on why we should be concerned about the possibility of the approaching ice age! I ask you! Does it really matter?'

'There's something wrong, isn't there?' Colin asked her once Polly had gone up to her room.

'How well you know me.' filling their glasses.

'I should by this time.'

'I suppose so,' she admitted, 'but honestly, Colin, I don't know whether there is anything wrong; it's just -' not knowing how to describe what she wanted to say.

'Just what?'

'You won't have heard yet, but a woman's body was found this morning in Riverside Lane -'

' – Good God; don't tell me we're in for another spate of disasters!' his glass half-way to his lips.

'I don't know, Colin; I sincerely hope not.'

'How did you hear about it?'

'From Letitia; we were having a coffee this morning and somebody had told her about it, but that isn't what's bothering me.'

'What is then?'

'I watched the six o'clock news this evening and they flashed up a photograph of the victim and I – and I recognised her.'

'Who was she?'

'She was called Katherine Peters, but I didn't know her.'

'I'm sorry, Rachel, you've lost me. If you didn't know her, how did you know who she was?'

'Because she was at the lodge on Sunday night, that's why. You remember I said to you that Eric Noble was talking to someone out there?'

'Yes, but you were some distance away; how can you be so certain it was her?'

'There's nothing wrong with my eyesight; that woman *was* Katherine Peters!'

'I don't understand why you're being so emphatic; is it so important, Rachel? Alright,' he went on slowly in what she recognised as his reasonable voice and one which never failed to irritate her, 'if you are right, she must have made her way back to the town later. After all, that's where she was found and presumably that's where she was attacked, in Riverside Lane.'

'You don't know that, Colin.'

'Of course I don't; I'm only trying to look at this logically.'

'I'm sure you are, but don't you think it is all rather – rather suspicious?'

'You're not suggesting Eric was responsible, are you?'

'Well, we don't *know* him!'

'You cannot go around accusing people of murder.'

'I'm not; it's just that – oh, I don't know. I really don't. It's as if this town had a jinx on it.'

'Come on, Rachel, you're letting your imagination run away with you. I admit that living on the edge of a town as small as Meadowbank has certain drawbacks in that when anything of a serious nature happens, like a murder for instance, everyone hears about it and when the victim was one of the community, as apparently was the case with Katherine Peters, any snippet of information about her can become distorted and before you know where you are, you can find yourself surrounded by rumours which often, even after the crime has been solved, leave a lasting and unpleasant impression.'

'You don't think we should say anything, then?'

'To the police you mean?'

'Well, yes, I suppose so.'

'Not unless they ask you, Rachel.'

'You think they might come here?' appalled at the suggestion.

'It's always possible. If, and it is only if, they should find out that Eric was friendly with the woman, more than likely they will want to question him. Inspector Ash has already been to the lodge when Dad was killed and will remember how Eliza Grant was able to see our house from one of the lodge's windows.'

'I know.'

'Don't worry, Rachel, please. If it's any consolation, I know Graham Ford and he's a damn good police officer. The Winchester force will be missing him.'

'He's replaced Brenda Masters, hasn't he?'

'Yes, the formidable Chief Inspector Brenda Masters,' giving a dry chuckle, 'she was like a terrier and always seemed to manage to get to the root of the matter; Ian Ash as well, so don't underestimate him, Rachel. Meadowbank is fortunate in having such a capable police team.'

'Just as well; it appears we are going to need one.'

***

Beppe Bortoletto, resplendent in scarlet topcoat and tails, with gold trim, gold embroidered waistcoat, black breeches and knee-high boots and a tall top hat, strode to the centre of the circus ring to the opening chords of the "Entry of the Gladiators", his portly figure illuminated by the myriad of spotlights.

'Ladies and gentlemen and children of all ages .... ' his voice booming out above the drum roll as he announced the first act.

The show was about to begin; people from Meadowbank and surrounding villages, many of them having queued for almost an hour before filtering through the curtained alleyway to the arena of the big top when they had been directed to the tiered wooden benches by ushers and usherettes dressed in identical silk blue trousers, matching waistcoats and white shirts. The turnout was good and the children in the audience wide-eyed in awe of what was happening around them. To them, they had entered a magical world; lights brighter than they had ever seen before, sounds louder, the sudden introduction of the trumpet fanfare making them jump, the whole spectacular in front of their eyes dazzling and fantastic and one they would always remember. The speedy appearance of the circus' three clowns, Bernie, Oscar and Jack, accompanied by the opening chords of "Danke Schoen", performed their juggling and somersaulting, with Oscar, the shortest, leap-frogging and dancing erratically, finally sliding full-length on the stream of water emerging from a hosepipe, all of which brought spontaneous shrieks of laughter from those among the spectators still young enough to enjoy such slapstick.

A muted trumpet filtered in with "A Nightingale Sang in Berkley Square", lights were dimmed, the audience's attention now being drawn upwards by the three large spotlights, heralding the imminent appearance of the trapeze artists, the music now being replaced by "Over the Waves".

There were two platforms for the trapeze artists; the highest one would only be used by Beverly during the circus' six days in Meadowbank. While the other two girls, Maria and Juliana, went into their act swinging between the lower platforms, Beverly nimbly climbed the last flight of steps. At this stage she was not highlighted by any of the spotlights, the intention being to focus the audience's attention on the two girls below her. Afterwards, when questioned, nobody was able to say with any accuracy how the accident occurred. Apparently, one second Beverly was on the steps, and the next she had gone until she re-appeared, her feet dangling free, her arms out-stretched as she tried to hold on to the side of the steps, but she was incapable of sustaining her grip, her body careering to the ground and although the safety-nets were in position, she wasn't close enough to them to save herself.

The band leader, Marcus De Marco, saw Beverly's hands slide from the steps and immediately directed the band to change the tempo of the music, "Over the Waves" now being replaced by "The 12th Street Rag" to alert the clowns to re-appear; Maria and Juliana, trained to recognise every musical signal, immediately brought their act to a close by sliding down the ropes; simultaneously, the lighting changed to focus fully on the clowns. By this time, each circus worker was aware there was something wrong and was on standby awaiting instructions. With only five minutes remaining until intermission, Beppe Bortoletto, aware by this time of the seriousness of the accident, waited until then to make the announcement to the audience that regrettably due to a tragic accident, he had no choice but to bring that evening's performance to a close, reassuring them they would be fully reimbursed. The evacuation of the tent was conducted systematically, each worker well versed in such an emergency, directing them to additional temporary ticket offices where they could arrange their refunds. Beppe solemnly walked to his caravan to make the call to Meadowbank Police Station. He had briefly been to the area where the body of Beverly Clements lay; someone had placed a sheet over her and he had pulled back a corner and looked at her face, making a silent prayer before replacing the sheet. Beverly had been with them for three years and had been a proficient and skilled trapeze artist; he was finding it hard to accept she had missed her footing on one of the rungs of the ladder; she had known, as all trapezists knew, how every movement they made during their performance was crucial. She had only been twenty-three and had learned her craft when no more than a child. His main concern now was to make sure the morale of everyone who worked for him didn't suffer, in particular the morale of Maria and Juliana. It was with a heavy heart he waited for the police to arrive, trying to quench an unexplained sense of foreboding. Beppe was superstitious, as many in the circus world were; he had never known any other kind of life, his career following on naturally and instinctively from his parents and grandparents. They had all had their own set of superstitious; he had never known what they were; it was just something none of them ever talked about; to do so would be unlucky. A vicious circle, he sighed. A vicious circle and one he would never in his lifetime be able to break.

***

Sergeant Allan Williams had been on duty the night before and had taken the call from Beppe Bortoletto. He had accompanied the pathologist to the scene of the accident where Dave Burrows confirmed the woman had died as a result of a fall from one of the upper rungs of the trapeze ladder; later, once the body had been taken to the police mortuary, he was able to verify that there was no evidence of any intake of drugs or alcohol. Allan Williams asked the engineer to examine the ladder; he subsequently discovered that the third step from the top had been removed. He said he had personally inspected the two flights of steps leading to the top platform, including the fixture of the safety nets, this having been carried out that afternoon in preparation for the performance and everything had been in order and in compliance with all safety regulations. Forensic were called and carried out a thorough search of the area, including all fingerprints on the relevant structure. For elimination purposes, the engineer's fingerprints were taken, forensic confirming there were no other prints. Allan made out his report and knowing that Inspector Ash would not be in the office until later, gave it instead to the Chief Inspector.

Graham's first reaction on reading the report was disbelief that the death of Beverly Clements, which was now being treated as murder, was not connected with Katherine Peters, remembering what Ian had said yesterday about there possibly being more to her murder than they had at first thought. It would seem he wasn't far wrong. Why should a young trapeze artist meet her death less than twenty-four hours after Katherine Peters? Was the link to their killer, assuming there was only one killer, the man from the circus she had met on Sunday? Already, in such a short time into their investigation, there were too many unanswered questions.

On reaching the circus grounds, Graham parked close to the entrance to the big top. The band, consisting of a trumpet player, drummer, keyboard player and clarinettist were rehearsing; the familiar strains of Johann Strauss' "Tritsh-Tratsch-Polka", resounding eerily around an arena devoid of any audience. What happened last night within yards of where he was standing would not deter these people, he thought; they were professionals, their adage being that the show must go on regardless of how they were feeling about the loss of one of their own people. The music came to an end and as though the band leader sensed his presence, he turned round to face him.

'Can I help you, sir?'

'I'm looking for Mr Bortoletto,' Graham said, showing him his identity card.

'Of course, Beverly.' his voice quivering as he tried to contain his emotions, 'I'll take you to Beppe, Chief Inspector.'

As was to be expected Beppe Bortoletto's caravan was the largest and most luxurious among the dozen or so others parked to the left of the main tent and at the edge of the park overlooking the stretch of river at the side of Saint Steven's.

Beppe Bortoletto, a stocky figure, with thick black hair, greying at the temples, and except for the jeans and denim shirt, looked every inch of what he was: a circus ringmaster, someone accustomed to stage-managing a performance, except this morning it was obvious to Graham by the sadness in his expression he was taking the death of his trapeze artist very hard indeed, also, judging by the dark shadows beneath his eyes, it was doubtful whether he'd had any sleep the night before.

'Come in, Chief Inspector,' he said as soon as Graham had introduced himself, 'this is a sad day for us all.' he added, gesturing for him to take a seat. Inside, the caravan was surprisingly spacious; not at all what he expected and bore no resemblance to the caravan he'd stayed in years ago when he'd been on holiday with his parents. This one, Graham thought, was the epitome of luxury: solid wood fitments, upholstered settles and vertical blinds at the windows.

'I've been in touch with Beverly's parents;' Beppe said, 'and they will be here this afternoon. They expressed the wish, Chief Inspector, to see her - ' faltering, unable to say any more.

'- if it would make it any easier for them,' Graham said, helping him out, 'I'll make arrangements for her body to be taken to the small Chapel of Rest.'

'Thank you; I know they will appreciate that. Meanwhile,' he added, 'we must continue with our performances; it will be expected of us. I trust you have no objection, Chief Inspector.'

'None whatsoever, Mr Bortoletto. I have read Sergeant Williams' report and as it would appear that one of the rungs on the trapeze ladder had been deliberately removed, we are now treating Miss Clements' death as murder.'

'I realise that.' he said quietly.

'We, at the Station, Mr Bortoletto, will be doing everything in our power to find the perpetrator and to do this it will be necessary to question a number of people -'

'- do you think whoever is responsible was — was one of us?'

'It's too early to say,' Graham answered, 'but first we need to find the motive for her death.'

'Regrettably, Chief Inspector, I have to face facts and say that the person who tampered with the ladder must have been employed by me; anyone else would surely have been spotted.'

'Yes, on the face of it, I agree. That is if he, or she, had been seen. Your engineer has confirmed he examined the equipment yesterday afternoon.'

'Yes, he did. This was shortly before four o'clock; I saw him there myself.'

'Were there many people in the tent around that time?'

'Very few; there had been earlier because of the various rehearsals, but they were over by then. The band was packing up and the engineer and I were the last to leave.'

'So this means the tent would have been empty from about four until — ?'

' — about thirty minutes before the performance started which was at seven.'

'So, it does indicate the possibility of someone going in there, perhaps unnoticed, during those times.'

'Yes, I suppose it does, Chief Inspector.' but with very little conviction in his voice.

'I had every intention of coming here this morning, Mr Bortoletto, but this was before news of Miss Clements' death reached us.'

'Oh?'

'Yesterday morning,' Graham started to explain, 'the body of a woman was found in Meadowbank and during our initial enquiries into her death, it transpired that on Sunday evening she had a drink with someone who worked for your circus. Unfortunately, we have no name for him, only a description.'

'May I ask how you knew he worked here, Chief Inspector?'

'Because he mentioned this to the landlord of the pub he was in, also he said he had only worked for the circus for a year and that prior to this he had been a stuntman.'

'You said you had a description of him.'

'Tall, about six foot, thin, possibly in his early forties and with a London accent.'

'Sounds like Jack Corbett. Most of my workers have been with me for well over a year.'

'I would like to have a word with him, if that's possible, Mr Bortoletto.'

'You don't suspect him, do you?'

'Not at this stage, no. We believe there is a possibility he may have known the victim, perhaps several years ago, and if he did, talking to him would give us a clear picture of her background.'

'I understand. He'll be in the tent at this time of the morning,' Beppe said, glancing at his watch, 'if you'd like to come with me, Chief Inspector, I'll introduce you to him.'

Walking over to the big top, Beppe stopped to speak to a woman standing beside the ticket office who reminded him of the actress Gina Lollobrigida; she had the same dark hair and the sultry expression.

'This is my wife, Cordelia, Chief Inspector.'

'Good morning, Chief Inspector.' even her voice reminded him of the actress and wondering where she fitted into the nomadic existence of these people; she was probably in her mid-forties, too old to be one of the acrobats or trapeze performers; her presence, surrounded by the paraphernalia of the circus, struck him as incongruous. 'You are going to solve the mystery of who is responsible for what happened to Beverly.'

'We will do our best, Mrs Bortoletto.' recognising the trace of mockery in her voice. She was making it quite plain to him, whether her manner was intentional or not, that she wasn't interested one way or another. Cordelia Bortoletto lacked the warmth generally associated with the people from her own country.

'Beppe,' she said, turning to her husband, 'I'm going to take a drive up to the Royal Oak for lunch; I'm finding this gloomy atmosphere depressing.'

There was no change in Beppe Bortoletto's expression as he looked at her, no way of knowing whether her words had affected him, no doubt well accustomed to her insensitivity.

'*Guidare con attenzione, cara mia.*' he said to her, leaning over and kissing her lightly on the cheek.

'I always drive carefully, *cara mio.*' she answered, glancing over to Graham with a challenging expression, implying perhaps that he lacked the knowledge to interpret the few words her husband had said to her.

Chapter Four

Maitland Holdings, a prestigious suite of offices on the second floor, overlooked Holland Park in Kensington. The receptionist, reminiscent of so many Ian had seen on his trips to London, languidly looked up from polishing her nails and, taking a brief glance at his identity card, buzzed through to her managing director's office. Within minutes, and with obvious reluctance, she was escorting him along the thickly carpeted corridor until they reached the smoked-glass door with a polished brass plaque bearing the inscription:

HAROLD G. MAITLAND, A.C.A., B.Com.

Harold Maitland was standing at the window with his back to the room when he went in, his stature and build immediately reminding him of someone he had seen before, but as soon as he turned round to face him, the likeness had gone, the way fleeting impressions were inclined to do. He was older than Ian had expected; close to sixty, he reckoned, a good twenty years older than Katherine Peters had been; grey hair receding from a high forehead, tall, about six foot, heavy build; pale eyes behind rimless spectacles which were equally appraising him.

'Your visit is about Katherine, I expect, Inspector.' he said quietly.

'Yes, that's right,' Ian said, 'I appreciate you taking time to see me, Mr Maitland.'

'Not at all. Won't you sit down;' gesturing to one of the upholstered chairs in the centre of the room, 'less formal than facing each other across a desk?'

'The purpose for my visit,' Ian explained, 'is an attempt to fill in Miss Peter's background. She had only been living in Meadowbank for a couple of years and prior to that what we have is somewhat sketchy with periods in her life where we've been unable to trace her whereabouts, although we did learn yesterday she had been living in Notting Hill up until 2005, but that's all. Up to now, Mr Maitland, there is no apparent motive for her death.'

'I see,' he said, leaning forward in his seat, 'well, as you are apparently aware we were married, although only for a short time; from the 2nd April 1999 until the 17th May 2002, but then you probably knew that already?'

'We did, yes. And during that time,' Ian went on, 'she was with the Esther Summers Theatre in Guildford which she left at the time of the divorce, but from then until she arrived in Meadowbank on the 8th February 2005, there is no record of what she was doing; this has yet to be looked into. Did you keep in touch after the divorce, Mr Maitland?'

'No, we didn't, Inspector; there was no need. The divorce wasn't entirely amicable, besides Katherine and I had nothing further to say to each other.'

'We have details of the divorce settlement,' noticing the way his mouth tightened; the movement was only momentary, but it was there, indicating perhaps he was finding the recollection distasteful, but he had to press on, 'the reason for acquiring these was because of the substantial alimony payments.'

'It was a court decision, Inspector; it was either that or pay out a lump sum which would have been considerable if you take into account Katherine was only thirty-three then and under normal circumstances,' he added dryly, 'her life expectancy would have been at least another thirty years.'

'After the divorce,' Ian asked, 'did you know where she was living?'

'No, I didn't. She had moved out some months before then and didn't tell me where she was going.'

'And you didn't ask her?'

'No, any communications were made through our lawyers. It was not a particularly pleasant period of my life and as you've read the settlement details you will realise that, apart from these regular payments, Katherine was granted full ownership of a property I purchased overseas many years before we met; this had been as an investment and provided a commendable additional income. Yes,' he sighed, 'she benefited alright.'

'I understand.' Ian said, but for some reason unable to feel sorry for him, but given what they had gleaned up to now about Katherine Peters, it would appear that here was someone else who had experienced her knack of getting what she wanted.

'Well,' he said, bracing his shoulders, 'she's gone. And nothing can be gained by opening up old wounds by a display of bitterness.'

'I have to ask you this, Mr Maitland, but would you mind telling me where you were on Sunday night?'

'Not in Meadowbank, Inspector.' he said, but the short laugh he gave was a forced one, 'As a matter of fact I spent the evening at the Saville Club in Mayfair. I had a meal and afterwards a couple of games of snooker, returning home around ten.'

'And do you live on your own, sir?'

'Oh, yes, Inspector; as they say: "once bitten, twice shy!" '

***

Jack Corbett matched the description they had been given, particularly the worn, haggard features and the lugubrious expression on his face as Beppe Bortoletto introduced him.

'The Chief Inspector would like a few words with you, Jack.'

'Purely routine, you understand,' Graham put in and, Beppe taking the hint, excused himself, 'but we're hoping you may be able to help us clear up a few points concerning the murder enquiry we're currently conducting –'

'– you mean what's happened to Beverley?' he interrupted.

'Not primarily.'

'I don't understand.'

'I'll explain,' Graham said, trying to put him at his ease although realising it was unlikely he would be able to do that, 'yesterday morning the body of a woman was found in Riverside Lane and it's our understanding you had a drink with her on Sunday evening –'

'– Kitty?' his face ashen.

'Is that what you called her?'

'Yes –'

'She was called Katherine Peters.'

'I know, but when I knew her everyone called her Kitty. How did –' stumbling over what he was trying to say, 'how did she – die, Chief

Inspector?'

'She was strangled, Mr Corbett.'

'My God! I can't believe it! I really can't! Kitty dead; it's hard to take in.'

'I'm sure it is,' allowing him a degree of sympathy, but Graham wasn't finished yet; there was still more he wanted to know, 'however, we have to face facts. Miss Peters met a violent death and our main criteria is to find the assailant –'

'– and you suspect me!'

'At this stage in our enquiry, we have no suspects, Mr Corbett. We need to know more about the victim and this is where you could perhaps help us.'

'How?'

'Were you surprised to see her on Sunday evening?'

'Very.'

'Why?'

'I had no idea she was living in Meadowbank; it didn't seem to be her sort of place. I would have thought it would be too quiet for her; she always used to prefer city life.'

'When did you last see her?'

'Years ago. Fifteen. We were both with a stage agency in Islington, although she didn't stay with them long. I didn't see her after that; she told me on Sunday that she had joined Guildford Rep.'

'How well did you know her?'

'Well, I reckon you could have said we were a unit, but neither of us were all that committed; too young probably to think seriously about anything as long term as marriage.'

'Did she have other boyfriends?'

'Not that I knew of.'

'Does the name Eric Noble mean anything to you, Mr Corbett?'

'No, I don't think so. Should it?'

'Not necessarily, but apparently he was someone else she used to know a number of years ago, that's all. So,' Graham persisted, 'after she left the agency, you didn't see her again?'

'That's right.'

'You weren't sorry about the break-up?'

'Not unduly.'

'And on Sunday, would you describe the conversation with her as an amicable one?'

'Of course; she told me a little about where she'd been during those years and then after she'd finished her drink she said she had to go.'

'Did she say why?'

'Only that she was meeting someone.'

'Not the person's name?'

'No, and I didn't expect her to; it would have been extremely unlikely whether I would have known him.'

'You say him.'

'It could have been a woman I suppose; just a figure of speech, Chief Inspector.'

'Where did you go after you left the pub?'

'I came back here.'

'Is this the first time you've been to Meadowbank, Mr Corbett?'

'Yes; why do you ask?'

'I was wondering how well you knew the town; the names of the various streets for example.'

'Well, I've only been here a few hours and I can't say I've looked at any of the street names.'

'Do you know where Riverside Lane is?'

'Probably by the river.'

'Quite. Katherine Peters lived in Riverside Lane and when you returned to the circus that night you would have had to walk past her cottage.'

'I wouldn't have known that, would I?' a tiny spark of annoyance making its appearance.

'Wouldn't you?'

***

It was only a short walk to Lansdowne Terrace and, noticing a pub on the corner, Ian wondered whether being so close to where Katherine Peters had lived it had been her local, but before going in decided to take a look at the mews house, not with any particular idea in mind, but more out of curiosity than anything else. Graham had described the interior of the cottage in Riverside Lane where, apparently no expense had been spared to transform the property from a terrace house to a stylish and ultra-modern dwelling, and having seen the full extent of the divorce settlement, there was no doubt she would have had ample funds.

Number Thirteen, the Mews, one of half a dozen two-storey houses was little different from its neighbours; brick-built, high sash windows, the front door with a half-moon stained glass window, leading straight from the pavement. The street was quiet, with only the muffled drone of traffic from Portobello Road. He was about to walk away when a taxi drew up alongside him. An elderly woman climbed slowly out and with the aid of a walking stick, made her way to the door of Number Eleven. She looked at him enquiringly, as though expecting an explanation of why he was there.

'I don't believe I've seen you here before, young man.' she said sharply, 'But if you've come hoping to see Miss Peters,' she went on before he had a chance to speak, 'you're going to be disappointed because she's abroad and won't be back until next month.'

'I hadn't realised.'

'You ought to have telephoned her first; that would have saved you a wasted trip. I'm told everyone has a mobile these days and I know Miss Peters has.' and without saying another word, turned her back on him and, reaching her front door, inserted the key in the lock.

That was interesting, he thought, retracing his steps back to the corner of the terrace, Katherine Peters had held on to the mews house and it looks as if he and Graham were right in thinking she had led a double life. Also, it would seem not everyone who had known her had watched the news last night.

"The Hog's Head" was unlike any of the London pubs Ian had been in before. While fairly spacious, the décor had managed to create a more intimate atmosphere. The bar area; umber-coloured quarry flooring tiles, a traditional mahogany panelled bar running the whole length along one of the walls with a highly polished brass rail and behind, smoke-glassed mirrors and rows of shining optics. The area was separated by a red brick archway leading into the restaurant where dark red carpeting, high-backed chairs and circular tables completed a general ambiance of comfort. There were a few customers standing at the bar, but being not yet midday, he hoped it would be a good time to have a word with the barman.

'Yes, Inspector,' he said, lowering his voice, after Ian had introduced himself, 'we all heard about Katherine. Very sad; she was a nice woman and one of my regular customers.'

'Did she have many friends in the area?' Ian asked him, measuring out just how much he wanted to say.

'I don't know about friends as such,' he said, 'what I mean, I don't know whether she ever met up with any of the people she used to talk to when she was in here. She may have done, of course, but perhaps not; she was away quite a bit, several times a year in fact.'

'She had only been living in Meadowbank for a couple of years and we're trying to establish what she was doing before then.'

'I see,' shaking his head, 'it's strange. She never mentioned to any of us she had another home. You see, most of the people she used to drink with were in here last evening when we saw the television news and they were all saying the same.'

'We understand she had a house in The Mews.'

'That's right, she did. I can remember when she moved in; it was about eight years ago, around the time I took over the pub; that's why I can remember. She told me she'd been living in the States and had just returned to England.'

'Do you know whether she bought the house?'

'No, she was renting. I'm fairly sure about that,' he said, 'because I'd already noticed the For Rent sign outside.'

'You've a good memory,' Ian complimented him, but he meant it; he did have a good memory considering that in the course of a day he must see and talk to a number of people and it was eight years ago, 'did you happen to see the name of the estate agents who were handling the rental?'

'They were Gregory & Stevens; their office is in Portobello Road.'

'I'm impressed.'

'Don't be, Inspector,' he smiled, 'I've used them myself in the past. Philip Gregory is a fairly regular customer; I've got one of their cards here.' he added, taking out a small pile of business cards from the shelf below the counter, and sifting through them, came to the one he was looking for. 'There you are, Inspector.' he said, handing it to him.

'Thank you,' Ian said, 'you've been very helpful, but I've taken up enough of your time.'

'That's alright; Katherine was well-liked around here; good company, very gregarious and I really hope you find the person who killed her, I really do.'

'We will. And the more information we can get at the beginning of a murder enquiry, the better. One last question, though.'

'Yes?'

'When did you last see her?'

'It must have been a couple of weeks ago; she'd been abroad somewhere, she didn't say where, but she only got back that afternoon. It was a Friday, the –' hesitating for a moment as he thought back, ' – the 18th of this month; that was when it was. There was a party in here that evening; one of my customers had won on the lottery and a crowd of them were celebrating.'

'And she was with them?'

'Yes, that's right.'

'Was she on her own?'

'Oh, yes, she always was; at least I never saw her coming in here with anyone.'

The bar was beginning to fill up and thanking him, Ian took his beer over to one of the tables by the window; he needed to make some notes before deciding what his next step should be before heading back to Meadowbank. At some point Harold Maitland's' alibi would have to be verified, but not yet. It was perhaps too soon in their enquiry; a lot depended on what would transpire in these first couple of days. Also, he wanted to confer with Graham over the wisdom of openly asking questions concerning a man as high-profile as Katherine Peters' ex-husband. Before he had spoken to him this morning his main reason was to find out as much as possible about her, but unwittingly he had supplied him with a possible motive, wondering whether he had realised this. The explanation he had been given for the way the divorce settlement had been agreed, while reasonable enough in that a single payment would have cost him a considerable sum of money, the fact that she had died prematurely immediately relieved him of making any further payments. It was a pity Dave Burrows had been unable to arrive at a closer calculation for the time of death, although going back to what Gerald Maitland had said about where he had been on Sunday night, it could still have been feasible for him to have spent the evening in his club, thereby providing an alibi, and instead of returning home, had driven to Meadowbank, calling in at Bramble Cottage. Graham and he had already mentioned she may not have been murdered in Riverside Lane, but somewhere else, her body being brought to the spot where it had been found. A lot depended on what Graham came up with after talking to Eric Noble and to the man she'd had a drink with earlier in the evening. By the end of the day, they could have three suspects on their hands. He looked at the card the barman had given him and, as he had said, the office of the estate agents was in Portobello Road, not far from where he was at the moment, but first he should give Graham a call, taking out his mobile and dialling the number.

'I was on the point of calling you, Ian,' Graham said, 'there's been a new development here, but it can wait; you've obviously got something important to report.'

'I believe I do, sir, but I thought you should know that Katherine Peters had continued to hold on to her house in Notting Hill. Apparently, she had been renting and I'm about to go along to the estate agents to have this confirmed.'

'Well, well, if that's true, Ian, it would certainly suggest she had been leading a double life.'

'I know,' he agreed, 'I had a look at the house and her next door neighbour informed me that Miss Peters was abroad; she didn't say where, probably didn't know, but that she would be back next month.

Also,' he added, 'I've spoken to the landlord in the pub she frequented; he'd watched the news last night so knew about the murder; he, and according to him, his other regular customers, said they had no idea she had also lived in Meadowbank, the last time she'd been in there being Friday, the 18th, when she told them she had just returned from abroad.'

'Strange behaviour.'

'Very.'

'Anyway,' Graham said, 'as soon as I hear back from you after you've spoken to the estate agents, I'll give New Scotland Yard a call and ask them to organize a search warrant. It would seem we will have to work in conjunction with them anyway, especially after what has happened here.'

'Yes?'

'Another murder, Ian; one of the circus' trapeze artists fell to her death during the performance last night; one of the rungs on the ladder she was climbing had been removed.'

'Connected with the Katherine Peters' case.'

'It could be, but at the moment it's all looking, for the want of a better word, bizarre. Two violent deaths within a matter of hours, not good.'

'I should be back by four, sir, but I'll give you a ring before I leave here.'

'That's fine. I'm hoping to see Eric Noble this afternoon. I feel the sooner we speak to him, the better.'

They brought the call to a close and Ian, finishing off his lager, made his way to Portobello Road, only a short walk away. Gregory & Stevens Estate Agents was easily spotted; their logo, deceptively simple, painted in bright primary colours and depicting what resembled a child's drawing of a house; one-dimensional, box-shaped, square windows, a twisting path to the front door. Taking a quick glance at the properties advertised for sale in the windows and mentally reeling at the extortionately high prices being asked, he went in. His first impressions were how different from Town & Country Estate Agents in Meadowbank, so much so, there was no comparison at all. In here, the hushed atmosphere was daunting; his feet made no sound on the beige carpeting as he walked over to the reception desk, beige vertical blinds blocking any natural light, this being provided by concealed ceiling lights. Surprisingly, there were no photographs of any property to interest or attract a prospective customer and the only splash of colour to break up the insipid and blandly clinical effect, was a glazed pot of chrysanthemums, the yellow and orange flowers almost startling. The girl at the desk, a carbon copy of the one he'd seen earlier, watched silently as he walked towards her.

'Have you an appointment?' she asked when he showed her his card, asking to speak to one of their partners; apart from the question being unnecessary, Ian thought irritably, it made him wonder why she was there in the first place when, presumably, if she was meant to be the receptionist, she would have known whether he had an appointment.

'Is it possible to see either Mr Gregory or Mr Stevens?' deciding to take a firmer line.

'I will find out if Mr Gregory is available.' She said sulkily, and with exaggerated slowness, picked up the receiver.

She didn't say anything further to him and within minutes, Ian heard a door opening somewhere along the passage and, presumably Philip Gregory, came striding up to him.

'Good afternoon,' he said, 'my secretary tells me you are with the police.'

'Yes, that's right; Inspector Ian Ash.' once again displaying his identity card.

'I see, Inspector;' frowning as he read the card, 'you are with the Meadowbank Police Constabulary.'

'I'll explain, sir,' curbing his impatience; at this rate he would be lucky to leave London before four, 'but perhaps we could use your office.'

'Of course. Of course. How remiss of me; if you will follow me, Inspector. I apologise, but I have neglected to introduce myself. Philip Gregory.' he added and somewhat belatedly shaking hands.

Philip Gregory's office was an improvement; a large room and although with the same blinds and lighting, it had considerably more colour and could almost be described as comfortable. The desk was oval and gave the impression he did actually work there with the blue flickering screen of his computer, the scattering of files and a pile of glossy property photographs in evidence.

'As you can see;' smiling apologetically, 'I'm not a tidy worker.' pushing the paperwork to one side and gesturing for Ian to take a seat.

'Now,' he asked, 'how can I help you, Inspector?'

'Before I explain, Mr Gregory, I would like to verify that one of your properties in Lansdowne Terrace is being leased out to a Miss Katherine Peters.'

'Lansdowne Terrace,' he repeated, 'we're handling more than one in that street, but I'll check,' pulling the keyboard towards him, and pressing a number of keys, scrolled down the screen, 'yes, Katherine Peters, I remember the name now, she took up the lease of number thirteen on the 4th January 1999.'

'Mr Gregory,' Ian said, 'it would seem you are not aware of Miss Peters' death.'

'She's dead!' making an automatic movement to stand up, then changing his mind, a look of bewilderment on his face, 'but – but how?'

'Her body was found yesterday morning; she had died by strangulation.' there was no way of softening the blow; he had to be told.

'My God! How absolutely awful!'

'It was on the television news last evening, Mr Gregory.'

'Believe it or not, Inspector; I very seldom watch the news, I tend to rely on my copy of "The Times" each morning. Where did this happen; not – not in –'

'- in Meadowbank; she was living there and had been for the last couple of years.'

'But – but, she was living in Notting Hill. And Meadowbank,' a look of enlightenment replacing his former expression of shock, 'that is why your police force is involved.'

'Yes, although this murder case has now become more complicated in that she actually had two properties. We are conducting further searches of the house she owned in Meadowbank, but the mews house will also have to undergo a search.'

'Of course, I understand.'

'I've already spoken to my Chief Inspector about this additional development and he will be contacting New Scotland Yard for their assistance. Until such time as they have completed what they have to do, I'm afraid the property will have to remain empty.'

'This is such a shock, you understand.'

'I'm sure it is. There are one or two questions I'd like to ask you about the time Miss Peters took on the lease, Mr Gregory.'

'Yes.'

'You would no doubt have carried out a credit check on her to satisfy yourself she had sufficient funds or income to support the monthly rent.'

'Oh, yes,' looking at the screen again, 'she was with the Esther Summers Theatre in Guildford and while her salary as an actress was reasonable, it was not enough to meet the required rental figure, but she did have more than sufficient in savings.'

'You have proof of these savings?'

'Yes, she showed me the relevant bank statement,' referring back to the screen, 'her salary from the theatre was paid into her current account with Lloyds Bank and the balance on the savings account she had with Lloyds gave us the necessary information we needed.'

'I see, how much is the rent?'

'When she took out the lease, the monthly rent was £900; this has increased by a small percentage each year, the current rent being £1,102 each month.'

'And is the property furnished or unfurnished?'

'Unfurnished, Inspector.'

'That seems clear enough. Finally, Mr Gregory, presumably she would have given you her former address.'

'She had been staying at "The Mandalay Hotel" in Guildford for two years since she returned to England after spending a few years in America.'

'That ties in with what we've been able to trace on her background.' Not dissatisfied with what he'd found out today, not only from the estate agents, but from the landlord of "The Hog's Head" and Gerald Maitland, and now, having learned that Katherine Peters had taken on the lease before she married him, and continuing with it right up to the time of her death, and for him not to have found out, or perhaps more significant, not being told by her, was hard to believe.

They were gradually and systematically trawling back through her past and it may just be possible by talking to the staff at "The Mandalay Hotel" and at the theatre in Guildford, they may discover something about those years she was in the States, including what happened to her first husband. Ian, like Graham, was coming round to the idea her murder had something to do with her past. As far as he could see, there were only two alternatives; either Franklin Bacall had died or there had been no divorce. If the latter, it would certainly put a different slant on how they had been viewing this murder enquiry; her marriage to Gerald Maitland would have been null and void which would have meant there could be no divorce and no settlement. What a conundrum, he thought, and now with the added complication of a second murder, even more so.

***

Graham was back in Meadowbank from Winchester before Ian, his meeting with Eric Noble not an entirely satisfactory one. He hadn't taken to the man, finding his brooding non-communicative manner irritating. From the moment he was shown into his office, Graham recognised what he was up against; whether Eric Noble had something to hide or not, his open resentment, probably deep-rooted, would surface. As he drove out of Winchester, he was asking himself whether he couldn't have handled the interview differently, from another angle, but it was too late; too much animosity existed between them. By the time he was on the slip road and joining the M27, he had begun to mentally salvage from what Eric Noble had permitted himself to say, something positive to add to what they had collected up to now.

"I would like you to know," Eric Noble had said, his first words the only greeting, "I have an extremely heavy workload and I strongly object to anyone calling in without making an appointment."

"And I would remind you, Mr Noble," Graham had been quick to retaliate, "I am conducting an enquiry into the murder of Katherine Peters, where time is of an essence, we do not have the *time* to arrange appointments with people we wish to interview. Your secretary has shown you my identity card which should have made it clear that as a senior member of the police force I am not anyone and that applies to my fellow officers when, in the line of duty, are questioning members of the public."

"What do you want to know, *Chief* Inspector?" he'd emphasised rudely, swivelling his chair and neglecting to offer him a seat.

"How did you spend Sunday evening, Mr Noble?"

"You ask me that!"

"At this stage in our enquiry, questions of this nature are purely routine."

"Only if you suspect someone."

"We have no grounds at present to suspect anyone, and until we do, for the purpose of elimination, we have to ask questions. How did you spend Sunday evening?' he repeated.

"What I would like to know is why, from all the men in Meadowbank, you're asking me?"

"We have reason to believe you made arrangements to meet Katherine Peters on Sunday."

"Well, I didn't meet her."

"Shortly before midday on Sunday, she made a call to you."

"What if she did?"

"We have heard every word of that call, Mr Noble, also to your, albeit reluctant, agreement to meet her."

"I changed my mind and if you've heard what was said, you will realise I had no wish to see her."

"But she made it abundantly clear she wanted to see you."

"Did she?"

"I would describe her tone as somewhat threatening, Mr Noble."

"Rubbish!"

"In what way could she have made life difficult for you?"

"I have no idea; she *was* an actress, everything was always high drama to her."

"Did she have some information which could, if she so wished, use to discredit you –"

"– do you really think that *I* would allow that to happen?" his voice rising.

"What was it she wanted, Mr Noble, and why wait almost ten years?"

"How the hell should I know!"

"I suggest you did know," Graham pressed on, verbally forcing him to speak without considering every response as he had been doing so far. "I suggest that whatever it was, relates to an earlier time, when you and she were together perhaps."

"You're suggesting I murdered her; because if you are –"

" – I'm not suggesting anything of the kind,'" interrupting him, choosing to ignore the implication behind his words, "but somebody did and unless her killer was some psychopath who just happened to be in Riverside Lane on Sunday night at the same time, he would need to have had a reason, and a very strong one to go to such lengths."

"Ah," sarcasm now in evidence as he glared across the desk at him, "so that's the way you work; first find the motive and then slap it on to the person you consider the most likely to have committed the crime!"

"Once again, how did you spend Sunday evening?"

"I had dinner at the Royal Oak Hotel."

"What time was this?"

"I'd booked a table for seven-thirty."

"Alone."

"Yes."

"And after the meal?"

"I spent some time in the bar?"

"What time did you leave the hotel?"

"About ten-thirty."

"Did you go straight home, Mr Noble?"

"Of course."

"When was the last time you saw Katherine Peters?" noticing by the way his eyelids flickered how his change of tack had surprised him.

"Nine years ago."

"You hadn't been in touch since then?"

"I've already told you when I last saw her."

"Which would have been in 1998?"

"That's right; I can't remember when exactly, but it was towards the end of the year, November or December."

"And how long had you known her?"

"For about three or three and a half years."

"How well *did* you know her, Mr Noble?"

"Extremely well; for most of the time we lived together."

"Where was this?"

"In London."

Graham looked more closely at the man sitting opposite to him; there had been no change in the supercilious expression he had adopted from the beginning. Either he was a consummate liar or he considered himself irreproachable. The profile the office had come up with on his background had, as with Katherine Peters, contained a number of years unaccountable and would need further investigation.

"Look," he'd said, leaning forward, both hands spread out on the desk, every line of his body signifying his growing impatience, "how much longer is this – this *interrogation* going to continue. I have work to do."

"And so do I, Mr Noble." Graham snapped, "You have told me you were living with Katherine Peters for at least, shall we say, three years."

"Near enough."

"And this was in London?"

"I am not in the habit of repeating myself, Chief Inspector. That is what I said and that is what I meant."

"And I would refute that, Mr Noble;" ignoring the splutter of indignation, "we have evidence to support that Katherine Peters was living in America from June 1994 until when she returned to England in January 1997. She did not return to England during this period." waiting for his reaction, even looking forward to hearing how he would handle that one.

"Are you calling me a liar?" not quite shouting, but his voice must have increased in volume by a few decibels. He was not far short from losing his temper which was what Graham was aiming for.

"Our source of information is irrefutable; therefore, unless you are mistaken about those years, I would have to say, yes."

Disappointedly, he didn't jump to his feet in fury, neither did he make any attempt to retract what he'd said, but remained quite still, shoulders hunched, a deep scowl creasing his forehead, his lips pressed tightly together. It was obvious he was exercising every effort to control his temper, although it wasn't clear to Graham who he was actually mad with; could be with himself. For being found out, but it didn't make him a murderer, only increased their suspicions.

"Meadowbank is a relatively small town, wouldn't you say," Graham went on conversationally, and for the second time, the way he changed the subject, hit its target just as he had calculated it would, "in the respect that, unless one is a hermit, the majority of people who live there will see the same faces, often on a daily basis; whether they know them or not makes no difference, eventually they will know who they are."

"What the hell are you getting at?"

"We realise you have only been living there for a few months," sidestepping his aggressiveness, "and haven't yet had sufficient time to get to know many of the residents, but Katherine Peters had lived there for two years, also from what we've learned of her character, spent a good part of her time socialising. There aren't many places in Meadowbank where one *can* socialise, Mr Noble, as I'm sure you will have found out already; there are only the two pubs, the Salmon's Rest restaurant, The King's Arms' hotel and, of course, The Royal Oak, many of which the majority of the people in the town frequent. I find it hard to accept that Katherine Peters hadn't bumped into you and yet," Graham went on relentlessly, "she told you on the phone that she knew your address. Didn't you wonder how she found out?"

"Not really."

"You weren't curious?"

"No, she could have been bluffing, but it doesn't matter."

"I think it matters a great deal, Mr Noble. She was apparently a regular customer of The Bridge, which doesn't mean she didn't visit the other pub, where I understand you were when she phoned you on Sunday."

"I can't give you any answer to that; surely that's your job to work out, certainly not mine."

Touché , Graham muttered under his breath.

He hadn't prolonged the interview as much as he would have liked to have done, but what he had managed to extract from him was enough for the present, realising he would be seeing him again and hopefully with more ammunition. He went over once more of how Katherine Peters had been able to discover where Eric Noble was living now and hadn't accepted the pathetic suggestion that she could have been bluffing, for the simple reason it wasn't true. It was quite feasible to assume someone could have phoned her at Bramble Cottage; she had been at her desk, jotted it down quickly and then neglected to enter it into her address book. Her missing car continued to niggle him. It had to be somewhere. But where? Graham firmly believed she had gone up to the lodge on Sunday evening, probably after she left The Bridge, or if not then, later. On the other hand, if she had gone there, found there was no-one at home, she'd waited until he returned.

By the time he pulled into Market Square he had decided it was time to take a look at the lodge; he'd heard of the Tilsly family from when Major Tilsly was murdered a couple of years ago, and from being familiar with the case, knew how close the Old Manor was to the lodge. It was just possible someone may have seen or heard something on Sunday night.

There was no sign of Ian's car in front of the Station, but instead of going inside, Graham carried on through the square, turning left at the bank and carrying on until he came to the Old Manor. The double gates were open and driving through on to the gravel driveway he glanced at the lodge on his right-hand side, making a mental note of the position of the building in relation to that of the main house directly in front of him. He noticed how the terrace at the rear of the lodge encroached on to the lawn at the end of the drive, with no hedge or bushes to separate the two properties and to provide any real privacy for either of them.

He pulled up outside the front door alongside a dark blue open-top Renault and, climbing the flight of stone steps, rang the bell. Judging by her expression, the woman who came to the door didn't appear too happy at the disturbance. She would be in her early forties, he guessed; medium height, slim, dark brown hair cut short, and if it hadn't been for her look of petulance would be considered attractive.

'I apologise for bothering you, but I wonder if you could spare me a few minutes of your time.' showing her his identity card.

'Chief Inspector Graham Ford;' she read aloud, 'I don't understand.'

'You are Mrs Tilsly?'

'Yes, that's right, -'

'- it's nothing for you to worry about, Mrs Tilsly,' trying to reassure her, 'there are just a few questions I would like to ask you.'

'Oh, well, you'd better come inside then.' opening the door wider, and leading him across the hall, opened a door on the right. The dining room was spacious, wood panelled, crystal chandeliers and two high sash windows overlooking the lawns and giving, he noticed, a clear view of the lodge. She gestured for him to sit down, surprising him by offering him coffee, although he didn't miss the relief on her face when he refused. No doubt remembering her social graces, he thought uncharitably.

'You will, I'm sure, have heard about the recent murders in Meadowbank?' deciding to come straight to the point sensing she was the type of woman whose attention span would be short-lived.

'You mean there's been another one?' her eyes widening in shock as she stared at him.

'I'm afraid so;' attempting to put her at her ease, considering her response excessive, although it was possible such a reaction would be normal with her, 'last evening a young woman who was a trapeze artist with the circus fell to her death during her act. It was discovered that the ladder she was on had been deliberately tampered with.'

'How awful! Two murders in Meadowbank and more or less at the same time. Are they connected, Chief Inspector?'

'At this stage in our enquiries we have nothing to prove they are, Mrs Tilsly, but the reason for my visit is because we believe Katherine Peters could have driven up here from Meadowbank on Sunday evening.'

'Oh, dear; this is rather awkward,' biting her lip, obviously finding it difficult to carry on, 'I really don't know how to say this.'

'You saw her?'

'Yes, I did.'

'What time was this, Mrs Tilsly?'

'I think it must have been about half past ten; it was still fairly light and I was upstairs closing one of the bedroom windows when I saw her out on the terrace of the lodge.' and pointing in the direction of the lodge.

'Can you be certain it was her?'

'Yes, I can, but I didn't know that at the time; it wasn't until I saw her picture on the news last night that I recognised her.'

'Was she on her own, Mrs Tilsly?'

'No, Mr Noble was with her; he's our new tenant.' she explained.

'Have you any idea how long she was there?'

'No; I went back downstairs.'

'Did you hear the sounds of a car afterwards?'

'No, my husband and I spent the remainder of the evening in the kitchen and that's at the back of the house. Neither of us would have heard if there had been any car leaving.'

***

'Did you enjoy your lunch, *cara mia*?'

'Not much fun eating on your own, Beppe;' annoyed by his banal question. Always with Beppe he put the circus first, there was precious little time left for her, 'I'd hoped you may have followed me up to the hotel and we could have had lunch together.'

'Surely you realise, Cordelia, at such a tragic time, it's impossible for me to get away, far less be seen to be enjoying myself.'

'Of course,' sighing deeply, '*Beverly*;' spoiling for an argument, 'how could I have forgotten.'

'Cordelia, please, I have a great deal to contend with at the moment.'

'What I don't understand,' ignoring his plea, 'why Meadowbank's Chief Inspector of police should have been here this morning. I would have thought that any questions which needed to be asked were dealt with last night.'

'I wouldn't know about that;' he said, 'but the Chief Inspector wanted to speak to Jack Corbett.'

'Jack Corbett,' becoming even more confused than she was already, 'why should he want to speak to him?'

'You won't have heard about the woman who was murdered on Sunday night, Cordelia; her body was found in Meadowbank yesterday morning.'

'Another murder! What is going on in this town, Beppe?'

'I wish I knew, *cara mia*, but it seems that Jack may have known her at one time, had a drink with her, in fact, on Sunday –'

'– and they think he killed her?'

'All the Chief Inspector said was that Jack could be helpful in giving them a clearer picture of her background.'

'Didn't she live in Meadowbank then, because if she did everyone would know all about her?'

'I've no idea, Cordelia; he didn't say.'

'We don't know much about Jack, do we?'

'Enough to know he's good at what he does, also, considering he's never worked for a circus before, he's adapted very well.'

'If you say so, Beppe.'

There were times Cordelia thought when Beppe could be too trusting; he was a man completely without any curiosity, treating every single person who worked for him as family. To her, this was positively unhealthy; the way he was reacting to the demise of Beverly Clements being a prime example. He had viewed her as the daughter he never had, shrugging off any lingering feelings of inadequacy. It wasn't as if she had ever wanted children, but although he had never said as much, she knew Beppe felt differently. She had only been twenty-three when she'd married him and eager to escape the restrictions placed on her by over-protective parents. They had been aghast when she told them about Beppe; to them, marrying into a circus family was tantamount to becoming a gypsy, but back then, she had been excited about what she saw as a glittering life, surrounded by people whose object was to entertain others, along with the accompanying razzmatazz associated with the big top. She wasn't dissatisfied; he was a generous husband, gave her the freedom she needed and if he suspected she was being unfaithful, never challenged her; that wasn't his way. He was too much of an ostrich to risk having his pride damaged and realising this, she took full advantage, safe in the knowledge, provided she was discreet, of enjoying her various liaisons, all of which had been no more than light-hearted affairs. What she felt for Eric differed from the others; she was in love with him, an intense, passionate and all-consuming love, made more so by the length of time between when they could be together, but so far she coped with this the best way she could.

Chapter Five

Carol Cliff's column on Wednesday morning didn't quite make the front page, another violent flare-up in Northern Ireland taking precedence, but the bold way she conveyed the news of the murders was such that anyone who bought a copy of the newspaper couldn't fail to read it. True to form, she stated the facts, interlacing them with suggestions which no-one else had spoken out loud, skilfully avoiding saying anything which would land her paper in the law courts for libel.

'I suppose you've seen this?' Graham asked, still holding the copy he'd bought at the newsagents on the corner of the square.

'I have, sir,' Ian nodded, his expression grim, 'she's got a double whammy this time, hasn't she?'

'You could say that and I know we can expect the rest of the pack descending on the town trying to sniff out anything else, although judging by this,' pointing to the newspaper, 'she's already done a thorough job.'

'Well, she did have a head start and was actually here when Beverly Clements was killed; that certainly gave her more to go on.'

'You're right, Ian.' he agreed, glancing at the article, picking up on the salient points and wondering how long it would take before "The Warrior" would be demanding positive results. Superintendent Bill Simms wasn't the most patient of men and to many who had experienced his wrath considered his nickname had been well-earned. Bill Simms' reputation had even filtered through to police headquarters in Winchester, and together with how Brenda had described him, Graham had at least been prepared for when he first met him. Now, he thought resignedly, it looked as though it was going to be his turn to experience first-hand the onslaught of his short temper. It would make no difference they had been working full out to make speedy headway into what had turned out to be a double murder enquiry, with the added draw-back of not knowing whether the two murders were connected or not. And, he thought with frustration, here was this woman journalist hell bent in aggravating the situation.

"Meadowbank," she had written, "a deceptively innocent looking market town in the heart of Hampshire, is now once again in the throes of suspicion and intrigue. Before the inhabitants of the town had time to recover from the shock of hearing about the violent death of Katherine Peters, whose body was found in Riverside Lane on Monday morning, later that day, Beverly Clements, a trapeze artist with the Beppe Bortoletto circus, fell to her death during her act. This was no accident. Forensic have since proved that one of the rungs on the ladder Beverly was climbing had been removed and at the time of writing has not been found.

"Surely," she went on, systematically throwing each loaded point into the metaphorical cauldron, "it is too much for anyone to accept that these two tragic deaths are not connected in some way; that would be stretching credibility too far. It should perhaps be noted that Riverside Lane is in close proximity to Riverside Park where the circus is situated, and to reach the park one has to pass Bramble Cottage where Katherine Peters had lived. What could these two women have had in common? A question which should be asked. They had both been entertainers; Katherine Peters an actress and Beverly Clements a trapeze artist. One could say they had both lived in similar worlds, and one which is unreal to the rest of us. Murder is certainly real, particularly so, when it happens against the backdrop of a once tranquil town like Meadowbank ....." and so she continued, winding up with a veiled criticism of the lack of policing.

'Heavy stuff, sir.' Ian commented dryly.

'She knows how to pull her punches; I'll say that for her. However, we'll press on. There isn't much more we can do inside the big top, but Allan Williams and Anne Brothers will be there this morning to question the circus workers; a tedious job, but it's got to be done. They'll be asking each of them where they were on Sunday night and Monday afternoon in the hope someone may have seen anything which could be relevant.'

'We're hindered by not really knowing what we're actually looking for.'

'True, but there's one thing, Ian, we'll recognise it when we do.'

'As we were saying, as things appear at the moment, we can view Eric Nobles as our number one suspect.'

'And one never knows,' Graham put in, 'we could have another one, once we've read what the office comes up with on Jack Corbett.'

'I'll be going up to "The Royal Oak" now, sir, and I don't need much imagination to know what sort of reception I'll get from Sandra Watson.'

'I'm sure you won't let her browbeat you, Ian.'

'She used to, a few years ago, but not anymore. She just likes to throw her weight around, remind us that her hotel's reputation is of paramount importance.'

'I bet Brenda was a match for her.' Graham chuckled.

The buzzer on the intercom, followed by the brusque voice of "The Warrior" permeating around the office, immediately wiped the smile from his face.

'Yes, sir.'

'I want you in here, Graham. Now please.'

'I'm on my way, sir.' standing up and, giving Ian a rueful shrug, made his way to the superintendent's office.

Bracing himself for what he expected was likely to be a stormy interview, he walked briskly along the corridor, tapping lightly on the door.

'Come in, Graham.' the voice reaching him clearly and, turning the handle, he went in.

'You've read this?' he asked, stabbing the newspaper spread out on his desk and glaring up at him.

'I have, sir.'

'The woman is a menace,' he complained loudly, impatiently pushing the paper to the far end of the desk, 'and how is it, I would like to know, she has managed to gather together so much information in such a short time. Do you have any idea, Graham?'

'I would say by being here in Meadowbank and talking or listening to what the local people have been saying. That, I understand, is the way she operates.'

'Ah, you've obviously heard about her, then?'

'Yes, I have. She's earned herself quite a reputation and having been in Meadowbank a number of times knows her way around, visiting the usual haunts frequented by many of the residents.'

'When did she get here?'

'Inspector Ash saw her arriving at "The Royal Oak" on Monday afternoon.'

'Monday afternoon.' he repeated, a look of puzzlement on his rugged features, 'this was before Katherine Peters' identity was made public and before the death of the trapeze artist on the Monday night. She's a London journalist, isn't she, based in London?'

'That's right, sir.'

'Has she a hotline to Meadowbank?'

'We believe it is feasible someone from Meadowbank could have informed her, perhaps shortly after Katherine Peters' body was found.'

'Logical.' he commented, 'So, given her apparent fascination for anything which disturbs as she so eloquently expressed it, "a deceptively innocent looking market town", she made a beeline down here as soon as she got the tip-off.'

'It would seem so.'

'You must at all costs, Graham, keep more than one step ahead of her. She's already suggested a possible connection between the two deaths. With her, it can only be guesswork, but hampering us all the same. And this reference to the lack of policing; I don't like that particular inference one little bit.'

'Neither do I, sir.'

'What sort of headway have you made so far?'

The question he'd been waiting for as soon as he stepped into the office and one he was unable to answer satisfactorily. It wasn't that they hadn't made any progress, because they had, but there was nothing of any real substance which would satisfy the superintendent.

'Inspector Ash was in London yesterday,' making a start, doubting whether he would have the patience to hear him through, 'in an attempt to find out more about Katherine Peters' background because the profile we had on her left a number of years unaccounted. He interviewed her second husband, who provided him with an alibi for Sunday night which will duly be checked out. Also, he visited the area where she had lived prior to moving to Meadowbank to find she was still renting the property in Notting Hill.'

'I see; you mentioned her second husband; what happened to the first one?'

'We are making attempts to find out, sir.'

'Alright. And what about the murder of the young woman from the circus?'

'Very little to go on yet, sir; Sergeant Williams and Sergeant Brothers are up there this morning questioning the circus workers to establish where they all were on Sunday night and Monday afternoon. '

'What's your opinion about these two murders, Graham; do you consider they're connected?'

'I would say it is a strong possibility.'

'Alright,' lifting his hands from the desk which could be taken as a lessening of his earlier approach, 'it is not my intention to put any undue pressure on you, or anyone else on your team, and I'm the first to admit, to quote the much-used phrase, that it's early days. However,' he added, 'in respect to the intrepid Carol Cliff and all those other journalists and reporters who will no doubt be descending on us as we speak, I suggest you call a press conference for tomorrow afternoon.'

'I'll make arrangements, sir.'

'I'll leave it to you to feed them with as little or as much as you think necessary to hopefully keep them off our backs for a few more days; that should give you the chance to get on with your enquiry without being constantly hampered by their continuing presence, although from what we know of the Cliff woman, it will take more than a press conference to appease her terrier-like instincts.'

***

There was no sign of Sandra Watson when Ian arrived at the Royal Oak, but he realised it would only be a matter of time before she spotted him. It was unfortunate, he thought, walking through reception to the bar, that all too often when he came here he was on duty and, to her, this invariably meant her hotel was once again the focus of unwanted attention, both by the police and the media.

He was Ted's first customer which was what he had hoped; he didn't want anyone to overhear what he had to ask him, his antenna on alert for any member of the press, remembering some of them, including Carol Cliff, had stayed here more than once, following in the wake of Meadowbank's spate of murders, each of them eager to glean what they could from snippets of conversation, enabling them to pad out their articles to an apparently sensation-hungry readership.

'Good morning, Inspector.'

'Good morning, Ted; I'll have half a lager, please.'

'What did you think of our antique auction the other evening?'

'Interesting, only we were outbid for what we wanted.'

'That's too bad,' he sympathised, passing the beer to him, 'perhaps next time.'

'Perhaps,' taking a sip, 'meanwhile,' he went on, 'I'm more interested at the moment in two of your customers who were in here on Sunday evening.'

'Oh, dear, it's about the murder, isn't it?'

'Afraid so, routine questions, you understand, Ted.'

'Of course.' his voice serious, no doubt remembering those other times when he'd helped them. Not only was he a good barman, he had proved himself to be discreet and had an excellent memory for faces in spite of the fact he must see several new customers coming into the bar over the weeks and months.

'I noticed that Mrs Bortoletto was in here on Sunday in the company of a man who has fairly recently come to live in Meadowbank.'

'Eric Noble; that's right. He's become one of our regular customers, mostly at the weekends.'

'So, Sunday was no exception?'

'No, he's usually here both Saturday and Sunday evenings.'

'Friendly chap?'

'I wouldn't say so; he's pleasant enough, Inspector, but not what you would describe the gregarious type.'

'Did you notice what time he left here?'

'I think it was around ten; I remember the time because we had a sudden surge of customers from the auction which wound up about then.'

'And Mrs Bortoletto?'

'She stayed on for a short while, but no more than fifteen minutes or so.'

'Thanks, Ted; as always you've been a great help. Incidentally,' he went on, 'had you ever seen Eric Noble before, before he came to Meadowbank I mean?'

'I have as a matter of fact; it was a few years ago –' pausing for a second as he attempted to recall when, '- yes, I remember; it was in 1998 and then again, a couple of years ago. Both times he was staying here.'

'The last time, Ted; can you remember which month?'

'Yes, it was in February, around the 14th, St. Valentine's Day. He was here for that weekend.'

'I realise 1998 is some time ago, but if you can remember roughly when it was.'

'It was in November, the beginning.'

'That's near enough. On these two occasions, was he with anyone?'

'Only the one, Inspector,' he answered, 'Mrs Bortoletto was with him the first time; I don't know whether she was married then.' he added with a complete lack of any guile in his voice.

Sandra Watson was in reception when Ian walked through on his way out of the hotel. She showed no surprise at seeing him which probably meant either she had noticed him talking to Ted or someone had told her; either way, it didn't really matter, at some point during this investigation it was more than probable they would meet.

'Inspector Ash, once again it would appear my hotel is being subjected to police presence.'

'I'm sorry if you find these visits an intrusion, Mrs Watson, but it is important in a murder enquiry for us to interview anyone whom we consider could assist us and we do make every endeavour to be discreet.'

'As I've mentioned on previous occasions, I really do not understand why you always make a beeline for my hotel. I read the article in the paper this morning and of course I recognised the name of the journalist. Carol Cliff!' she said scathingly, her voice rising an octave, 'I honestly don't know how on earth she gets away with the things she says. In my opinion,' obviously on a roll today, venting her spleen on the first person who would listen to her, 'her innuendos lower the tone of the newspaper; her column would be far more fitting in one of the tabloids!'

'Unfortunately,' Ian said, doing his utmost to halt the flow, 'there's nothing we can do to curb what any journalist submits, provided there is nothing libellous in the content.'

'That may be so, Inspector,' she commented dryly, 'however, that is no particular comfort to me and my husband; we are exercising a great deal of effort and energy in attempting to run a prestigious country house hotel, with up to now, an untarnished reputation. Also,' she added, her lips tightening in a thin red line, 'I have given my staff strict instructions not to openly discuss the recent events in Meadowbank.'

Having presumably conveyed to him everything she had set out to say, and with a dismissive nod, she moved away.

He wondered what her marriage was like; he'd only met her husband a couple of times, but he didn't think he would put up with her autocratic and demanding manner. Chris Watson had struck him as being the assertive type, certainly not one to be browbeaten.

He was thoughtful on the short drive back into town. Ted had been more than helpful; he had opened up a new lead in their enquiry which could suggest a link with the two murders. It had been a spur of the moment decision to ask him whether he had seen Eric Noble before and it had paid off. The relationship Eric Noble had been having with Katherine Peters ended in 1998 and could have been caused by his affair with Cordelia Bortoletto. And, equally important, according to Ted, when he had stayed at The Royal Oak around the 14th of February in 2005 he had been on his own. Katherine Peters had taken over the lease of the flat in Market Square on the 8th of that month; had he known this and if he had, would he have contacted her? Given his reluctance on the phone to meet her, Ian was inclined to doubt it. But, he further reasoned, if she had seen him in Meadowbank, wouldn't she have used the opportunity to approach him then and if not, why wait a further two years? Remembering her manner during the telephone conversation, could it have been she had only recently discovered something she could use to discredit him? As with most murder enquiries, there were far too many imponderables, all of which meant, as Graham had said the other day, more spade work.

***

Graham waited until five to put the call through to Oakland in California, taking into account the seven hour time difference. After his meeting with Bill Simms, he had put out a search into Franklin Bacall's background which had proved productive. Franklin Bacall had died in August 1997, reportedly from a drug overdose. From 1993 until the time of his death he had been a director of Stuart Computers in Oakland. The date of his marriage to Katherine Peters tallied with what they had already, but there was no mention of any divorce. There was something odd here, he thought, going over the various dates again. Eric Noble had led him to believe the last time he'd seen Katherine Peters had been at the end of 1998 and that they had lived together for at least three years or perhaps slightly more which, if true, meant that he must have been in the States around 1994 or 1995 up to the time she returned to England in January 1997, also returning and continuing to live with her until the breakup of their relationship the following year and yet he hadn't admitted he'd been there. Why? He must have realised he wouldn't be able to talk his way out of what he'd said, and if anything, insisting they had both conduced their affair in London even when it had been pointed out that Katherine had been in California for a good part of that time. He must have a strong reason for not wishing to disclose where he was living then. The résumé the office had come up with had been sketchy: he was born in Manchester in 1953 and, graduating from Manchester University with a degree in Computer Science in 1975, worked for IBM in Hampshire for seven years before taking up an appointment with the Standard Chartered Bank in Hong Kong and, according to the Personnel Manager, he left their employment in 1990 and it was at this point there was no trace of where he had been until 1997 when he started up his own business as a computer consultant and software specialist in London. Computers had to be the operative word, Graham decided, looking again at the report on Katherine Peters' first husband. Franklin Bacall had been a director of a computer company and, like Eric Noble, he also had graduated in Computer Science. If Eric Noble had worked for Stuart Computers it was feasible to suggest he met Katherine while he was over there.

Jean buzzed through to tell him she had the Managing Director of Stuart Computers on the line.

'Good morning, Mr Stuart,' he said, once she had put him through, 'good of you to take the time to talk to me.'

'That's no problem,' the distinctive Californian accent reaching him clearly, 'I thought it must be pretty important when your secretary told me who you were; we don't often get calls from the English police. How can I help you, Chief Inspector?'

'I'm hoping you can,' Graham said, 'we're conducting a murder enquiry here, Mr Stuart and there are a number of anomalies which have cropped up. First of all, I have to tell you who the victim was as there is every likelihood you would have known her.'

'Yes? I'm listening. This is beginning to sound ominous.' he added and Graham could recognise the concern in his voice.

'She was called Katherine Peters, Mr Stuart.'

'Katherine? Good Heavens! That's truly dreadful.'

'It is, yes. I apologise for having to break the news so suddenly, never easy over the phone, especially long distance.'

'Don't apologise, Chief Inspector. I won't say that hearing this hasn't been a shock because it has been. How was she killed?'

'She died by strangulation; this happened late on Sunday night,' Graham went on, deliberately giving him time to recover, sensing his distress, 'she had been living in Meadowbank for the last two years which has meant there was not a great deal known about her, resulting in extended searches being carried out on her background. We know she was married to one of your directors, Franklin Bacall, and had lived in

California for three years, returning to England in the January of 1997.'

'That's right.' he said, 'I don't suppose you knew, Chief Inspector, but Franklin was my brother-in-law.'

'We hadn't realised. We were aware only that he had died, Mr Stuart.'

'As you know that, presumably you will also know how.'

'A drug overdose.'

'Yes, all very sad; he had been diagnosed four months earlier with acute depression, only a matter of months after Katherine left him.'

'You say when she left him; does that mean they continued to live together up until she came back to England?'

'Oh, yes, my wife and I knew all too well their marriage wasn't going well, so neither of us were all that surprised, but Franklin just refused to admit there was anything wrong.'

'There was another man involved, wasn't there?'

'Yes, Eric Noble, he was on our payroll; the pair of them were not discreet, so it came as no great surprise when they both went.'

'We know of Eric Noble.'

'Ah.'

'And you're saying he worked for your company, Mr Stuart?'

'He certainly did. Not all that popular, could never understand what Katherine saw in the guy, but as far as we were concerned he knew his job alright.'

'How long was he with you?'

'About four years; we took him on in 1993, the year before Franklin and Katherine were married.'

'When he left, had he worked the requisite period of notice?'

'No, he didn't. One day he was here, Chief Inspector, and the following day he wasn't.'

'Which presumably meant he wouldn't have been given any reference covering the years he was with your company?'

'Too true, but all things considered, even if he had given us notice of wishing to terminate his contract, we wouldn't have supplied a reference, written or otherwise.'

'Although you were satisfied with his work?'

'This is all a bit delicate, Chief Inspector, but one or two of us on the Board had begun to have certain reservations about him. Nothing tangible, you understand, because if there had been we would have dismissed him. They were really no more than rumours; at least they started off like that, but it was only after he'd gone we began to suspect -'

'- yes?' prompting him, recognising his reluctance, but this could be something they should know.

'- er – suspect him of being involved in hacking into a number of our clients' accounts, but we've never been able to prove anything, so we had no alternative but to drop it. This sort of crime is unfortunately too common in our business, Chief Inspector.'

'And after he left your employment,' Graham asked, 'did the hacking come to an end?'

'Not immediately.'

'You mentioned that one or two on your Board had reservations about him.'

'Yes, that's right.'

'Was your brother-in-law one of them, Mr Stuart?'

'Not at first, even although a number of our clients had made complaints to him about their investment files being tampered with, but then Franklin was like that; he was always reluctant to actually point a finger at anyone. He was a bit of an ostrich in that way.' he added.

***

Ian took the call from Inspector Mason in Stockbridge shortly after five to tell him that Katherine Peters' car had been found.

'I'll be emailing our report through to you, Ian,' he said, 'but thought you would want to know immediately.'

'I appreciate that, Phil; I must admit it's been puzzling us for the last few days.'

'I bet it has; cars as a rule don't simply disappear.' he chuckled dryly. 'Anyway, you'll be interested to hear we've got the culprits. I've just finished interviewing the pair of them and their stories tally.'

'That was quick.'

'We were lucky, Ian; one of them carelessly left his student bus pass where he must have dropped it. He's called Robert Gaunt and the other one is Victor Glenn, both of them living in Stockbridge. Apparently, they were drinking in the Bridge Inn in Meadowbank last Sunday evening and missed the last bus back here. They had decided to walk to the main road and hitch a lift and, not knowing the geography of Meadowbank, had assumed they could take a shortcut along Riverside Lane to reach the Stockbridge Road, and when they found that wasn't possible, retraced their way back towards the centre of the town. They'd already noticed the Audi parked outside Bramble Cottage and when they passed it the second time it was still there but the lights had been switched off inside the house, and considered in their so-called infinite wisdom to take it. They were indignantly insistent they only wanted the car to get them back here, as if that made any difference to the indisputable fact they were still stealing.'

'So, did they just abandon the car, then?'

'In a manner of speaking, yes.' another chuckle, 'They ran out of petrol and were forced to leave it on a piece of wasteland about a mile short of Stockbridge.'

'Served them right.'

'Exactly. It's a quiet stretch of road along there; not many people about, probably explains why it has taken so long for it to be spotted, but at two this afternoon, a Mr Ralph Townsend was taking his dog for a walk, saw the Audi and became suspicious when there was no sign of any driver, and making a note of the registration number, gave us a call.'

'You're obviously aware of the results so far on this case, Phil?'

'Yes, we've been receiving regular updates here; it sounds like another complicated one for you all, Ian.'

'It's turning out that way,' he agreed, 'anyway, I'm glad the car turned up. It does explain something.'

'Yes?'

'Not much, but we know she went out on Sunday night, quite late as it happens, also where she went and would have taken her car, but although it arrived back at Bramble Cottage it doesn't prove she had been driving it.'

'I suppose not, Ian, but if it had been her killer they would have needed a key to get into the house.'

'Because of those two saying there had been a light on when they first went by?'

'Yes.'

'The key to the Audi and the ones to Bramble Cottage were all on the same key ring and were in her handbag, which she'd had with her when she was murdered.'

'I see,' Phil said, 'two steps forward and one step back, eh?'

'That's what it feels like.'

'Would it help if we checked the car for fingerprints and for anything which appears untoward before we arrange for it to be returned to Meadowbank?'

'If you would, Phil.'

'I daresay if there are any which didn't belong to Katherine Peters, they will have been obliterated by those young idiots.'

'I thought students were supposed to have more sense,' Ian remarked, 'our future generation and all that.'

'Hmmph. Unfortunately, we don't live in an ideal world and you'll always get one bad apple amongst them, although I must admit it was heartening to see they were more than a little taken aback when we took their fingerprints this afternoon; that shook them out of their swaggering bravado.'

'Perhaps they've learned their lesson.'

'Don't bank on it, Ian; from what I've seen since joining the service, youngsters of that ilk never do. They start early.' he added sourly.

***

'Katherine Peters' car has turned up, sir.'

'At last; where was it?'

'Stockbridge; on the outskirts.' Ian said, going on to give him the gist of what Phil Mason had told him and giving him his report which had come through a couple of minutes earlier.

'So,' Graham commented, having quickly scanned down the print-out, 'what sort of connotations do you put on this, Ian?'

'I think we have to accept that Katherine Peters used her car to drive up to the lodge, but although it made its way back to Bramble Cottage this doesn't necessarily exonerate Eric Noble; he could have either murdered her up at the lodge and, using her car, brought her body to Meadowbank ,or he could have waited and gone down later, having previously found out where she lived, rang her doorbell, persuaded her to come outside, perhaps using the pretext of having a further talk, suggesting they have a short walk along Riverside Lane and strangled her exactly where her body was found.'

'If the latter was the case,' Graham suggested, picking up from where he'd left off, 'it must have been before those two lads returned along Riverside Lane and noticed there were no lights on in the house.'

'And she would have already been dead, and as it was dark, they wouldn't have noticed the body. It wouldn't have given him much time to get as far away from Riverside Lane as possible; they wouldn't have stolen the car if there had been anyone about.'

'No, I'm sure they wouldn't. Forensic gave Bramble Cottage a thorough going over, finding only Katherine Peters' fingerprints which makes me believe there had been no-one else in there. If she had agreed to go out it would be natural for her to switch off the lights, I suppose.'

'Unless her killer, whether Eric Noble or someone else, arrived much later after the car had gone, he wouldn't have known it had been stolen assuming it was in the garage, all of which brings us back to the time of death.'

'I know, Ian; The Bridge Inn closes at eleven, add ten minutes drinking-up time and five minutes or so for those two to discover they'd missed the last bus and decided to take a shortcut, I reckon it would have been shortly after eleven-thirty when they first passed Bramble Cottage. We don't know what time she left the lodge, but she would have probably arrived home before then, but that's only a guess. But if so, she must have been inside Bramble Cottage when they first spotted the car, add a further twenty or twenty-five minutes before they passed it again. They are obviously well-practised at breaking into cars and starting up engines without the aid of keys which means it wouldn't have taken them long. I realise we're getting close to Dave's estimation of no later than twelve-thirty, but it's feasible.'

'Also,' Ian suggested, 'if it did happen that way it would have given her killer more time with the additive that the later it was, less chance of anyone either walking or driving along Riverside Lane.'

'I have to say that after talking to Andrew Stuart, who incidentally was Franklin Bacall's brother-in-law, Eric Noble is not emerging in a favourable light. We shall have to take a heavier line with the man, officially this time, but it will have to be later in the afternoon tomorrow after the press conference.'

'Do you think we should be considering Jack Corbett in a different light now we have the report on his background?'

'Perhaps. Up to now, he's been very much of a nonentity with no apparent motive, but it appears he's led a variable existence, spending more years unemployed and in prison than being gainfully employed in spite of a promising beginning; his father a lawyer, mother an opera singer, educated at Cheltenham Grammar School, and accepted as a student at the Guildhall School of Music and Drama before joining the stage agency in Islington where he met Katherine Peters. The downhill spiral seems to have started from when she left him; from then onwards one offence after the other: drugs, assault, theft, you name it, Ian, he's done the lot.'

'Perhaps the breakup of their relationship acted as a catalyst.'

'You mean it upset his equilibrium?'

'Yes, incapable of going straight; it could be significant that since leaving the stage agency in 1993 and starting with the circus a year ago, he's only had one job, working for another stage agency as a stuntman.'

'That's right; I see he reached the age of twenty-six when he served his first prison sentence, hardly classed as a young offender. It does make one wonder of what else the man could be capable. We don't know what was going through his brain when Katherine Peters made her appearance in "The Bridge" on Sunday.'

'Or how strongly seeing her again affected him; it could have pushed him mentally over the edge.'

'Possible; either way, he's someone else we can't dismiss, Ian. According to Allan Williams' report from today's interviewing, Jack Corbett did return at the time he told me when I spoke to him yesterday and spent the evening playing cards with three of the other circus workers, but who's to say he didn't go out later.'

'Perhaps no-one, sir. I see that he was the first to leave the tent where they were playing cards, this being corroborated by the three of them, saying he was going to have an early night, but this was about eleven, he would have had time to make his way to where she lived, strangled her, dragging her body to where it was found the following morning, and still get back to his caravan before midnight without the two guys he shares it with would have wrapped up the card game.'

'And,' Graham put in, 'we only have his word for it that Katherine Peters didn't tell him where she was going, also,' he added, 'that she didn't say where she lived. That's something we'll probably never know.'

'I realise this is all hypothetical, sir, but it could be credible.'

'I know,' he nodded, 'and it looks as though there is someone else we should be considering as I've no doubt you've noticed, having read Allan's report.'

'Cordelia Bortoletto.'

'Exactly,' turning to the relevant section,' she said it had been late, almost midnight when she arrived back at the circus and that she had spent the evening at The Royal Oak attending the antique auction first and then in the bar for the rest of the evening.'

'Ted was quite definite about when she left, sir. Also,' he added, 'I can vouch for the accuracy in part of what she's said about being at the antique auction and was already there when Jennifer and I arrived and did come into the bar. Ted said she only stayed on for about fifteen minutes after Eric Noble went, that was at ten. It wouldn't have taken her any longer than fifteen minutes to reach the circus grounds.'

'So,' Graham said, 'where was she?'

'It wouldn't have been the lodge, sir; otherwise Rachel Tilsly would have noticed her when she saw Eric Nobles and Katherine Peters out on the terrace.'

'She may have been there all the same, Ian.'

'Oh, you mean, she could have gone there and remained outside.'

'That's what I've been thinking, yes. You mentioned that Jennifer described her as being very Italian, and having met her, I would say she has the typical Latin temperament; passionately jealous, hot-blooded, perhaps hot-tempered as well.'

'Her friendship with Eric Noble isn't platonic.'

'Would you say she was capable of having such a relationship?'

'No.'

'We're agreed on that, then.' he smiled, 'Of course what we're saying, suggesting even, can only be hypothetical, but nonetheless, it should be considered. One solid fact remains though; there is the matter of almost two hours unaccounted for here. Where was she and what was she doing?'

'You would have thought, sir,' Ian put in, 'someone from the circus would have seen her returning. There was her husband of course, but I meant anyone else.'

'You're thinking of Beverly Clements?'

'Well, yes, I was. We don't have any motive yet for her murder and the chance of it being carried out by anyone not connected with the circus is a fairly remote one. She may have noticed someone, not necessarily Cordelia Bortoletto, but someone else acting suspiciously and, whoever it was, decided to silence her before she could, in the event of any possible police questioning, say anything incriminating –' pausing for a moment, trying to sort through what he was thinking, ' – sorry, sir, I'm not making much sense.'

'No, Ian, I think you are making a lot of sense. And,' he smiled encouragingly, 'I believe what you're saying about a possible motive is probably very close to the truth. Unless we discover anything to the contrary, it would be reasonable for us to think along the lines you've just mentioned. Given the unlikelihood of us having two murderers to deal with here, the killer, having already disposed of one person, may have been pre-empting just such an occurrence should the police decide to question the circus people in the course of their enquiry into Katherine Peters' murder.'

'Not everyone would have the technical knowledge of how to remove that rung on the ladder, would they, sir?'

'I would say no,' Graham nodded, 'the apparatus they use is designed exclusively for the circus; only those trained professionally would be permitted to assemble and dismantle the equipment in accordance with the rulings on safety which are, I understand, quite rigid. Also,' he went on, 'not only does this involve skill, but a certain amount of agility.'

'They would have to be pretty fit.'

'Yes, they would. Have you ever noticed when the circus arrives, how quickly the big top is in evidence, and within a matter of hours everyone has completed the work of erecting everything, including the tiered rows of seats and presumably other parts we don't even know about.'

'It certainly didn't take them long on Sunday; apparently they arrived at eleven-thirty and shortly after six-thirty that evening, Jack Corbett was in "The Market Inn".'

'Must be thirsty work, Ian.' he smiled. 'Going back to the Sunday night again,' he added, 'and your theory that Beverly Clements may have seen someone acting suspiciously.'

'Yes?'

'Well, there would have been a number of people walking about, say returning to their caravans; therefore it would have been quite normal to have seen them there, so whoever it may have been must have looked suspicious in some way.'

'Perhaps they were coming or going from a different direction.' Ian suggested.

'Yes, let's assume for a moment that Cordelia did go up to the lodge that night; she would have been driving of course, and had seen Eric Noble with Katherine Peters, then followed her back into Meadowbank. She would have seen where she lived, but wouldn't have stopped the car there, but driven the short distance to the circus grounds, left her car, and walked back to Bramble Cottage, dealt with Katherine Peters, and returned to the circus.'

'It's a pity Rachel Tilsly hadn't been able to hear what they had been talking about.'

'I know, Ian, but if someone had been standing fairly close to the terrace, they would have heard.'

Chapter Six

'I guess this morning was a total waste of time, Jimmy.'

'Only to be expected, considering the circumstances. You should know that we aren't exactly the flavour of the month. Press to many people, Carol, is a very dirty word.'

'Talk about closing ranks,' she continued to complain, remembering the expression of distaste on Beppe Bortoletto's face when she'd introduced themselves, 'he was positively hostile.'

'I know,' he grinned, 'anyway, I'll get us a couple of drinks.'

They had called into the Bridge Inn on their way back from the circus grounds with only some photographs Jimmy had taken to show for their efforts. She couldn't help feeling disgruntled; she had hoped she would have been able to glean something more of Meadowbank's recent events. At this rate, she thought, she would be lucky to scrape enough together to fill one column, never mind the usual three. If it wasn't for the press conference at three, she would have suggested to Jimmy that they head back to London.

'There's always the press conference.' Jimmy said, bringing two lagers over to their table.

'I wonder what this new guy will be like.'

'The formidable Chief Inspector Brenda Masters' replacement?'

'Yep.'

'You have to admit, Carol, you met your match with her.'

'I guess you're right.' smiling as she recalled the many spats she'd had with her. Although Carol had lived in England for over ten years she had never lost her edge; a New Yorker, living and working in a city where you had to quite literally think on your feet and never ever be without a speedy retort. Even being married to Rocky, who was English through and through, had done nothing to diminish what she knew to be her brashness, but then he was also a journalist, although she had always accepted a far superior one in the way he handled the craft of eloquently writing up his articles each week for 'The Sunday Times'.

'Jimmy,' she said taking an appreciative sip of her beer, 'would you describe me as a fanciful kinda person?'

'You, fanciful!' he laughed, 'You're the most down to earth person I know, Carol. What made you ask?'

'Because,' she answered, amused in spite of herself, 'each time I come to this town, I get the distinct impression of antipathy, an undercurrent, as though people were quite literally holding their breath, waiting until we'd gone, and they could get their town back to themselves. Oh, I don't know, I guess it's just small-town insularity, but I know one thing,' she added, 'if I had to live here, I would either go mad or die!'

'You're a city girl, Carol, but if it's any consolation, I feel the same way. We've overheard enough conversations to know that these people have an in-built dislike of 'foreigners'; it's as if we frightened them in some way, we're probably a threat to them.'

'In that our continual presence could change their otherwise predictable lives, you mean?'

'Yes,' he nodded, 'perhaps the younger generation feel differently and if they do, no doubt they move away.'

'You're probably right. These two murders, Jimmy,' she went on, 'they have to be connected, wouldn't you say?'

'It's stretching coincidence to think otherwise,' he agreed, 'even given Meadowbank's crime record over the last few years when a dozen people have been murdered and in each case they were connected.'

As on previous occasions, one of the interview rooms at the police station had been allocated for the press conference. Chief Inspector Graham Ford and Inspector Ian Ash were already there when the desk sergeant escorted them along the corridor. Carol recognised the reporters from the nationals, also the two from the Winchester "Chronicle" and Meadowbank's "Courier".

'Ladies and gentlemen,' Graham began, once they were all seated, Carol managing to position herself directly facing him from where she knew he would find it difficult to avoid eye contact, 'the reasons for calling a press conference this afternoon is two-fold,' pausing slightly as he glanced at each of them in turn, his eyes lingering for a fraction of a second on her. A good-looking guy she thought and by the firm set of his jaw a tough cookie, 'the first being,' he continued, looking away from her, 'is to give you a brief summary of what has transpired so far in our investigation into the two cases of murder; namely, Katherine Peters, a Meadowbank resident and Beverly Clements, a performer with the circus. We know how these two women were murdered, but we have yet to establish why; in other words we are looking for motives –'

' – Chief Inspector,' Carol interrupted, raising her hand to catch his attention, 'you've said *two* cases, does –'

' – Inspector Ash and I are conducting this meeting,' he said smoothly, the acerbity in his voice not lost on her, which she interpreted as a metaphorical slap on the wrist, 'any questions any of you may wish to ask will duly be dealt with, not in the middle of when either of us are talking. I trust that is understood. As I was saying, we need to find motives for why these two murders were committed which means our enquiries have to be extensive, entailing numerous interviews with anyone who may have known both victims. This takes time, which brings me to the second reason for calling this meeting, which is the continual 'overlapping' by members of the press quite literally following in our footsteps or, on occasion, pre-empting what has yet to be established, resulting in misleading reporting. Now,' Graham said, gesturing towards her, 'if you would like to continue with your question.'

'Thank you, Chief Inspector,' she answered, 'what I wanted to know is, although you mentioned two murder cases, does this mean they are not connected?'

'Until such time as we have conclusive proof we will be continuing to treat each one separately.'

'Is it true, Chief Inspector,' a reporter from one of the nationals asked, 'that one of the circus people had a drink with Katherine Peters on Sunday evening?'

'How the hell did he find that out?' Carol muttered under her breath, giving Jimmy a nudge with her elbow.

'Yes, we confirm she did.' he answered, overlooking Carol's raised hand, to point to the Winchester "Chronicle" reporter sitting behind her.

'Do you suspect this man to have been her killer?' he asked.

'At this stage of our enquiry there is nothing to indicate his guilt; he met the deceased early and we have witnesses from the circus to say he spent the remainder of the evening with them before retiring for the night.'

Determined he wouldn't ignore her this time, Carol put her hand up before he had finished, 'How do you know he didn't go out later, Chief Inspector?'

'He may have done, but so could a number of other people.'

'Do you have anyone specifically in mind?'

'What was the time of Katherine Peters' death, Chief Inspector?'

And so the questions continued, each one being answered briefly, either by the Chief Inspector or Inspector Ash, and Carol thought irritably, supplying nothing they didn't know already.

'Not satisfactory, Jimmy,' she said to him as they all filed out of the room, 'he gave nothing away.'

'Could be he hasn't got anything else.'

'Don't you believe it! Of course there's more. What did you think of the little pep talk, eh; I felt like a school kid being told off!'

'You don't look like a school kid,' he grinned, 'too much to say for yourself!'

'Okay. Okay. I was only talking metaphorically. He's a bit high-handed though. Talking down to us like that; we're only trying to sell newspapers and the public want to know what's going on.'

'I bet you were mad at being pipped at the post.'

'You mean by that guy from "The Telegraph" coming up with her meeting someone from the circus?'

'Yes, probably been ear-wigging in one of the pubs.'

'That's what *I* do, Jimmy and,' she added indignantly, 'I'm damn good at it!'

***

Eric Noble was standing in the open doorway of the lodge when Graham pulled up outside. He'd phoned him earlier to say there were further questions he needed to ask and having already met the man, knew in advance what his immediate reaction would be, but after considerable voluble protests of police harassment, he agreed.

'Good of you to take the time to see me, Mr Noble.'

'It would seem I didn't have a great deal of choice, Chief Inspector; you'd better come in.'

A man devoid of any social graces, Graham thought, following him into the lodge and towards the kitchen, preparing himself for a stormy few minutes.

'Since talking to you on Tuesday, a number of inconsistencies have emerged which concern much of the information you gave me.'

'You have nothing to support these so-called inconsistencies; if you have, they are pure fabrication.'

'On the contrary,' Graham said, keeping his voice level and looking closely at the man standing opposite; his rigid stance indicative of righteous indignation; the lower lip jutting out in defiance, 'the various facts we have collected over the last couple of days are conclusive evidence of these inconsistencies and I would suggest, Mr Noble, it would be in your best interests to comply, rather than going on the obverse. Do you think we could sit down,' he added, pointing to the chairs around the kitchen table, 'more conducive to conducting an interview of this nature.'

'Of course, Chief Inspector, feel free.'

'Thank you.' taking the seat nearest to him, 'First, I will refer to when you told me on Tuesday that you hadn't kept the meeting with Katherine Peters; your words being:' checking on the notes he had with him, 'you had changed your mind.'

'Which I had.'

'You may very well have changed your mind, Mr Noble, but it doesn't alter the fact that you did see her on Sunday. Was she waiting for you when you arrived home from "The Royal Oak"?'

'Whatever gave you that idea?'

'It's not an idea; you were seen, Mr Noble.'

A dismissive shrug was his only response.

'I have a witness who saw you and Katherine Peters together outside on your terrace; this is something you will find impossible to dispute.'

Another shrug.

'Mr Noble,' Graham said, 'there is nothing to be gained by you adopting this attitude and if you persist I have no alternative but to take you in for official questioning which will be recorded with the possibility of a charge for obstructing the police in their line of duty. Is that understood?'

'I don't see what I'm expected to say; what I told you on Tuesday was quite true; Katherine Peters called me and, as you already know, I agreed reluctantly to meet her, but afterwards I changed my mind. I didn't want to see her.'

'But she wanted to see you. Why? What was so important to her that she had, after a number of years, decided to get in touch with you?'

'I have no idea.'

'Surely she must have told you on Sunday night.'

'I didn't see her on Sunday night.'

'Very well,' Graham said, refusing to rise to his stubbornness because he felt that was what it was; the man knew that on this issue he was cornered; at some stage he would be forced to admit Katherine Peters had been here, 'in the event of you being questioned in a court of law, I would remind you that my witness is prepared to sign a statement to the effect you were both seen together on Sunday night, which will be treated as evidence.'

'You've only *your witness's* word against mine, Chief Inspector,' he emphasised.

'When did you first meet Katherine Peters?'

'What's that got to do with any of this?'

'Mr Noble, just answer the question.'

'I've already told you, but if you've forgotten, it was at the beginning of 1995.'

'And you met where?'

'In London.'

'I don't think so, Mr Noble; perhaps you would like to think again.'

'Why should I?'

'For the second time I'm going to remind you that Katherine Peters was not in London then; she arrived in the States on the 20th June 1994, having married Franklin Bacall on the 8th and didn't return to Britain until the 5th January 1997.

'There's something wrong there.'

'The dates I have given you are accurate, confirmed by Immigration, also by Stuart Computers in California.'

'Stuart Computers?' affecting a puzzlement which Graham thought wouldn't have fooled a ten year-old.

'Yes, the same company who employed you from 1993 until your abrupt departure in the January of 1997, at the same time as Katherine Peters left the States.'

'What's so important?' openly belligerence in his tone now.

'Everything I've mentioned so far, Mr Noble, has an importance and is relevant to our investigation into the murder of Katherine Peters. To withhold information as you have done has hindered us considerably in what we are aiming to achieve. The reasons why you left Stuart Computers when you did may have had nothing to do with your relationship with her, and your reluctance to misdirect us could have been because of your concern to avoid the re-opening of what was occurring during the time you were with them, but that doesn't come under our jurisdiction in England.'

All the time he had been talking there had been no change in his surly expression. He had remained where he was, his arms folded across his chest, the broad shoulders slightly hunched forward as he glared across the table at him. Graham had seen that look before many times, and the hostile body language spoke volumes, but it still didn't mean Eric Noble was the murderer. And if, as Ian and he had agreed, the same person had killed Katherine Peters and Beverly Clements, he or she would have needed to possess the technical knowledge of how to remove the rung and be sufficiently agile to climb up the ladder without being seen by any of the circus workers. Graham couldn't see him being either, but conversely it didn't indicate he was in the clear.

'We'll return to Sunday night,' he pressed on, 'as we know Katherine

Peters was here, I'll ask you once more, Mr Noble, why did she want to see you?'

'As she wasn't here, Chief Inspector, I can't tell you.'

'I presume you do realise the seriousness of your situation?' Graham asked him.

'I have an excellent lawyer.'

'I'm sure you have. Well,' getting to his feet and walking towards the door, 'I suggest you get in touch with him and he can then be present when we continue with our questioning.'

He said nothing, didn't even stand up and escort him to the front door. Another unsatisfactory interview, Graham thought, driving back into town. For the present it was stalemate and time to re-question Cordelia Bortoletto. He had deliberately chosen not to mention her name to Eric Noble; if he had, it was likely he would tell her and he wanted to avoid that, although it still wasn't clear what sort of relationship they had. All they did know, by picking up the threads from when Eric Noble returned from California in 1997, unless they had known each other further back, it was probable the affair had started during the months when he was still living with Katherine Peters. It could be they were thinking along the wrong lines here by believing there was only one murderer. Eric Noble and Cordelia Bortoletto could both be involved; certainly she would be more capable of tampering with the ladder. And the night Katherine Peters was murdered? Perhaps the first part of Sunday evening had been orchestrated by the pair of them; he had booked a table at "The Royal Oak" in advance, had eaten alone before going into the bar, thus making the meeting with Cordelia Bortoletto appear unplanned, while she had attended the antique auction as no doubt she had told Beppe, even going so far as to purchase a couple of items and then joining Eric in the bar. They had left separately as confirmed by the barman, except that instead of returning to the circus Cordelia drove to the lodge and, seeing another car parked outside, held back until Katherine Peters had left before going in. Eric told her the reason for Katherine's visit which could have been threatening to them both; to expose, not only their affair which would affect her marriage to Beppe Bortoletto in severing her lucrative lifestyle, but to reveal his business activities while he was with Stuart Computers. Knowing already where Katherine Peters lived in Riverside Lane, he went there, persuaded her to come outside, strangled her and partially concealed the body at the side of the lane. Had Beverly Clements seen him that night? This was something they might never know, but if she had, and to prevent the girl ever saying this if and when she was questioned by the police, Cordelia said she would deal with her.

A plausible hypothesis, Graham thought, but no more than that; the forthcoming meeting with Cordelia Bortoletto, provided she was taken by surprise, may throw up something to substantiate what they had collected so far. It was now too late to drive up to the circus grounds, realising they would all be preparing for the opening of that evenings' performance. The show must go on, he thought cynically, as he pulled into one of the parking spaces in front of the Station. With only a couple of days left before they moved on, Ian and he would have to move quickly while they were still in Meadowbank.

Graham hadn't wavered from his belief that Katherine Peters' murder was linked to her past. In spite of what they had learned about her, there were pockets in her life remaining a mystery, recalling what Ian had said about her clothes. Should they be considering them differently; not only as an indication she had lived a double life, but to something more sinister? A strong word, but he instinctively felt there had been something sinister about her. Blackmailer? More than likely. But what else had she been up to? This case, he decided, was sluggish; one step forward and two steps back. Not good, and with "the Warrior" breathing down his neck, frustrating.

Even the report they had received earlier from New Scotland Yard had held no surprises. The property Katherine Peters had rented in Notting Hill was little more than a *pied-à-terre*; apart from a backlog of statements for her current and deposit accounts with Lloyds and a few clothes, there was nothing else of a personal nature. Why had she kept on the mews house during the time she was married to Harold Maitland and had she gone back there after the divorce in 2002? She may have done; as far as the landlord of "The Hog's Head" and those regulars she used to have a drink with believed, she had been living there all the time. Ian had mentioned a neighbour; it could be worthwhile going back to Lansdowne Terrace, having another talk with her; she appeared to know when Katherine was expected to return, perhaps she knew more than that. A germ of an idea was beginning to grow in his mind; not a pleasant one, but what he was thinking could explain what she had been doing after she left the theatre in 2002 and may well have continued while she had been in Meadowbank.

And there was Harold Maitland to be considered. His alibi for Sunday evening had been checked; the head waiter and the bar steward both confirming he had been in the club all evening and had left, according to the concierge at ten, but as Ian and he had said, it would have been possible that instead of going home he had driven on to Meadowbank. Although, as New Scotland Yard had reported, his property in South Hampstead was in a relatively quiet road, but a neighbour may have seen or heard him when he arrived home. He couldn't be ruled out as a possible suspect for Katherine's murder; he would have had the motive for wanting her out of the way, but to suggest he was responsible for what happened to Beverly Clements was really out of the question. Nevertheless, they needed to check, as far as they could, when he returned home that night, whether around ten-thirty or some time later, before they could be entirely satisfied of his innocence. Easier said than done.

***

'This makes a change from the Bridge Café.' Letitia smiled, looking up from the menu she had been studying for the past five minutes.

'I used to come here often when we were living in Winchester.'

'You miss Winchester, don't you, Rachel?'

'Not as much as I did when we first moved to Meadowbank, but I look forward to when we can come back. Mind you, both Colin and Polly appear to be enjoying the change.'

'But not you?'

'Not really. Certainly my life is less hectic now; no housework, thanks to a tremendously efficient housekeeper, and with only the evening meals to cook.'

'You're sounding a bit down this morning.'

'Sorry, I don't mean to be; it's just – oh, I don't know – a number of things I suppose; these murders for a start, Letitia. What on earth is going on in that town?'

'I know what you mean,' she agreed, 'as you know I've been living there for almost three years and in that time – I counted them up the other day – there have been twelve murders altogether since I arrived.'

Twelve! Good Lord, I hadn't realised; that's a frightening thought, isn't it?'

'If you think about it, Rachel, yes, but best not to dwell on it; as my son would say: it would do your head in.'

'He would be right. Anyway, shall we order?'

They had spent the morning, once Letitia had collected some art materials she'd ordered, wandering around the specialist shops in The Square and Great Minster Street, finally stopping for lunch at "Roberta's Bistro", an elegant yet unassuming restaurant tucked away in one of the many cobbled streets overlooking the cathedral. It was a relief to get out of Meadowbank for a few hours; she had meant it when she'd told Letitia the effect the recent events were having on her; realising she was, as Colin had said, over-reacting, made no difference to the way she was feeling. She was obviously spending too much time on her own and silently vowed to make an effort to snap out of what was bordering on depression.

Letitia chose the salmon with a prawn and lemon herb sauce with new potatoes and vegetables and, while it sounded delicious, she chose instead the chicken breast with white wine, cream and mushrooms. The restaurant was beginning to fill up with lunchtime customers as it usually did at that time of day, and looking across the room she caught a glimpse of Eric Noble seated in one of the booths. She wasn't sure whether he had noticed her, but then for a fraction of a second their eyes met before he turned his head away. She had fully expected him to either come over to their table or at least give some sign of recognition, but he did neither.

He remained where he was, appearing to be engrossed in the menu.

'How strange.'

'What is?'

'Our new tenant, Eric Noble he's called; he moved into the lodge at the beginning of April; he's over there in the booth next to the mirror. I'm positive he saw me, Letitia, but perhaps I was mistaken.'

'I'm sure he did, Rachel.'

'How do you know?' taken aback by her tone, also by the sudden change in her expression.

'I can't be certain of course,' Letitia answered, 'but I would say he did see you; you are sitting directly across from him after all. No, Rachel, it wouldn't be a wild guess to say that I was the one he wanted to avoid.'

'You know him?'

'Unfortunately, yes.'

'Oh, dear; this doesn't sound good.'

'I don't intend to be so dramatic, Rachel;' she said quietly, 'it was all so long ago, and I never expected to see him again. Knowing he is now living in Meadowbank fills me with the utmost distaste. Quite frankly, the man is a shit!'

'Are you going to tell me what he did to make you feel so strongly?' placing a hand on her arm in an attempt to console her; it was apparent that whatever had happened must have been traumatic for her to react so intensely to his presence after a space of several years.

'I will tell you, Rachel,' she said at last, 'but after lunch if you don't mind. I don't want to spoil our meal; he's not worth it.'

Their lunch wasn't spoiled; by mutual agreement they kept their conversation light; inconsequential topics and avoiding all mention of the recent murders or even Meadowbank itself. It was obvious to her that Letitia was making every effort to act as she normally did and telling her about the latest email she had received from her son who seemed to be enjoying the time he was spending in Thailand along with a group of other backpackers. The food was excellent and they managed to round it off with the bistro's vanilla and lemon cheesecake which they both agreed was scrumptious.

'Coffee, Rachel?' she suggested as the waiter was taking their plates away.

'Please.'

Eric Noble, Rachel was relieved to see, had gone; his table now occupied by new customers. Had she been right, she wondered, in her reasons for not wanting to socialise with him when Colin had suggested inviting him over to the house for a drink. Perhaps. She hadn't mentioned to Colin that she hadn't taken to the man on the one and only time she had met him the day he moved into the lodge.

'The last time I saw Eric,' Letitia said when their coffee had been brought over, 'was in 1988.'

'Nineteen years ago.'

'Yes, that's right. We were living in Hong Kong then, Timothy was only five. We'd been there for six years, my husband was working for the Standard Chartered bank out there. They were good years; an extravagant colonial lifestyle, long before the handover of course, not that any of us ever considered how that would affect us; we were all young,' she added, stirring the coffee with a faraway look in her eyes, 'Eric worked for the same bank and it was inevitable in the relatively small expatriate community our paths would cross. Perhaps they wouldn't have though,' she added thoughtfully, 'if it hadn't been for a close friend of mine having an affair with him. Everything changed, for most of us, after that. Valerie was already married, but that didn't make any difference to her. Looking back, I doubt whether she could help herself; it was though he had cast a spell over her. It wasn't as if he ever demonstrated his feelings towards her, not in public anyway. I don't know whether their relationship could have been described as a passionate one, at least as far as he was concerned and the inevitable happened; her husband found out, which was hardly surprising; he would have had to be blind not to have noticed what was going on. When he confronted her, instead of denying she was involved with Eric, she owned up, told him she intended moving in with him.'

'Oh, dear.'

'I know,' shaking her head, 'Valerie was not behaving normally, also she was so confident that Eric wanted her, she completely ignored anyone's advice, even mine and I was her closest friend, her confidante I suppose you could say.'

'Sounds as though she was besotted by him.'

'Oh, she was. Anyway,' Letitia went on, 'she left Pete and, unannounced, arrived at Eric's apartment, complete with luggage.'

'You mean she hadn't discussed it with him?'

'No, apparently not. However, he invited her in, not with the intention of letting her stay, but to tell her to go back to her husband.'

'He didn't want her.'

'No; that was the last he wanted. Eric Noble was a womaniser, probably still is,' she added, 'and having a live-in girlfriend would have definitely cramped his style.'

'What a sad tale,' Rachel put in, trying to imagine what it must have been like, 'so what happened, did she go back to her husband?'

'It gets sadder, Rachel,' her voice so low she could hardly hear her, 'there had been another woman in the apartment, and this may have been what pushed her over the edge; experiencing rejection from a man she was passionately in love with, believing he returned that love, coupled with the evidence of being replaced by someone else. She phoned me and told me what had happened, also that she was going away for a few days to think things over.'

'She didn't go back to her husband, then?' Rachel asked, intuitively sensing the outcome.

'None of us knew where she went, Rachel, but three days later, her body was found on Lamma, that's one of the islands close to Hong Kong —'

'- how absolutely awful. How did she die?'

'The verdict was suicide, a drug overdose. She had been staying in a flat on the island; the police found this out by talking to the neighbours, but nobody seemed to know who owned it.'

'Presumably she must have known?'

'Yes, she must have done.'

'And they never found out?'

'No, I think the authorities lost interest once the verdict of suicide was confirmed; I don't know, Rachel and never will I'm sure.'

'She couldn't have stayed there indefinitely, could she, but then if she had intended to take her own life, that wouldn't have concerned her.'

'I suppose not. Even after all this time it still remains a mystery. Even although she was in an emotional state, Valerie was a practical person; I've always found it hard to accept she would have just given up like that.'

'What about Eric Noble; did he look remorseful at indirectly being responsible?'

'I've no idea,' she said, 'none of us saw him again; he left the bank the day before her body was found and apparently took a flight back to England on the same day.'

'Guilt?'

'I don't know.'

'But you think so, don't you?'

'You're very perceptive.' she smiled.

'Sometimes.' returning the smile.

'As to what I think; well, it's another I don't know. He had a good job with Standard Chartered with all the usual perks, including a luxury apartment in Mid Levels, in the same road we were living actually, with fantastic views across the water to Kowloon. He would have had to start again and, without any references that wouldn't have been easy. There was one strange thing which did emerge though.'

'Yes?'

'Valerie's luggage; it wasn't in the flat, in fact there was no luggage at all.'

'Could have been stolen.' Rachel suggested.

'Yes, we thought that might have happened, but her handbag was there; Pete told me that he didn't think anything had been taken; her passport was still there, also her wallet with a couple of credit cards and about five hundred dollars.'

'Strange.'

'Very.'

'It can't be all that comfortable for you knowing that Eric Noble is living in such close proximity.'

'No doubt I'll get used to that,' she said, 'perhaps he won't stay in Meadowbank for all that long. And,' she added, 'as it appears he has chosen to ignore me that suits me fine.'

'Letitia,' Rachel said, 'I've found what you've been telling me rather disturbing, not only because of what happened to your friend, but about him.'

'Yes?'

'It concerns Katherine Peters.' finding it awkward to explain without unnecessarily alarming her.

'Go on.'

'Well, on Sunday night I saw them both; they were out on the terrace at the back of the lodge. I had never met her, but when I watched the news the next evening and her picture flashed up on the screen, I recognised her.'

'My God!'

'I've been really worrying about this, you know, and couldn't decide whether I should mention it to the police or not, but then on Tuesday I had a visit from Meadowbank's Chief Inspector. He didn't say a great deal, except that he believed Katherine Peters could have driven up to the lodge on Sunday night and when I told him I had actually seen her with Eric Noble, he didn't sound all that surprised.'

'You're not still worried are you Rachel?'

'I don't know whether I should be. Colin thinks I'm overacting, and he could be right.'

'I really don't know what to say; maybe I shouldn't have told you about Valerie.'

'I realise this is not a sensible question, but would you consider Eric Noble to be a dangerous person?'

'It's quite a good question, actually; I suppose it depends on circumstances. What I mean is, a perfectly well-balanced and mild-tempered man, or woman, could react in a way which could harm someone else if they considered they were being placed in a compromising or a threatening position. As far as he is concerned, well, to dislike the man as much as I do, doesn't mean he would be capable of carrying out an aggressive act such as murder.'

Chapter Seven

By mid-morning the newsagents on the square had sold out on "The Courier", Meadowbank's weekly newspaper; not that there was anything new about the murders they hadn't already read in the nationals, most of which had been discussed at length by the regular customers who frequented the two pubs. It was as if, Brian thought, fastening back the shutters of the Market Inn at eleven-thirty, people couldn't get enough to feed their insatiable appetite for what to him was tantamount to peeping through keyholes and preparing himself for more home-spun philosophy from his band of cronies. He could have written the script for them, so predictable were they with their varying degrees of indignation at, as one of them had come out with the previous evening, having their lives violated again by being publicly exposed.

There they were; standing patiently outside waiting for the door to be opened, Friday mornings being no different from any other morning to them, each of them having already enjoyed at least a good ten years of retirement. Not that he was complaining. They were good fellows, appearing quite happy to spend their days they way they did; lunchtimes, the first to arrive and the last to leave, afternoons spent either in their allotments or getting their heads down before the evening session when their never-ending speculations would occasionally be interrupted by a game of dominoes.

'I told you, didn't I,' one of them said as soon as their beers were placed in front of them and they had taken their first appreciative sips, 'that no good would come of this circus coming here?'

'What's the circus got to do with the price of chips?'

'Bert, that was a crass remark, if you don't mind me saying so.'

'I wasn't being crass,' for a fraction of a second a look of hurt on his weather-beaten face, 'you know what I mean anyway.'

'Bert's right, though, Fred,' the other one put in, 'what has the circus got to do with these murders?'

'In my opinion,' Fred replied before taking a second sip of his beer, 'I think it has a lot to do with them.'

'How?'

'How?'

'Yes, Fred, just because you object to them being here, doesn't mean what's been happening is their fault.'

'I don't know about you two,' he said, 'but there are times when I don't think you see any further than your own noses! Not only was that young trapeze artist murdered, but according to what I heard, one of the circus workers was in The Bridge last Sunday evening having a drink with Katherine Peters. So, what I'm saying is, if they hadn't been in Meadowbank, it probably wouldn't have happened, at least not here, giving our town a bad name.'

'Who told you about them having a drink, Fred?' Bet asked him.

'Bill Knowles, he's a regular customer in The Bridge, has been for years.'

'You should have been in the police force, Fred.' George quipped.

'I think a lot, I do; you should try doing that sometime. Anyway,' he went on, 'talking about the police, I saw that new Chief Inspector drawing up alongside where the circus vehicles are parked this morning and that, according to Bill, is the second time he's been there.'

'Well, as the girl was murdered there, he would have to investigate the crime, wouldn't he?' Bert calmly pointed out.

'Police procedure, Bert. Police procedure. *Normally*,' he emphasised, 'routine questioning, searches, that sort of thing, would be done by a sergeant and his team together with an inspector, but Chief Inspector Graham Ford, is of a higher rank.'

'When Brenda Masters was our chief inspector, Fred,' George reminded him, 'she was always present at the scene of the crime. So, why is he so different?'

'The answer is obvious.'

'Is it?'

'Yes,' Fred said, 'these two murders are connected which means it is probably being treated as a major crime.'

'Talking about major crime,' Bert said, interrupting his rhetoric, 'those two reporters from London have just come in.'

'Thought they would have gone by now,' Fred grumbled, 'there can't be much else for them here.'

'You would have thought so,' Bert said mildly, his tone indicating he was losing interest in what members of the press may or may not be up to, his attention being caught by the gnarled figure of their old friend, Charlie Hobbs, standing in the open doorway.

'Over here, Charlie!' waving to him.

Charlie Hobbs, gardener on the Tilsly Estate for a good forty years, having adjusted his eyes from the brilliant sunshine out in the street, strode over to them.

'Surprised to see you here at this time of day, Charlie.' Fred remarked, making room for him at the bar.

'Had to pick up some plants at the nursery for Mr Tilsly, then thought as it was my dinnertime I'd call in here for a beer before getting back.'

'We've just been talking about what's been going on in Meadowbank this week.' George said conversationally.

'Not just in the town either,' Charlie nodded his head, 'that new Chief Inspector's been to the lodge; last evening it was. I was about to finish when he turned up.'

'I wonder why.'

'It doesn't take much guessing, Fred; you've said often enough that Eric Noble was a quiet one.'

'You mean he's a suspect?' Bert answered, and for once lowering his voice.

'Now, Bert,' he answered, 'that sort of suggestion could be taken as slanderous, you know.'

'What do you think, Charlie?'

'Don't know what to think,' Charlie shrugged his shoulders, 'seems a decent sort. Nothing wrong with keeping yourself to yourself, Fred. Best way sometimes.'

***

'So, Chief Inspector,' Cordelia Bortoletto called out to him as he pulled up beside a brand new Peugeot off-roader, which he reckoned could very well belong to her, 'who have you come to interrogate this time?'

'Good morning, Mrs Bortoletto,' Graham said, walking over to her, 'it is to be hoped that the questions I've been asking are not being interpreted as such. They have all been,' he added, 'purely of a routine nature.'

'Really?' the tilt of her head and the speculative expression on her face clearly displaying her disbelief.

'Mrs Bortoletto,' he said, there are a few questions I would like to ask you regarding last Sunday.'

'Why Sunday; I thought you were investigating what happened here on Monday?'

'Is there somewhere we could sit down,' he asked, ignoring her question, recognising it for what it was; an attempt to mislead him. Her husband would have told her the reason for the first visit and he had no intention of encouraging her, 'more comfortable than standing in the middle of a car park.'

'We can use the ticket office;' pointing over to where she had been on Tuesday morning, 'it will be empty at this time of day.'

Once they were seated, Graham wasted no more time in skirting round the edges with her for what he wanted to know, deciding a more direct approach would be best.

'I understand you told Sergeant Williams when he was here on Wednesday that you spent the evening at The Royal Oak Hotel and that you had returned here at midnight. Is that correct?'

'Of course.'

'It is only a fifteen minute drive back to Meadowbank from the hotel, Mrs Bortoletto.'

'I suppose it is.'

'You were having a drink with Eric Noble in the hotel bar and after he left at ten, we have it on very good authority that you also left about fifteen minutes after he did.'

'Eric Noble.' she repeated, 'Was that his name, I didn't know.'

'You had never met him before? I would suggest,' he warned, 'you carefully consider the importance of being accurate.'

'I don't understand.'

'Had you met Eric Noble before?'

'I am a married woman, Chief Inspector.'

'You haven't answered my question.'

'The answer is no, I hadn't met him before. He was just someone in the bar and we got into conversation, that was all, and he didn't tell me his name and I wasn't sufficiently interested in asking.'

'Where did you go when you left The Royal Oak?'

'I've told you;' a chink in the little game she was playing, the switch in the questioning surprising her, 'I came straight back here.'

'In that case,' he persisted, taking advantage of the quick flash of anger, 'why did it take you so long?'

'It didn't; whoever told you I left shortly after ten was mistaken.'

'Did you go somewhere else first?'

'Although I've been to Meadowbank a few times, I don't know anyone who lives here and I'm not in the habit of frequenting pubs, so there would have been nowhere for me to go.'

'When you returned to the circus grounds at the time you've said, were there many people around?'

'A few.'

'Did you speak to anyone?'

'I may have called out to one or two to say goodnight.'

'Was one of them Beverly Clements?'

'Beverly?'

'Yes, Beverly; she had apparently been watching a video with two of her friends and would have been returning to her caravan around that time.'

'No, I didn't see her.'

'Who did you see, Mrs Bortoletto?'

'Oh, I'm not sure; it was dark.'

'There would have been some lights on though.'

'Of course.'

'So you can't remember?'

'There was only Marcus; he was just leaving our caravan, he and Beppe had been playing chess for most of the evening and the only other person was Jack.'

'Jack Corbett?'

'Yes, but then you've already met him, haven't you, Chief Inspector?'

'Whereabouts was he when you saw him, Mrs Bortoletto?'

'He was actually in Riverside Lane.'

She was lying. The woman was no actress. Graham had interviewed too many people not to recognise when he was being deliberately fed with a cobbled together explanation, all too often in an effort to extricate themselves from a tight spot. It was impossible to ignore the signs which were providing him with precisely what he wanted. He could now increase the pressure, something he hadn't done so far in this investigation, even when interviewing Eric Noble, but he instinctively felt that the woman sitting across the table from him had a totally different agenda from him. According to what he had learned from Stuart Computers, Eric Noble had been systematically infiltrating their clients' portfolios, presumably for his own personal and financial gain, while, given the Latin temperament of Cordelia Bortoletto, and from what she had divulged so far, he didn't think he was wrong in saying she operated on a high emotional level, not for money, but the need to possess and in this case, Eric Noble; a man who had reached the age of fifty-odd without committing himself. He had dumped Katherine Peters at a point where she probably thought he would marry her, his next move had been to take up with Cordelia, their affair such as it was, appearing pretty one-sided. She appeared to be comfortably well off; a husband who possibly had chosen to overlook her indiscretions and sufficient free-time to indulge in them. Could it be, he wondered, she guarded this situation jealously, suspicious of any woman he might show any interest in, especially if they happened to be an ex-girlfriend. If he was right and she had followed him back to the lodge and had seen him with Katherine Peters, had this affected her to such a degree as to physically remove her from the scene permanently? Just how unbalanced would a person have to be to go to such lengths? But then, that wasn't their domain; only the psychiatrists would be able to supply the answer.

'Where exactly was he in Riverside Lane,' picking up from where he'd left off, 'can you remember?'

'I can't remember *exactly*.'

'Well, it is quite a long lane; how far away from the circus grounds was he when you saw him?'

'For goodness sake, does it matter?'

'It could. As you are aware there are a number of houses, the last one ending about quarter of a mile before the beginning of Riverside Park; that may help to jog your memory.'

'Oh, about half-way along, I would say.'

'He was walking?'

'Of course he was.'

'And coming back to the circus grounds?'

'Yes.'

'But you didn't stop to give him a lift?'

'Why should I have; he didn't have much further to go.'

'Mrs Bortoletto,' Graham said, 'would you be prepared to sign a written statement to that effect?'

'Surely I won't be expected to do that.'

'It's inevitable you will be asked.'

'This is positively ridiculous; don't you believe me?'

'It is not a question of disbelieving you; it is part of normal police procedure during a murder enquiry.'

'How much longer do you intend to *hold* me here, Chief Inspector? I have other things to do, you know, than sit here all morning being subjected to this barraging.'

'There are a few more questions I would like to ask you.'

'Go on, then, I'm listening.' shrugging her shoulders.

'You have told me you had never met Eric Noble before last Sunday –'

'– which was true.'

'I would dispute that, Mrs Bortoletto. Nine years ago, you spent a weekend in his company at The Royal Oak.' watching as the colour drained from her face; she hadn't expected that, wondering how she was going to react, but this time she remained silent, 'Although you didn't share the same room, you were seen together in the restaurant and in the lounge bar. What I would like to know,' he went on when she still didn't say anything, 'why you denied knowing him.'

'I had my reasons.'

'Which were?'

'They were personal.' she snapped, the colour gradually returning.

'In a murder enquiry whether they were personal to you is immaterial.'

'I've been – I am having an affair with him –'

'– Mrs Bortoletto,' his turn now to interrupt, 'at this stage of our enquiry that is of no interest to us. On Sunday night you followed him back to the lodge, didn't you?'

'I may have done.'

'Did you?'

'Yes,' a further flash of defiance as she looked at him, 'but when I reached the gates, I decided it wouldn't be such a good idea, so I came back here. As I've said it was late.'

'It still doesn't account for the length of time it would have taken you to drive back into Meadowbank; as you know, the lodge is only minutes further along the road from the hotel. I would suggest, Mrs Bortoletto, when you saw there was someone with him that evening, you waited until she was leaving and followed her to where she lived. I shouldn't need to add that the woman you had seen was Katherine Peters who, in less than a couple of hours later, was murdered.'

'You're saying that I murdered her! That is preposterous!'

'I'm not saying that, Mrs Bortoletto, but did you? Were you so eaten up with jealousy, you took it upon yourself to dispose of her? Is that what happened?'

'I will not allow myself to be browbeaten in this way.'

'It is not my intention to browbeat,' Graham said, 'I am merely trying to get some truthful answers from you.'

'I have told you the truth. I have no reason to lie. No reason at all.'

'Did you know Katherine Peters?'

'Of course not.'

'Perhaps you knew of her?'

'How?' not realising she was falling into the trap he'd set for her.

'Eric Nobles may have told you. Prior to meeting you, it is our understanding he had been in a relatively long relationship with Katherine Peters, therefore it would be reasonable to suggest he may have mentioned her name to you.'

'Well, he didn't.'

'On Sunday night,' he pressed on,'did you overhear what Eric Noble and Katherine Peters were talking about?'

'No.'

'Why not; they were both outside on the terrace; I would have thought anyone standing reasonably close enough to them would have been able to hear their voices.'

'Well, I didn't.'

'Were they whispering then?'

'No; I just couldn't make out what they were saying.'

'So you did see them?'

'I must have done if I was there.'

'Were you there, Mrs Bortoletto?'

'I've already told you I was.' she snapped back, showing the first signs of being careless; up to now every word she'd uttered had been measured, every response calculated, without actually admitting or committing herself to anything which could be used against her. Was she beginning to weaken, he wondered.

'You have only told me you reached the gates of the lodge and, having changed your mind, carried on back to Meadowbank. You didn't say you got out of the car and walked up the drive towards the lodge.'

As with Eric Noble, an answering shrug.

'What were they saying?' he repeated.

'I don't know. I wasn't interested, besides I felt I was eavesdropping and didn't want them to see me.'

'If that was the case why did you bother walking up to where they were?'

'Curiosity, Chief Inspector. Surely, even you have been curious at times.'

'A signed statement will be required from you, Mrs Bortoletto, covering the time when you left The Royal Oak until you came back here; as I said a few minutes ago this is routine police procedure. Could you therefore call into the police station sometime this afternoon; it shouldn't take more than half an hour to complete.'

'I suppose so.' another shrug, 'So tedious.'

'Anything of a routine nature invariably is, but especially in a murder investigation, crucial.'

'How pompous you English police are!' standing up and pushing her chair back irritably.

The irony in her parting words wasn't lost on him, wondering how she would describe her own country's police.

***

Déjà vu, Ian thought, driving into Lansdowne Terrace and, parking in front of number thirteen walked up to the house next door and rang the bell. She took a good five minutes to come to the door, but he waited, remembering she wasn't too nimble on her feet.

'You were here on Tuesday, weren't you?' frowning up at him over the rim of her spectacles, a copy of "The Times" in one hand, folded open at the crossword page.

'I apologise for disturbing you, madam,' quickly giving her one of his cards before she had the chance to close the door in his face.

'Meadowbank Constabulary,' she read out, 'Meadowbank was where they found Miss Peters.'

'That's right, madam; I'm involved in the investigation into her death and the reason I was hoping to have a word with you was in the hope you may be able to tell me a little about your neighbour.'

'You'd better come in,' opening the door wider for him, 'I had just made some fresh coffee, Inspector, would you like a cup?' leading him into her kitchen; a sunny room, double glass doors opening out to a stone-flagged terrace.

'I had no idea what had happened to her,' she said, once she had introduced herself, 'I think I must have been the only person in the neighbourhood who didn't; in fact, it wasn't until yesterday when I had lunch at "The Hog's Head" as I usually do on a Thursday, that I heard.'

'How well did you know her?'

'Apparently not as well as I had thought, Inspector.' she said dryly.

'You mean because of her having a second home?'

'That is exactly what I mean. Obviously she must have had her reasons for not mentioning it, but I can't help feeling it's all rather odd.'

'Were you living here when she moved in next door?'

'I was, yes; but only two months before; I bought this house at the time of my retirement in November 1998.'

'She had only been living in Meadowbank for the last two years,' Ian explained, 'and although we have been able to piece together a good part of her background, there still remains a period of three years from the time of her divorce in 2002 to when she arrived in Meadowbank.'

'You say she was divorced, Inspector?' a puzzled expression on her face as she thoughtfully stirred her coffee.

'She hadn't told you she was married?'

'She did, yes, but she said he'd died.'

'That would have been her first husband, Miss Bennett; he died in 1997.'

'So obviously she re-married; when was this, Inspector Ash?'

'In April 1999.'

'How very strange; yet, she continued living in Lansdowne Terrace and it looks as though nobody around here was aware of this.'

'She had, through both her marriages, continued to use her maiden name. During in particular, from when she married in 1999 up until her divorce in 2002, was she living on her own, Miss Bennett?'

'As far as I'm aware.'

'Did she have many visitors?'

'I suppose you mean men friends?' giving him an old-fashioned look and one he had no difficulty in reading. Elspeth Bennett may not be agile physically, but during the short time he'd been talking to her, it had become quite apparent she had a keen brain.

'Well, yes.'

'I would say Miss Peters had a great number of them; of course I have no idea what kind of relationship she had with any of them, but she was an attractive woman –' leaving her sentence unfinished.

'You knew she was an actress?'

'Oh, yes, she was with the Esther Summers Theatre in Guildford, had done for a while.'

'Miss Bennett, she left them in 2002.'

'The same year as her divorce.'

'Do you remember noticing any change in her routine from that time?'

'Rather difficult to say, you know; she had always been away a great deal which after a while seemed normal behaviour, but there was something I did notice around then.'

'Yes?' prompting her, but without putting on any pressure; what she was going to say could be one of the missing links they had been looking for.

'Well,' she started to explain, 'it was when sometimes she wouldn't take her car.'

'But you knew she was away?'

'That's right,' she nodded, 'a car would come for her and then bring her back later.'

'The same car?'

'Occasionally.'

'What about the driver, Miss Bennett? Were you ever able to get a glimpse of him?'

'Not really,' she admitted, for the first time showing reluctance to say much more, but he had to press on, 'you see they were actually limousines, always black with the windows darkened, making it practically impossible to make out who was inside them, they were no more than outlines actually.'

'Were they chauffeur-driven, Miss Bennett?'

'I should have known better than to attempt to hold anything back from you.' smiling for the first time.

'You know where they came from, don't you?'

'Yes,' she sighed, 'I'm afraid I do, Inspector Ash; they were from Whitehall; in other words, government owned.'

'May I ask how you can be so certain?'

'Because I used to work in Whitehall; I was a secretary in the foreign minister's office for over twenty years, Inspector and I recognised them. Although it is ten years since I retired, some of the older models continue to be in use.'

'I expect you have drawn your own conclusions by now, Miss Bennett?'

'Sadly, yes, but you don't need to concern yourself about me ever mentioning this to anyone; you will realise of course that I had to sign the Official Secrets Act.'

'Yes, I realise that and thank you for being so frank; what you've told me has been helpful.'

He was not expecting the next part of his morning to be as fruitful, all too aware of the need to exercise discretion; the last they wanted was an irate Harold Maitland putting in an official complaint to Bill Simms.

The drive to South Hampstead was not an easy one, but within half an hour of leaving Notting Hill, he was approaching Fairfax Road and, as New Scotland Yard had reported, the street where Harold Maitland lived was a quiet one; tree-lined with a small park for residents facing the half dozen properties. The house on the right-hand side of Harold Maitland's appeared to be empty; a For Sale notice was fixed to the gate, but there was someone in the garden, hearing the sound of a lawnmower from behind the tall beech hedge which shielded the property from the pavement. Making a pretence of jotting down the name of the estate agents, he waited in the event of whoever was there would notice him. It didn't take long; two, three minutes, no more, and a woman about his own age drew level to where he was standing and, turning off the lawnmower, walked over to the gate.

'Hello;' she smiled, 'are you interested?'

'I could be.' Ian said.

'It hasn't been on the market for very long, actually; we only moved out on Wednesday, so I thought I had better make an effort to tidy up the garden.'

'It should get snapped up; it's in a great position, especially for London.'

'I hope so.'

'What are the neighbours like?'

'Don't really know them,' she said, 'everyone keeps themselves very much to themselves.'

'No rowdy parties, then?'

'No, nothing like that. In fact, I hardly ever saw the man who lives next door to us,' pointing to Harold Maitland's house, 'all we knew was that he was somebody frightfully important, something to do with investments; way above my head.' she added.

'You've been lucky I would say,' he fabricated, 'one of my neighbours keeps very late hours, waking me up practically every other night when he comes back from wherever he's been.'

'Poor you,' she sympathised, 'Mr Maitland isn't like that. He does get home quite late sometimes, but he's always very considerate; no banging of doors or anything like that. For instance,' she went on as though she was in no hurry to get on with her mowing, 'it was so warm on Sunday night I found it impossible to get to sleep and I heard his garage door closing when he came home; I don't know whether you've noticed, but his house is the only one near here with an up-and-over garage door and I would say it is practically impossible to close without making any noise, however slight.'

'It was a warm night, wasn't it?' Ian said, keeping his voice casual and scarcely believing what she had so freely given him.

'I know, even at that time, at three in the morning.'

'You didn't think it might have been a burglar; not that they would have been able to drive into the garage?' he asked jokingly.

'Actually,' she smiled, it did cross my mind and I must admit I did take a peep out of the window, but it was Mr Maitland alright; he had to walk back down the path to close the gate. Anyway, as I've said, he's okay, so anyone who buys this place certainly won't have any problems with him, or with any of the other neighbours either.'

***

Cordelia's main concern after Graham had gone was not primarily for herself, but for Beppe's reaction once he learned she was being considered as one of their suspects; this was something she wouldn't be able to conceal from him, but first, before she told him, she must get in touch with Eric. Although the Chief Inspector hadn't said, she was sure he would already have been in touch with him as, apparently, the police were aware Katherine Peters had been at the lodge on Sunday night; Eric needed to know what she'd been more or less coerced into admitting. He wasn't going to be pleased but she was confident in being able to quench the inevitable anger. She had known him long enough to realise that Eric was, at the best of times, on a short fuse; the slightest aggravation could rapidly flare up into one of rage, often taking hours to totally extinguish. She'd always found a certain irony in their two personalities; she, Cordelia Bortoletto, a hot-blooded Italian was expected to have outrageous bursts of temper, not an Englishman, who she considered should have the traditional traits of being cool, calm and collected. There had been times when he had behaved like one of her own countrymen; she had once remarked on this to him and had been surprised to find he didn't share her amusement at the anomaly.

When she had seen Eric with her on Sunday night, his body language had been sufficient to indicate he had been quite literally approaching boiling point and as she had stood at the side of the lodge, partially concealed by one of the lilac trees lining the edge of the lawn, she had wondered how long it would take for him to lose his temper, but he hadn't.

The Chief Inspector had not been far away from the truth when he had practically accused her of being there and although she had finally admitted it, he didn't know everything. He hadn't been there after all, but she had. He hadn't listened to what they had been saying, but she had, and that was something he would never learn from her. It could be that to him, she represented a neat conclusion to what had every appearance of being a double murder case. She remembered what her father used to say in his pontifically archaic way: "everyone has a boss, Cordelia; you should always remember that." and no doubt it was the same with senior police officers; Chief Inspector Graham Ford would have a boss, someone he would have to report to, which ultimately meant there would be pressure put on him to wind up his investigation as quickly as possible. Well, she decided, he's not going to use me as his scapegoat. She wasn't a murderess. And for him to further suggest that she could have been compelled by jealousy was positively offensive, wondering how he had fared with Eric if, as she thought, he'd questioned him.

Eric hadn't been like himself when she had met him on Sunday; his mind had obviously been elsewhere. More than once when she said something to him, he was uncharacteristically slow in answering. It had been his idea to have a drink when she'd finished her bidding at the auction, but then after only about fifteen minutes or so, he said he had to get back as he had an early start the following morning. She hadn't believed him, convinced he was meeting someone else and to her that could only be one person; Katherine Peters. She had known for two years that she had moved to Meadowbank and when Eric told her earlier in the year he was taking his business out of London and was in the process of renting a property in the same town, the first seeds of her suspicions were sown. She had tried to ignore them; his manner towards her hadn't changed and commonsense told her that it was unlikely he and Katherine Peters would get back together again having listened to his reasons for leaving her all those years ago, but they were like persistent little demons, refusing to budge and when she had seen the pair of them together out there on his terrace, they were instantly confirmed; that was, until she heard what they were saying.

"You can throw as much dirt as you like about me, Katherine," he had said, "you know as well as I do you have nothing to substantiate about my activities in Oakland -"

" – you're bluffing; all I'm asking is for a share of your dishonest gains."

"I am not bluffing." Even although she couldn't see his face, the searing impact of his words sent a shiver down her spine, not wanting to hear any more, but she was transfixed, physically incapable of moving away.

"In case it has slipped your memory, I work alone and that's why I know you're lying. Now," he'd continued, lowering his voice, but she could still make out what he was saying, "if you know what's good for you, you'll leave; I didn't invite you here –"

"- you agreed to meet me –"

"- and I have no intention of making any deal with you;" continuing as if she hadn't spoken, "to me, Katherine, you are a pest."

"You'll regret this, you know."

"Not as much as you will when I make it known your attempt at respectability in this town is a complete sham."

"What *are* you talking about?"

"You want me to spell it out for you; well, I will; when I first met you, Katherine, it didn't take me long to realise you had a personality problem, bordering in fact on schizophrenia and that was the reason I decided to end our relationship -"

" – you ended it because of that Italian woman!"

"You will leave Cordelia's name out of this. What I've said is true and you know it. What you don't seem to realise," he went, speaking quickly now as if wanting to come to the end of what he was saying, "people talk and some years ago I heard your name mentioned and what they were saying, although perhaps predictable, was not pleasant. It would seem you have been moving in some highly influential circles over the past number of years, starting from when you took out the lease on the mews house in Lansdowne Terrace, using the property as your base for earning considerably more than you did as an actress. How would you describe yourself these days, Katherine; a bit too old to be using the title of call girl, how about a high-class prostitute? And," he had added, not allowing her to interrupt him this time, "please do not insult my intelligence by denying it. What I'm saying are the facts, all of which I can prove; also, I know who is procuring your clients. I wasn't exactly thrilled when I learned that you also had a home here, but I hoped if we had at any time seen each other you would behave in a civilised way."

A shuffling of feet on the wood decking of the terrace muffled any response she may have made, and stepping further back into the shadows, Cordelia made her way to the car. In less than five minutes, she heard a car door banging, followed by the crunching of tyres on the gravel. She waited until the car emerged on to the road, turning right into Stockbridge Road, before starting up her engine and, keeping a reasonable distance between them, followed her into Meadowbank, turning right at Saint Steven's church along Bridge Street and right again into Riverside Lane, slowing down as the car turned into the short driveway of one of the houses on the left-hand side.

Almost a week ago, Cordelia thought, dialling Eric's mobile number, and she hadn't been able to dismiss from her mind the ironic parallel with Christine Keeler who had made headline news in every English newspaper. The Profumo scandal in the early sixties had shocked and embarrassed the government when it emerged that a nineteen year-old aspiring model had a brief affair with the Secretary of State for War while simultaneously being sexually involved with a Soviet Naval attaché; both men being introduced to her by Stephen Ward, a London osteopath and socialite, who, at the time of his trial, believing he was being used as a scapegoat, committed suicide. Christine Keeler had lived in the two worlds of politics and the arts. Was that what Eric had meant, Cordelia wondered, when he'd accused Katherine Peters of moving in highly influential circles.

'Cordelia; where are you phoning from?' Eric asked as soon as he heard her voice.

'I'm in Meadowbank; we need to talk, Eric –'

' – you sound worried.'

'I don't know whether I should be, but it's about Sunday night; the Chief Inspector has been here –'

'- Chief Inspector Graham Ford?'

'Yes, that's right; he was asking me some questions.'

'Such as, Cordelia?'

'He wanted to know why I took such a long time to get back here on Sunday night.'

'Yes?' not making it easy for her.

'Well,' pausing, unsure of the best way to tell him, 'I'd already told one of their sergeants when he was here yesterday questioning everyone about that night, that I'd got back around midnight, which was actually true.'

'So, why are you so concerned?'

'Because someone at The Royal Oak, probably the barman, told them when I left there on Sunday.'

'So? When did you leave?'

'Shortly after you did, Eric.'

'You're being very mysterious, Cordelia; aren't you going to tell me?'

'You're not going to like this.'

'Look, my dear Cordelia, whatever it is, it can't be that dire.'

'Well,' taking a deep breath, 'when we were having a drink you seemed to be very distracted, as though there was something worrying you and when you left after only the one drink, I began to think you –'

'– that I had another woman.'

'Yes, I shouldn't have thought that, I know, but I've known that Katherine Peters was living in Meadowbank and I suppose I was putting the proverbial two and two together when you told me earlier in the year you were renting a property in the same town, and –' unable to go on.

'If you had only told me, Cordelia, I would have reassured you. You realise that, don't you?'

'I do now, yes.'

'Good. Anyway, where *did* you go on Sunday night?'

'You've probably guessed.'

'Followed me back to the lodge and discovered Katherine was here.'

'At first I didn't realise it was her, but when I walked closer to the house, having heard voices coming from the terrace, that's when I recognised her.'

'Presumably you heard everything that was said?'

'It was not my intention to eavesdrop; you must believe me, but I did hear most of it.'

'Don't think I'm mad with you, because I'm not, Cordelia. I do understand how you must have been feeling; in many respects it was probably good that you did hear. But,' he went on, 'why didn't you come in; I would have welcomed the interruption.'

'I felt bad enough about being there in the first place, so after she left, I drove back to Meadowbank. I took my time; I had a lot to think about.'

'You will, of course, have realised that I've also had a visit from the Chief Inspector.'

'He didn't tell me, but I was fairly sure he would have talked to you.'

'Twice in fact, neither of them particularly enjoyable experiences.'

'I can imagine. He tricked me into admitting I had been at the lodge on Sunday.'

'Don't worry about it; that's the way the man operates it would seem; find a likely suspect and stick the crime on to them.'

'There's something else; he knows about us.'

'How the hell did he find that out?'

'I would say from the same person who told him when I left the bar on Sunday.'

'You mean Ted?'

'Is that his name; I didn't know. In any case it must have been someone from the hotel because he had remembered you and me staying there.'

'Inquisitive lot.'

'Small town, Eric.'

'What about Beppe,' he asked, 'does he know about any of this?'

'I don't think so; I've been undecided whether to tell him or not, not about seeing you, of course, but about being questioned by the police. Incidentally, I've been asked to call into the police station this afternoon to make out a statement confirming what was said earlier.'

'Police routine, Cordelia, and presumably I'll have to do the same.'

'You're not worried?'

'Why should I be?' he was quick to reply and she heard the defiance in his voice, knowing if he was worried, he wouldn't admit it. He was shutting her off and for the first time since she had known him, she realised the truth; she had no real part in his life and never would have. She had been foolish to believe any differently. She had permitted herself to fall in love with a man who was incapable of making the commitment she longed for. She had given him too much and now it was too late. Somehow, she must find the strength to emotionally break away from him.

Chapter Eight

After Cordelia rang off, Eric sat for a moment and thought over what she had said. He wasn't unduly concerned, even that the police were aware of their relationship; he couldn't see how that knowledge could have any bearing on their investigation. It was obvious they had been asking questions about him; anything he thought bitterly which they could use to substantiate their cobbled together reasons for suspecting him. They probably thought he was responsible for that circus girl's murder as well. He'd give his lawyer a ring later; the forthcoming interview with the over-zealous Chief Inspector was one battle he wasn't prepared to fight single-handedly. Matthew Provost had for a number of years proved himself to be a capable and formidable legal adviser, but this time he would be representing him personally. He would be expensive, but Eric considered it to be money well spent.

For the first time since moving out of London he questioned whether this had been such a clever decision. Perhaps it would have been better if he'd either rented or bought a property in Winchester, rather than choosing such a parochial town as Meadowbank where apparently the people took inquisitiveness to its highest level. Seeing Letitia the day before only contributed to this feeling of claustrophobia and the fact she had been with Rachel Tilsly didn't help. Of course Letitia had seen him; also fairly certain Rachel Tilsly would have told her he was renting the lodge. He hadn't missed her look of surprise when he hadn't made any attempt to acknowledge her. Well, he shrugged, standing up and going over to the window to look down at the street below, what does it matter? In Eric's opinion, the past was the past and should never be raked up; if the authorities in Hong Kong had had any suspicions about him having had anything to do with what happened to Valerie, they'd had the resources to locate him, but they hadn't. Valerie had been a similar type to many other women he had known; highly emotional, overtly passionate and jealous to the point of obsessiveness. Cordelia was no different and following him back to the lodge on Sunday night only proved to him how intense her feelings must have been towards Katherine. Also, going so far as to find out where Katherine was living; what had been the point; he'd still been in London then? That really was verging on the paranoid and why had she taken so long to get back to the circus grounds on Sunday? This could be the time for him to back off, cool the relationship until such time he would sever all his ties with her. He had no intention of continuing in this way; he never had before and he certainly wouldn't in the future. Cordelia would have to find someone else who would be prepared to offer her what she wanted, knowing she would never leave Beppe until then. Whether unwittingly or not, Beppe made it too easy for her to 'play the field', secure perhaps in this knowledge, having been married to her all this time; one day his complacency may backfire, but it would have nothing to do with him and as to Beppe Bortoletto's feelings, he couldn't care less.

***

'Well, Ian,' Graham said, 'it would appear our theory about Katherine Peters living a double life was right and had been for some time; for exactly how long we don't know. Perhaps since she came back from the States and leased the property in Notting Hill, or even before then. Mention of the government vehicle would imply someone was behind her; she wouldn't have been able to arrange such meetings with, presumably top officials, on her own. It could explain these regular large deposits and if that registered package is anything to go by, whoever sent it must be involved.'

'Big business, sir.'

'Indeed, and to many a distasteful one, hence the reason perhaps for her to go to such lengths to present a totally different persona.'

'She was placing herself in a rather vulnerable position for being blackmailed, wasn't she?'

'Yes, that's right, which brings us back again to that conversation between her and Eric Noble on Sunday night. Cordelia Bortoletto who, as I've said, admitted she had seen the pair of them but emphatically denies hearing what they were saying. Too emphatically in fact; she was lying, which I take to mean, she is trying to protect him. If she had listened she will know why Katherine Peters wanted to see him.

'Which adds some credence to what we were saying about both of them being responsible for the two murders.'

'It does; he would have had the opportunity to deal with Katherine, while Cordelia, equally, would have had the opportunity to cause Beverly Clement's death. I cannot see the man having the ability to climb up and remove the rung from the ladder without being noticed by someone, not only in the big top, but in the circus grounds. It would have been far too risky, Ian; he no more looks like a circus worker than you or I.'

'The odds are certainly against an outsider being responsible.'

'I would say so. I continue to consider Eric Noble as our number one suspect for Katherine Peters' murder which means we have two murderers. I've put out some feelers this afternoon,' Graham went on, 'in respect to the time Eric Noble was in Hong Kong and we should have some feedback by tomorrow.'

'Because of his shady background when he was with Stuart Computers?'

'Partly, but since Cordelia Bortoletto came on the scene, I'm more interested in the man's personal life. He was involved with Katherine Peters for a number of years, their relationship coming to an abrupt end when he met up with Cordelia. He does appear to have a very strong effect on women, I was wondering whether anything dramatic happened, not necessarily to him, but surrounding him, when he was in Hong Kong. It's a long shot, Ian, a hunch even, but it might unearth something.'

'He may have made another quick exit from there.'

'That's certainly a possibility. I'll give Standard Chartered a ring later tonight and have a word with personnel; they should be able to tell me even although it is a number of years ago. His departure could have been, as you've said, a replica of what happened in California.'

'What are your views about Harold Maitland, sir, now we've learned he didn't get home until much later than he'd told us?'

'A three and a half hour discrepancy; it could go towards building up a stronger case against him, on the other hand, he may have had another reason for lying to you. I know you've given me a description of him, Ian, but what were your impressions of the man?'

'Not as I expected him to be, what I should say is, not the type of man I would have thought Katherine Peters would be attracted to, given her outward appearance and, according to those who knew her, both here and in Notting Hill, her gregarious personality. If anything, he came over as somewhat affected, a bit foppish.'

'In the way he was dressed?'

'Not really; it was more in his manner.'

'I think I know what you mean. They say opposites attract though, don't they? He sounds a little effeminate to me; not that that should concern us, but it could be important all the same.'

'They weren't married long.'

'No, they weren't, but then she wasn't with her first husband for long either. What really puzzles me about Harold Maitland is that he professes not to have known about the house in Notting Hill.'

'Perhaps he did know, sir. I should have asked the estate agents the name of the owner.'

'It's not too late, Ian; we'll give them a ring in the morning, they'll be open on a Saturday. Meanwhile, it's been a long day, although not altogether unproductive, I suggest we give it a rest until the morning.

***

Their last performance tonight before packing up and moving on to Petersfield the next day and Beppe would not be sorry to leave Meadowbank. Although everyone had made an effort to carry on with each evening's act, he realised that at the back of each of their minds was the inescapable fact of what happened to Beverly. Yesterday morning he had attended her funeral accompanied, not by Cordelia who made it abundantly clear she would not be going, but by Marcus, his band leader and friend. Although Beverly's parents had invited them for lunch they had declined realising that their presence would only act as a vivid reminder of where Beverly had met her death. Driving back to Meadowbank, the memory of seeing her body lying on the ground remained with him; to Beppe, as with all of his workers, she had been family and as with the loss of any blood relative, he continued to grieve for her.

Such was his absorption when Cordelia had told him she was going to spend some days in their London apartment, the disappointment of not having her around scarcely registered. It wouldn't be the first time she had felt the need to get away and he should have recognised the signs of her restlessness, but he hadn't. No doubt, when she was in London she would indulge in some retail therapy as she had done a number of times in recent years and fortunately, for the sake of their marriage, it always worked and she would come back re-vitalised and less prone to criticising anyone and anything which didn't meet with her approval. This week had obviously added to her chronic discontent and being questioned by the Chief Inspector must have literally been the last straw. She hadn't told him about his second visit until this morning over breakfast, telling him how degrading she had found it having to go to police headquarters to make a written statement. He couldn't understand her reticence; he would have expected her to want him to go along with her and the only explanation she gave him when he asked was she thought he had enough to contend with, which in many respects was true, but he couldn't help feeling hurt, realising with a jolt that these days his wife didn't need his support.

"I do find his manner officious, Beppe," she had said, "and please do not tell me he is only doing his job."

"I wasn't going to, *cara mia*, but from what you've said, a written statement would be routine procedure for reasons of elimination."

"I hope I'm wrong, but are you implying that they should think for one minute I murdered that woman, someone I had never even known!"

"Of course I'm not, but they need to find out whether anyone who was out that night had noticed anyone acting suspiciously."

"Well, I didn't and I told him that."

"That's alright then, *cara mia*, so why the fuss? Getting away for a few days should help you to see things in perspective."

"I hope so."

She had calmed down by the time she left for London later in the afternoon, saying she would call him as soon as she arrived; he had walked with her to the car, and leaning through the open window, kissed her on the cheek.

"*Guidare con attenzione, cara mia.*"

"*Naturalmente, cara mio.*"

He stood watching as she pulled away, accelerating as soon as she reached Riverside Lane, until he could no longer see the car with only the diminishing sound of the car engine as she turned into Bridge Street. He walked slowly back to their caravan; such was the strength of her personality he could feel her presence beside him and for a fleeting second experienced a stab of apprehension. He couldn't explain to himself why; Cordelia, he knew, could look after herself. She had proved long ago how self-sufficient and capable she was, so why this fretting about her safety? It was time he snapped out of this mood of introspection; it was doing him no good. Besides, he had work to do, wanting that evening's performance to live up to the reputation he and his family had devoted their lives in achieving, the rallying voice of his grandfather echoing down the years: "The show must go on, young Beppe, always remember that." And he had, with one exception. Monday night would remain embedded in his memory for the rest of his life and he hoped to God it would never be repeated.

Cordelia's call didn't come through until ten minutes to seven; Beppe had put the finishing touches to his costume and was about to make his way across to the big top when his mobile rang. She quickly explained she was phoning from a land phone as she had discovered when she reached London she had forgotten to recharge her mobile. Relieved to hear she had arrived safely, he had had to curtail the call, a little surprised she hadn't realised it was now only minutes away from the start of the performance. Already he could hear the opening chords of Merle Evans' circus march, *Symphonia*, the familiar beat conducted by Marcus reaching him clearly from where he was standing at the open door of the caravan and, placing his tall black hat squarely into position and straightening his shoulders, he strode across to the rear entrance of the tent to confront his audience, some of them still settling themselves on to the tiered benches.

For the next couple of hours he permitted himself to only think about what he had been trained to do; flamboyantly introduce each act, co-ordinating with the change in tempo as one performance smoothly followed on from the preceding one until the finale, accompanied by the roll of drums and crash of symbols as the music reached a crescendo to be superseded by the clapping and cheering from three hundred-odd appreciative spectators. Bowing deeply, he sighed with relief. Very soon now they would be leaving Meadowbank and the thought of moving to their next venue gave him a flutter of excitement as it always did, although this time, tinged with sadness that Beverly wouldn't be with them.

***

'I had a beer with Eric Noble when you were out this morning, Rachel.'

'Whose idea was that; yours or his?'

'His, actually; he asked me over to the lodge.'

'Friendly of him.' she commented dryly, thankful she hadn't been here, 'Did he mention he saw me on Thursday?'

'No, he didn't;' a frown quickly appearing on his forehead, 'where was this, in Winchester?'

'Yes, Letitia had to go there to collect some drawing materials and she suggested we have lunch at Roberta's. Eric Noble was in there, but he affected not to notice me, but he must have seen me, Colin.'

'Depends on how far away he was.'

'He saw me alright.'

'You don't like him, do you?'

'Not particularly.'

'Why, Rachel? It's not like you to take such an instant dislike to anyone; after all, you hardly know him. Are you still thinking about last Sunday night?'

'It isn't only that,' she tried to explain, but finding it difficult; to Colin, everything had to be logical, methodically thought out, gut-feelings and premonitions played no part in his make-up, 'but there's something about

146

him which I can't take to. Oh, I know what you're going to say, Colin, that I'm over-imaginative, and perhaps I am, but I can't help feeling the way I do, especially,' she added, 'after what Letitia told me.'

'This sounds like gossip to me.'

'You're quite wrong, you know; as it happens, Letitia knew Eric Noble years ago when she was living in Hong Kong and quite frankly what she had to say was not pleasant. I think she probably regretted telling me afterwards, but I'm glad she did. You see, when Eric ignored me in Roberta's, it surprised me, so much so, I mentioned it to her and that's why she told me because she was sure Eric had noticed her and she was the one he didn't want to acknowledge.'

'You really are too sensitive, Rachel; it couldn't have been that bad. I suppose Letitia said she didn't like him either?'

'She dislikes him very much and I think she probably has every reason.'

'What was he supposed to have done, then?' for once taking what she was saying seriously and not dismissing it all as another example of her imagination.

He listened to her without interrupting while she told him, making sure she remembered everything Letitia had said and when she reached the end where her friend had committed suicide in a flat which the authorities had been unable to trace the owner, including the missing luggage, his expression altered to one she had never seen before; a mixture of shock and puzzlement. She leaned back in her chair, mentally exhausted, although relieved she had been able to share what had been bothering her since Thursday.

'It all sounds so extraordinary, Rachel,' he said at last, 'Hong Kong, almost ten thousand kilometres away, another world and one with which you and I are unfamiliar; an expatriate community, many of them with too much idle time on their hands, an affair, while common enough in this country, had a sinister and tragic ending.'

'I know; that's how I felt when she told me, Colin.'

'And you say Eric left Hong Kong the day before her body was found?'

'Yes, without giving the bank any notice, he just went, apparently back to England.'

'He probably felt guilty.'

'It is to be hoped he did,' she retorted, sharper than she intended, but he didn't appear to notice, obviously trying to understand what must have happened so many years ago, 'but it was cowardly of him all the same, don't you think?'

'Oh, yes, you're right. All very unpleasant, Rachel, but it doesn't make him directly responsible for the woman's death.'

'That's debatable. What about the flat she'd been staying in; nobody knew who owned it. Letitia said she felt the police lost interest once the verdict of suicide had been confirmed.'

'It's possible; try not to dwell on all of this; it isn't doing you any good.'

'When you saw Eric Noble was anything said about these murders in Meadowbank?'

'No, why do you ask?'

'I told you I saw the Chief Inspector call at the lodge on Thursday afternoon, didn't I?'

'Yes.'

'Presumably he would have questioned him about Katherine Peters being there on Sunday night; I was wondering whether he had come to the conclusion that either you or I must have told him; he would have worked out that it couldn't have been anyone else.'

'I don't see that it matters, Rachel. If the Chief Inspector did mention to him they'd been seen, I'm sure he wouldn't have revealed the source, therefore,' he went on laboriously, 'Eric would only be assuming, so I shouldn't concern yourself.'

'Well, I suppose we're stuck with him for the tenure of his lease.' she sighed. For all Colin's reassurances, she felt no easier in her mind living in such close proximity to someone like Eric Noble.

'I have every faith in the police force here and when you think about it, Rachel, with all the recent cases they've had to deal with, they have an excellent track record. As I've said, I know Graham Ford and he will do a thorough job; in fact,' he added, 'I rather pity anyone who falls foul of him; you thought Brenda Masters was formidable, Graham is also, but I've been told he has the unsettling ability of adopting a laid back manner when he's questioning people which can instantly and without warning become razor sharp. And, if you remember, Ian Ash conducted himself admirably when he was involved in the enquiry when dad was killed, in fact, earned himself early promotion. No, Rachel, we can depend on the whole team in Meadowbank arriving at a satisfactory conclusion to both murders, so stop worrying and let them get on with what they're paid to do.'

***

The "South China Morning Post", Hong Kong's leading English-language newspaper dated Friday, the 15th July 1988, reported the suicide of one of the territory's expatriates ..... "The body of Valerie Blake, a British subject, was discovered yesterday in Yung Shue Wan on Lamma Island. The verdict was suicide, the pathologist confirming this had been caused by a drug overdose taken three days earlier, on the 12th July. Although there is an element of mystery in that the deceased had arrived on the last ferry from Central and according to the ticket officer on duty she had been carrying two large travel bags, neither of which had been in the flat where the body was found, the authorities are not treating the death as suspicious."

Brief and to the point, Graham thought, reading on further. Apparently, the flat had been unoccupied for several months, a local woman going in each week to air and clean the place; she had gone there as usual on the Thursday morning and finding Valerie Blake's body lying full-length on the sofa had immediately called the police station in Yung Shue Wan. When asked who employed her, she had given the officer the name of an Englishman called Mr Carter, but no more than that, no telephone contact numbers or address, and being Cantonese, she was unable to give an adequate description of the man, explaining to the officer that to her all western men looked alike. There had been no suicide note, but they were able to identify Valerie Blake as her handbag had been there containing her Hong Kong identity card. Valerie Blake's husband was also employed by Standard Chartered around the time Eric Noble was there, but this didn't prove he was in any way involved, the only possible suggestion he may have been, was the fact that he left Hong Kong on Wednesday, the 13th July, the day before the body was found. That could have been coincidental, except when he phoned the bank last night and spoke to their personnel officer, she confirmed that Eric Noble had severed his contract without giving any notice, his last day at the bank being the 13th July. As Ian had suggested, a replica of what happened in Oakland. They were hampered in that all of this happened nineteen years ago. The Hong Kong authorities had treated the incident as suicide; whether there was anything significant about the missing luggage was, after so long, anyone's guess; it could have been stolen but if it had been, why didn't the thief take the handbag also? Valerie Blake may have decided to dispose of it herself between the time it would have taken her to reach the flat from the quayside. There was nothing to be gained by thrashing around with 'what ifs'; it wasn't helping them in their investigation. He had no valid reason to believe Eric Noble was guilty of Katherine Peters' murder; suspecting him was one thing, but hard evidence was something else and so far they didn't have any.

They were at that stage in a murder investigation when they had reached the crossroads and to take the wrong route from hereon could further delay them reaching their conclusion. Ian and he had agreed when they started their enquiries that there was something just a little too pat in that pieces of evidence all appeared to indicate Eric Noble as being guilty. Up to now, he had done nothing to defend himself and had shrugged off as unimportant anything which was substantiated by a witness. He had lied more than once when he had questioned him, but then so had Cordelia Bortoletto and his continual insistence he had not seen Katherine on Sunday night was not exactly helping him. Something wasn't gelling here, but he couldn't work out what it was. Eric Noble had a motive if Katherine Peters had been trying to blackmail him; there was no doubt quite enough in his background from which to choose, also he had the opportunity, so why, Graham reasoned, was he hesitating in pulling him in for official questioning? The answer was there, travelling full circle, because he was too obviously guilty. Eric Noble didn't care. Because he enjoyed a fight to the end or because he was innocent? It wasn't as though he was their only suspect, but perhaps the one who had more stacked up against him. Jack Corbett, in spite of his criminal record, would have had no real motive if you ruled out the rather unlikely one of him harbouring deep feelings of rejection for fifteen years and seeing her again had disturbed him to such a degree as to resort to murdering her. No, Jack Corbett could be described as a 'red herring'; Katherine Peters' death was not, he felt certain, a *crime passionnel*.

Someone else had lied and one who at first they had not seriously considered as being a possible suspect; namely, Harold Maitland. He had emphatically denied keeping in touch with Katherine Peters after their divorce and, more importantly, said he had no knowledge of where she had been living in London, but now, following Ian's phone call to Gregory & Stevens, they knew differently; the mews house was owned by Maitland Enterprises, the crucial question being why had he withheld this fact when it had been a simple action of contacting the estate agents, all of which indicated Harold Maitland was aware of the reason why she needed such a prestigious address; she could hardly have 'entertained' her clients in a flat in Paddington. Not only had he known this, but the natural follow-on question had to be, was he part of the set-up, was he the person who procured these clients for her? Also, in respect to the time he returned home on the Sunday night, this also was questionable; did he drive on to Meadowbank or did he go somewhere entirely different when he left his club? Either way, whether he murdered her or not, a further meeting was essential, but first, he must confer with Bill Simms, preparing himself in advance for the inevitable warnings of not saying anything which could backfire on the Force being accused of browbeating a public figure of Harold Maitland's standing.

***

'I have Mr Gregory on the line, Mr Maitland.'

'Put him through, Amanda.' Gerald Maitland said, quelling a feeling of unease; it was seldom he heard from Philip Gregory but he didn't need any crystal ball to tell him why he should be calling him now. Ever since Inspector Ash's visit last week, he had instinctively sensed he hadn't been satisfied with what he'd told him. He couldn't be much more than thirty, but already in his career he had risen to the rank of Inspector and the way he directed his questioning, doggedly persistent, only went to prove his trained ability to reach the crux of the matter and now it would appear he was right, inwardly cursing his slip-up over that damned property in Lansdowne Terrace. God knows, he'd owned it long enough; he'd had ample time to transfer the deeds to one of his offshore companies.

'Hello, Philip; how are you?'

'I'm fine, Mr Maitland; sorry to bother you, but it's about Number Thirteen Lansdowne Terrace.'

'I rather thought it might be; I take it the police have been in touch with you regarding Miss Peters' occupancy?'

'Yes, they have; it's caused something of a disturbance actually, not frightfully good for business; we haven't been able to place it on the market yet because of a search having to be carried out by New Scotland Yard -.'

'- not by the Meadowbank authorities?'

'No, I believe they're working together on this dreadful business. I had an Inspector Ash call into the office last Tuesday; that was the first time I learned she had been murdered, however, we've got the keys back now, Mr Maitland, so we can place it back on our books, but that wasn't the reason for calling you.'

'No?'

'I didn't expect to hear from the Inspector again, so was somewhat surprised when he phoned this morning. He wanted to know who owned Number Thirteen, naturally I had no alternative but to tell them. I hope that was in order, Mr Maitland?'

'Quite in order, Philip; I wouldn't want you to commit perjury on my behalf.' attempting a joke; he had known Philip Gregory for years and had always considered he took life far too seriously as he was now; the man sounded a nervous wreck, imagining what he would be like if he was ever unfortunate enough to be called to the witness box.

'If it's any consolation to you,' trying to reassure him, 'they've also been in touch with me. As you know, I was once married to Miss Peters and for this reason, purely routine of course, they wanted to talk to me, so nothing to worry about, Philip.' metaphorically crossing his fingers and preparing himself for further questioning.

'The Inspector wanted to know whether Miss Peters was aware of the proprietors of the property, but I told him it was not the policy of Gregory & Stevens to divulge the name of the owner to the lessee.'

'And *vice versa?*'

'That's right, Mr Maitland; and *vice versa.*'

'A good company policy, Philip.' he said smoothly, but not altogether convinced Inspector Ian Ash would believe this. Maitland Enterprises owned more than one property in Lansdowne Terrace and it wasn't as if number thirteen would have been mentioned to him personally, but whether he believed Philip or not, was of no real concern to him. He was a businessman, for God's sake; he had more to do than waste his expensive time on such incidental matters which were efficiently handled by his staff.

Chapter Nine

Cordelia had lied to Beppe when she told him she was phoning from their apartment; she wasn't even in London, having joined the A30 at Stockbridge, driving west towards Taunton, but before reaching the town, she doubled back, spending a good part of the afternoon in Stockbridge and arriving on the outskirts of Meadowbank in the late afternoon. Avoiding the centre of the town, she carried along the Stockbridge Road until she reached the Royal Oak Hotel, parking the car at the rear of the building. She had reserved a room earlier, asking for the one she and Eric had been in on the second floor; the window facing the road from where she could see the roof tops of the Old Manor and the lodge, although she was too far away to see any more of the properties.

Since leaving Meadowbank she had felt numb; it was as though her feelings had been set in ice, her actions; driving, parking, walking round to the front of the hotel and going over to the reception desk had been automatic, even her voice had sounded distant to her, and now in the solitude of her room, she continued to feel the same. Her mind was made up. Even if she had wanted to return to what she was voluntarily leaving behind, she knew she couldn't. It was too late. She had no regrets. She had played a dangerous game and she had lost. Her religion should have rescued her, made her realise she was on the verge of committing the ultimate sin, but what, at one time, had been strong beliefs, had also deserted her; she was on her own, beyond help and certainly beyond redemption.

Eric arrived at The Royal Oak around seven-thirty. There were no spaces available at the front of the hotel which wasn't all that unusual for a Saturday, meaning he had to use the larger parking area at the back. He saw Cordelia's car immediately, surprised she hadn't told him she would be there. He knew this was the circus' last night and had fully expected her to call him for a farewell drink before she left Meadowbank. Reluctant to see her, he almost changed his mind about going in, but shrugged off such reluctance as pointless. If anything, he thought, walking through reception to the lounge bar, seeing her here could be the opportunity he

154

needed; she wasn't going to like what he intended to say, but she would hardly openly display any embarrassing reaction in such a public place which, judging by the high level of voices and the chink of glasses coming from the open doorway, was busy. While he waited to be served, he glanced round the bar, but she wasn't there. He could see part of the restaurant from where he was standing, but no sign of her. As Cordelia preferred to eat later in the evening it was unlikely she would be, which was even more puzzling, deciding to give her a ring on her mobile, but when he did, he got no response. On the off chance she had the phone on charge, he left her a text message.

'Good evening, Mr Noble; sorry to have kept you waiting.'

'That's alright, Ted; it is Saturday night after all, but you do seem to be busier than usual.'

'Mainly because of a wedding party, sir,' he said, 'it's always the same and this was a particularly large reception.'

'I'll have a campari, please. I saw Mrs Bortoletto's car outside,' he said casually, 'have you seen her this evening?'

'No, not yet, sir. She might be in the restaurant though, but I'm sure I would have noticed if she had walked through here.'

Fortunately his attention was caught elsewhere, forcing him to move away. Eric didn't want to pursue the conversation, especially if Ted had been the person who had obliged the police with information about Cordelia and himself. What was it that she had said to him when he'd complained about how inquisitive people were in Meadow Bank? "Small town, Eric"; that's what she'd said and she had been right. Too damn small for his liking, but the question remained; where was she? Eric disliked people behaving mysteriously, dismissing the possibility of there being a simple explanation for her car being out there. She could have been in at lunchtime and for whatever reason left it there, but he was sure Ted would have mentioned if she had been. Cordelia was a creature of habit; for her to visit any hotel, she would always make straight for the lounge bar, but this time it would seem she hadn't. Why? It suddenly seemed important to find out where she was. It never occurred to him she was involved with anyone else. He was too vain and self-confident to think along those lines. He had booked a table in the restaurant for eight, deciding he would have his meal and if her car was still there when he'd finished he would have a word with the receptionist. Eric Noble could never be described as an imaginative man; acting on instincts was not part of his make-up; he operated on hard facts, although over the years he had developed a strong sense of survival, but only when it directly concerned himself. If he experienced any unease about Cordelia's whereabouts, he was only concerned about his own position. More than once in the past he had found himself in a potentially vulnerable situation; years earlier in Hong Kong when Valerie made her dramatic exit and then later, although not so compromising, when Katherine's first husband, Franklin Bacall decided to end his life when she left him and now of course with the Meadowbank constabulary labelling him as their number one murder suspect. All in all, there was quite enough piling up against him; he didn't want anything else to tip the balance.

From where he was sitting in the restaurant he had a clear view of her car, but she didn't appear during the time it took him to finish his meal. It was only nine and still light when he went through to reception. The same girl he had seen earlier was still on duty and, waiting until she had dealt with some new arrivals, moved over to the desk.

'I was hoping to meet a friend of mine this evening,' he fabricated, 'a Mrs Bortoletto –'

'– oh, yes, sir,' she smiled up at him, 'Mrs Bortoletto booked into the hotel this afternoon; I had just come on duty and I remember her name.'

'I have tried to phone her on her mobile, but without any success. I noticed her car in the car park, but she isn't in either the bar or the restaurant.'

'She will be in her room, sir; would you like me to call her for you?'

'If you would.' watching as she dialled the number. What the hell was Cordelia playing at? Had she left Beppe? Was this secretiveness some form of revenge? If so, why had she remained in her room? Nothing was making any sense.

'I'm sorry, sir,' the receptionist was saying as she replaced the receiver, 'I can't get any reply.'

'I suppose she may have gone for a walk,' he suggested, but without any conviction; Cordelia did not like walking.

'I don't know,' the first sign of apprehension appearing, 'I would have seen her, I'm sure. She could be asleep, sir.' she suggested lamely.

'It's only just after nine.' he reminded her unnecessarily.

'Is there a problem, Julie?'

'Er – I'm not sure, Mrs Watson.' going on to explain to the woman Eric recognised as Sandra Watson, the manageress, having seen her a number of times.

'Good evening, Mr Noble,' she said, turning to him, 'this is somewhat irregular, you know. Mrs Bortoletto is a guest in my hotel and if she decides to have an early night and not answer her phone, well, that's really up to her, wouldn't you say?'

Tough cookie, but then he had heard about Sandra Watson's reputation of being something of a tyrant, wondering how she managed to keep staff. By this time, the receptionist, no doubt expecting to be blamed for creating the slightest form of disturbance in the prestigious surroundings of the Royal Oak Hotel.

'I agree with you, of course, but as Mrs Bortoletto and I had made arrangements to meet in the lounge bar this evening, I can't help feeling a little concerned.'

'Hmmph.' her only reply, 'Try to phone Mrs Bortoletto's room again, Julie.'

They both waited silently as the girl redialled.

'There's still no answer, Mrs Watson.'

'Very well,' nodding dismissively at her, 'you can't do any more. If you would care to follow me, Mr Noble, we'll go up to her room;' taking a duplicate key from the receptionist, 'I trust this isn't going to be embarrassing for Mrs Bortoletto.' she added, leading the way to the lift.

'If it is, Mrs Watson, I will be the first to apologise, but as I've said, my concern is for my friend.'

She made no comment; every line of her body rigid with barely suppressed resentment. Hardly the type of woman to be in the hospitality business, he thought uncharitably, although he had to admit the hotel was a splendidly run establishment and a pleasant oasis after the parochial confines of the two pubs in the town.

The corridor on the second floor was quiet, their feet making no sound on the dark red carpeting, and stopping at Room 222, she tapped lightly on the door, waiting for a couple of seconds before putting the key in the lock and slowly turning the handle.

'Mrs Bortoletto?' she called out softly, but there was no answer. The curtains hadn't been drawn and the last shreds of daylight filtered into the room, appearing to spread out to encompass the body of the woman who had been Cordelia lying on the bed, an empty glass tumbler clutched in her hand.

'Oh, my God! Oh, my God!' Sandra Watson gasped, her voice no more than a whisper, 'Is – is she dead, Mr Noble?'

Without saying anything, he walked up to the bed, leaned over, placing his fingers at the side of her neck to find the pulse, but there was none. Taking a deep sigh, he straightened up and turned away.

'There's no sign of life, Mrs Watson;' he said, taking her arm and leading her out of the room, 'we must telephone the police; they'll bring their own doctor and I think it would be best if we go down to your office.'

'Of course.' She was obviously having considerable difficulty in composing herself and he could almost feel sorry for the woman, the cynical side of his nature wondering how long it would take her to recover.

'Would you like me to phone them?' he asked her once they were in the office.

'No, it's alright. I have to do that.'

She wasn't on the phone for long and by the time she had finished she looked slightly better with more colour in her cheeks.

'They're on their way,' she said, 'and should be here in ten or fifteen minutes.'

'Your husband needs to know what's happened.'

'I know; he'll be in the restaurant,' she said, glancing at her watch, 'we usually have our evening meal at this time, so if you'll excuse me, Mr

Noble, I'll go and tell him.'

'No doubt the police will want to question me,' he said, not looking forward to another barraging, 'so I'll be in the bar if they should ask for me, Mrs Watson.'

'Mr Noble,' she said as she was leaving the office, 'I'm sorry about your friend. It must have been dreadful for you finding her like that.'

'It was a shock, Mrs Watson,' he said, 'quite indescribable in fact.'

***

Graham had still been in the office when the call came through from Sandra Watson and before leaving for the hotel he rang Ian, regretting he would be disrupting his Saturday night, but thought it best for him to be there also. He didn't stay long once Dave Burrows made his preliminary examination of the body, wanting to inform Beppe Bortoletto as soon as possible of his wife's death; an unpleasant task and a role he was not comfortable with, but having spoken to many fellow officers knew they all shared the same view. A dirty job, but someone's got to do it, he thought with resignation, driving along Bridge Street towards the circus grounds. He arrived as the evening's performance came to an end and the first members of the audience emerged from the big tent.

Beppe, recognisable by his scarlet jacket, looked across to where he was standing and as though sensing the reason why he had come, moved away from the man he had been talking to and came slowly towards him.

'It's Cordelia, isn't it; that's why you're here?'

The pain etched on his face as he listened was unbearable to witness, making him feel he was intruding on the man's grief, noticing how his hand was shaking as he took the letter his wife had left for him. During his career, Graham had read many suicide notes and each time he was reminded of the selfishness of those people who had decided to end their lives and were still able beyond death to inflict this additional burden of guilt and remorse on to loved ones.

'If you would rather read it later, sir, I will understand.'

'No, Chief Inspector,' he said, tearing the envelope open, 'we need to know why Cordelia has done this dreadful thing.' taking out the single

159

sheet of notepaper. It didn't take him long to read the few lines she had written, and ashen-faced, he passed it over to him.

"Beppe," Graham read, "I know there can be no forgiveness for me and I don't expect any, not only for ending my life, but for Beverly's also. Perhaps in your eyes, Beppe, that will be the greater sin. I give no explanation why I arranged her accident, only to say now that I made a mistake and one I have found impossible to live with. Cordelia."

No endearments, no apology and no remorse, Graham thought, folding the note in half: 'We shall have to keep this for the moment, Mr Bortoletto -'

'- I don't want it back, Chief Inspector; I never want to see it again. I am beyond words; I can't begin to tell you how devastated I am. We were married for over twenty years, you know, and it would seem I never knew my wife; that is what I am struggling to understand. I haven't asked you how she died.' he added.

'By a drug overdose;' Graham told him, 'our pathologist has yet to make an analysis.'

'Cordelia was on medication, at least she had an ongoing prescription to control a high blood pressure problem, but I have no idea whether she was continuing with the treatment. She disliked talking about sickness and always avoided mentioning ailments of any kind; even a headache, according to her, was a form of weakness.' he explained bitterly.

Graham didn't mention to him the other letter Cordelia had left although it was inevitable in time he would learn about it once the evidence relating to Beverly Clements' murder was brought to court, but now was not the time; Beppe Bortoletto had enough with which to contend without any premature additives.

***

Ian, after a few words with Chris and Sandra Watson, walked through reception into the lounge bar. The body of Cordelia Bortoletto had already been taken to the mortuary, followed by Dave Burrows and the forensic team. Much to the relief of both Sandra Watson and her husband there were very few people in reception when the stretcher was carried through to the police vehicle parked outside on the drive. Dave had told him he would have the autopsy report ready the following morning, the fact it would be a Sunday making no difference to any of them at the Station whether a sudden death was a suicide or not; routine enquiries would have to be carried out and, as always, time was a key factor. It was obvious to Graham and himself that Cordelia's decision to take her own life must have some connection with the two murders earlier in the week. Another twist, he thought, in their investigation which showed no signs of letting up; if anything, since Katherine Peters' body had been discovered on Monday, subsequent events and findings had gathered momentum.

Eric Noble was seated by an open window overlooking the gardens; it was a warm evening and many of the guests had taken their drinks outside on to the terrace, presumably unaware of the activity inside the hotel.

'Mr Noble,' Ian said, 'sorry to have kept you waiting for so long; I'm Inspector Ash,' showing him his card.

'You knew who I was, then?' only glancing at the card.

'I recognised you, yes.' having no intention of saying when he had last seen him. Graham had already warned him about his belligerent manner, but by the look of him, considerably paler than he had been on Sunday, it would seem that tonight's incident must have shaken him. 'I've only a few questions to ask you, sir,' he went on, 'but first,' taking a sealed envelope from his pocket, 'this is addressed to you; it was found beside the body.'

'She left a suicide note.' slowly stretching out his hand for it, 'I didn't see it when I was in there.'

'I understand she had been lying on it, that's probably why.'

'I see.'

'I'd like you to open it, Mr Noble.'

'If it's addressed to me, Inspector, it must be my property. I'll read it later – when I'm on my own.'

'What you're saying is correct; the letter does belong to you, but what has been written could have some bearing on the double murder enquiry we're conducting.'

'I suppose this is something else you can use to pin on your prime suspect.'

'Mr Noble,' Ian said, keeping his voice low, 'that is not the way we work. The content of the letter may have nothing to do with our enquiry, but this is something we must verify, therefore, would you please open it.'

With only the slightest hesitation, he opened the envelope and, taking his time, read what she had written. Without waiting to be asked, his lips in a thin tight line, handed it over to him.

'It doesn't make much sense;' he muttered, 'just that she'd had enough; probably meant she'd had enough of me.' he added, shrugging his shoulders.

"I don't know why I'm leaving this note for you, Eric," Ian read, "except to say when I spoke to you the other day I realised you were backing out of our relationship, so I guess I wanted to get in first. I've done too much for you and that was wrong of me. I have had enough." signing her name with a flourish at the bottom.

'Were you planning to break-off your friendship with her?'

'Probably.'

'She seemed to think so. What did she mean when she said she'd done too much for you?'

'How the hell should I know?'

'Apparently, you had made plans to meet this evening.'

'Who told you that – oh, I suppose you've been talking to the Watson woman.'

'Had you arranged to see Mrs Bortoletto this evening?'

'No, I had no idea she would be in the hotel and certainly not that she'd booked in.'

'Why did you lead Mrs Watson to believe you were meeting her?'

'For the simple reason, Inspector,' making no effort to suppress an exasperated sigh, 'I had noticed Cordelia's car outside when I arrived and as it was still out there when I'd finished my meal, I decided to have a word with the receptionist.'

'Why?'

'Why not; I was concerned. I couldn't understand why her car should be here and there was no sign of her. I thought it strange, that's all, and when the girl told me Cordelia had booked into the hotel this afternoon, I thought it even more so.'

'I see,' Ian nodded, acknowledging there was a certain logic in what he was saying, even if he had avoided giving him a direct answer.

'Have you quite finished, Inspector? This has been a harrowing evening for me; I'm tired and would like to get home.'

There were no further questions he needed to ask him and nothing further to be gained by going over the same ground. Ian remained where he was as Eric Noble stood up and, with a curt nod in his direction, walked away. It was at that moment he was reminded of Harold Maitland; when he had been shown into his office on Tuesday, Harold Maitland had been standing at the window with his back to the room. It hadn't been the man's features which made him think he'd seen him before; it had been more his build, his height and the way he held his head, slightly to one side which had struck him as familiar. He knew now he had never seen him before; it had been Eric Noble he had seen, the other Sunday, here in the hotel. The resemblance was only superficial, but sufficient to make him consider another possibility in their enquiry. The two men, Eric Noble and Harold Maitland, were of a similar height and build, even around the same age, both had their hair cut longer than the average businessman and rimless glasses added to the likeness. The Chief Inspector had yet to meet Harold Maitland and it would be interesting what his reactions would be; sufficient perhaps to support their growing suspicions of him and may explain the casual attitude Eric Noble was adopting. The note Cordelia had left for him was somewhat ambiguous but what her comments implied certainly couldn't be considered as any form of confession for Katherine Peters' murder. Without something further to go on, they could only speculate. Was there any real meaning behind her saying she had been wrong in doing too much for him, or had she been speaking metaphorically, over-dramatising their relationship? There were a number of connotations, but nothing to substantiate any of them. Cordelia Bortoletto could have been responsible for Beverly Clements' death if she believed the girl had seen Katherine Peters' killer and had therefore been a threat either to herself or to her lover, Eric Noble, and discovering he was planning to end their relationship, had decided to take her own life. Could it be as neat and simplistic? He didn't think so; they had already uncovered another side of Katherine Peters' life, but it wasn't enough. She had been working for someone and that person must be of sufficient social or political standing to provide her with the type of clients she apparently had if the evidence of her bank accounts was anything to go by, even discounting the monthly alimony payments. At what age he wondered did a woman following her particular career path decide to retire. Forty-five, fifty? Surely no longer than that. Katherine Peters had been within a few months of her thirty-eighth birthday; had this concerned her? Had this been the reason, anticipating an imminent drop in her income, she had resorted to blackmail?

It was important he conferred with Graham Ford, admitting he didn't have the older officer's experience to analyse salient points and arrange them in some semblance of order to make credible sense. He also realised if he continued the way he had been doing these last couple of days in pursuing each thread of evidence he felt he would be bound to end up in a mental corner.

***

News of the sudden death of one of the Royal Oak's guests reached Meadowbank in record time, causing a stir of excitement among the regulars in The Bridge Inn. Jeff Brown, a waiter at the hotel, had called in for a drink on his way home and needed no encouragement in telling his captive audience of the police activity in the wake of the woman's body being found; more than one or two of them mentioning similar circumstances a year and a half ago when Stephanie Collins was murdered in close proximity to the hotel and that she, also, had been a guest there.

'If she was a guest, she wouldn't have been from around here.' one of them said, nodding his head authoritatively.

'Have the police named her, Jeff?' Bill Knowles, Fred's friend from The Market Inn, asked.

'No, they haven't said.'

'Probably because of this next of kin thing.' another piped up.

'Funny though.' Bill said slowly, draining his glass.

'I don't see anything funny about what's happened.' the man next to him said.

'I don't mean funny ha-ha, Ted; I mean funny peculiar.'

'What d'you mean, Bill?' Jeff asked him.

'Well, we've had two murders in Meadowbank within a matter of days and here's another.'

'Nobody's saying anything about murder tonight.' Jeff corrected him.

'Perhaps not, but you have to admit it does sound suspicious all the same. Could have something to do with that circus. It was peaceful here until they arrived.'

This was the first time since he and Matilda had taken over the pub from Isobel Gallier he had seen them so animated, but then, although they had heard about the spate of murders around Meadowbank over the past couple of years, this was the first incident since their arrival. Now he knew what Brian Morrison had meant when he'd told him how his elderly regulars had reacted then; what they didn't know, each of them had been ready to put forward a theory which more often than not was pure fabrication, a product of over-active imaginations, but there had been times when they had come pretty close to the truth.

As he replenished their drinks he couldn't help wondering whether Bill Knowles was right; the circus being in the town for the last week seemed to have acted as a sort of catalyst; as he'd said, things had been quiet before then. Thankful he wasn't in the police force; they had a difficult job ahead of them and compared to being a landlord of a pub in a relatively small market town, far more onerous. Even coming from a town the size of Camden Town in London where the local populace was familiar with crime, the most he had had to contend with was the occasional drunken brawl at closing time and, if anything, the more common domestic altercation, most of which had never taken long to subdue, often without police assistance. So this, he thought wryly, was an introduction to the rural life.

***

The circus pulled out of Meadowbank shortly after midday the following morning and, as on their arrival exactly a week ago, drove through Market Square, a splash of colour on a dull overcast day, the spell of warm weather having come to an abrupt end during the early hours with a heavy thunderstorm, followed by torrential and relentless rain coursing along the gutters and splashing on to the pavements.

Beppe Bortoletto was not with the circus, remaining behind in Meadowbank to attend to the various formalities requiring completion, but would be in Petersfield the following afternoon in time for their first performance in the town. He had booked into The King's Arms in the square, electing for obvious reasons not to spend the night at The Royal Oak. Once Graham Ford had left him, he had spent the remainder of last night talking to Marcus, appreciating his friend's sympathetic, but down-to-earth advice. He no longer felt the utter shock and despair of what Cordelia had done; Marcus had helped him come to terms with what had happened, even the impact of Beverly's death was starting to dissipate. He knew that after Cordelia's funeral at the end of the following week, he would be on the mend and would be able to carry on with a lessening in the weight of the terrible sadness which had been with him since last Monday night.

Carol Cliff passed the long procession of circus vehicles as she joined the A3057 from the motorway. She knew they were heading for Petersfield and if necessary she would go there, but for now, she was more interested in Meadowbank and anything further she could glean to fill out her column for Tuesday morning's edition. Rocky had teased her before she left about 'her man in Meadowbank', but she hadn't minded; there was a time when they'd been first married, she would have retorted with one of her New Yorker quips, but being married to an Englishman had given her an understanding of the British sense of humour. Although in the same profession, working for rival newspapers, they never encroached on each other. Rocky had completely understood when she'd told him after she'd got the phone call last night that she was returning to

Meadowbank and hadn't asked why. She was lucky having a husband like him and these days hardly ever thought about the States, having adapted to the slower tempo of London, but as she'd said to him each time she spent any time in a town as parochial as Meadowbank, she would go mad if she actually lived there, but she shrugged, this was work and if another visit would give her what she needed, so what. She had already drafted out the piece; all she needed was some more local background to give it that extra bite her readers expected from her.

Here we go again, she thought, pulling into an empty space in front of The King's Arms and, taking her overnight bag and laptop from the boot, climbed the few steps to the front door.

'Good afternoon, Miss Cliff,' the receptionist greeted her, and not for the first time, Carol wondered why, in spite of her wedding ring, people invariably addressed her as miss, 'I've given you the same room you had before.' turning the register round towards her and handing her the room key.

'That's fine, thank you.' her hand poised for a fraction of a second over the page, scarcely believing her luck; the last person to book in this afternoon had been Beppe Bortoletto. This, she decided, would have to be handled tactfully; she would require more than her usual deviousness if she was going to succeed in extracting anything she could use for her column, remembering the man's open hostility when she'd seen him earlier in the week. She was not quite sure what sort of approach she should adopt, but in her unbreakable confidence knew she would think of something and by the time she reached her room she had decided it would be wiser just to use her instincts; there would be nothing achieved by approaching him, only succeed in making him more irate, trying to literally place herself in his shoes. Only, if the situation arose, would she give any sign she had noticed him. Beppe Bortoletto had recently lost his wife and if the information she'd learned so far was correct, she had died from a drug overdose; the chances of it not being a suicide could be negligible, but she had to be absolutely certain, constantly aware of potential libel charges. Why had the woman been staying in the hotel anyway, she wondered; according to Jeff she had been on her own, having arrived earlier in the afternoon, although there was a contradiction here and the more she thought about it, the more she believed it could be an important factor, possibly the 'hook' she was looking for. Jeff had mentioned that one of their regular customers; Eric Noble he was called, had planned to meet Cordelia Bortoletto and when she didn't turn up he became sufficiently concerned to speak to the management, resulting in him, together with the proprietress, going up to Cordelia's room and finding her body. Eric Noble, Carol frowned; she had heard that name before recently and then it came to her. It had been in The Market Inn; she and Jimmy had been in there on Friday lunchtime for something to eat before returning to London when the old gardener from the Tilsly estate had come in and they'd overheard him saying the Chief Inspector had been to see Eric Noble at the lodge the previous evening. Definitely food for thought there, she decided. Jeff had actually given her quite a lot, but it wasn't enough; she needed more, not only the bare bones with veiled suggestions, and this could be it.

Carol had first met Jeff Brown a year and a half ago; it had been during another double murder enquiry in the town and she, along with two of her colleagues from the paper, had been staying at The Royal Oak. Jeff had seen one of the victims shortly before she was killed and had been the person who discovered the body the following morning. He had been full of it in the restaurant that evening; he shouldn't have been of course, somewhat indiscreet of him, but she had immediately recognised how he might prove to be useful and had given him one of her cards, saying there would be a reasonable payment for anything she considered newsworthy. He hadn't failed her either, and then, when the Miller-Croft murders occurred at the end of last year, he hadn't wasted any time in getting in touch, which resulted, as it had done this time, in her being the first journalist to turn up. He had heard about Katherine Peters' body having been found early on Monday when he'd called into the newsagents on his way to work and had phoned her more or less straight away, which had given her even more of a head start, a fact which she didn't think had escaped Ian Ash, recalling his look of surprise when he'd seen her outside The King's Arms. By now, she realised, it must have become apparent that someone in Meadowbank must be tipping her off, but they could only guess who it might be. Jeff was sensible enough to realise the wisdom of not speaking out of turn; he wouldn't want to forfeit what had become regular increments to his wages, but by the law of averages these must dry up, although it would appear not yet with the suicide of a woman known to someone, namely Eric Noble, presumably having warranted police questioning in Meadowbank's latest murder enquiry.

***

When Harold Maitland received a telephone call from Chief Inspector Graham Ford of the Meadowbank Constabulary, he couldn't decide whether he should attach any importance to this or not. If the call had been made on any day except a Sunday he would have dismissed it as being routine police procedure in a murder enquiry and, as far as he was concerned, not to be taken too seriously. The officer had been pleasant enough; he had no complaints there, although he did object to his leisure hours being disturbed. Now, he thought peevishly, the remainder of the day was going to be spoilt with this nagging little irritant at the back of his mind. Surely they should have reached their conclusions by now and gathered in all the evidence they were likely to get. Harold couldn't imagine what other questions they wanted to ask him. The police authorities in that part of the country appear to operate in a very haphazard way; if he had to conduct his businesses along those lines, utter chaos would reign. And now, it looked as if there was going to be more time lost by repeating everything he had said to the Inspector the other day. Katherine is causing more trouble and disruption than she did when she was alive, grumbling under his breath.

He had first met her fifteen years ago; she had only been twenty-three and was with the Islington Stage Agency. She had only been at the beginning of her acting career and, although she did get work, they were small bit parts and the wages were low. She had shared a flat with two other girls; it had been in Islington and not far from the agency. When he offered her some occasional work, she hadn't hesitated; the extra money she earned made a marked improvement to the way she lived. She had only stayed with the agency for a year before joining the Repertory Theatre Company in Guildford and a couple of years later she married an American and moved over to the States. He had lost touch with her after that, until she turned up in London three years later, bumping into him in 'Annabel's' one night and, although this time, she was with the Esther Summers Theatre in Guildford, she was more than willing to work for him again on a part-time basis.

She mentioned a boyfriend, leading him to believe they'd met while she was in the States, but typically, Katherine was frugal with explanations which personally concerned her. It wasn't until the relationship broke up about the end of 1988 she'd told him his name and from what she had said, it appeared he left her for another woman, the extent of her bitterness had surprised him at the time; he had always considered she never took any of her affairs to such a high emotional level, but on that occasion, it had been plain to him she felt quite differently towards the man with whom she had spent some years. It wasn't as though they had made any attempt to set up home together, both of them staying in The Mandalay Hotel in Guildford and where she had remained until he arranged for leasing of the mews house for her through one of his companies.

Marrying her the following year had been a mistake, although at the time it had made sense; his businesses were thriving, especially Maitland's Investments, enabling him to establish himself as one of the city's key financial figures and believing a wife would add respectable solidity, also to quash disturbing rumours in London of his sexuality. He had spent a number of years building up the image he wanted to portray and he had no intention of allowing it to be tarnished and for him to become an object of after-dinner sniggerings. At first, the relationship, purely platonic, worked well; neither of them made any demands on each other with Katherine fulfilling her end of the bargain; accompanying him to numerous functions and acting as his hostess when they entertained. As far as he was aware, there had been no successor to Eric Noble, but he continued with the occasional casual affair, each of them conducted discreetly, or so he had thought, until one of them, a rather flamboyant young photographer who made no secret of being gay, had mentioned their relationship to one of their mutual friends, who, in turn, maliciously passed on to Katherine. Instead of dismissing what the woman had told her, surprisingly, she had gone on the obverse, accusing him of sullying her name and other equally uncalled for remarks, the volatile tirade ending in her demanding a divorce. She returned permanently to the mews house shortly before the divorce and once the settlement had been agreed, took the opportunity of resigning from the theatre, while continuing to work for him as she had always done, but even with her considerable income she still wasn't satisfied; she started putting pressure on him to 'pay her off' as she described it. Latterly, when he was still refusing, she became more demanding, even issuing a time limit for him to change his mind. It was when she resorted to veiled threats of exposing him, he realised something had to be done.

Chapter Ten

The warm weather had returned, the sky over Meadowbank now a clear brilliant blue, encouraging the residents of the town to abandon their Sunday chores and spend some time outdoors, many of them electing to call in at either of the two pubs and some hoping to catch up on the local happenings of the week, much of which was by now common knowledge. By one, the Market Inn was packed, with no free tables either inside or out on the pavement. Brian and Derek had their work cut out coping with the influx of customers, whose glasses appeared to always need refilling. Once Melissa had settled Caroline down for her afternoon nap, her additional help eased the situation.

'I can't make up my mind, Derek,' Brian said in between a slight lull of taking orders, 'whether it's the sun or the hope to learn more about what's been going on here that's making people thirsty all of a sudden.'

'A bit of both, I expect,' Derek grinned, loading the dishwasher for the third time since they opened at eleven-thirty.

'You're probably right and I shouldn't grumble; whichever it is, it's good for business.'

'Morning, Brian,' Simon called out, pushing his way through to the bar, 'you're obviously up to your eyes, perhaps I should have come later in the day, but I thought you and Melissa might like to have a look at the proofs of the christening before you open up again this evening.'

'No, it's alright, it's beginning to ease off a bit, but it was pretty hectic right from the moment we opened the door this morning. Good to see you; we're looking forward to seeing the photographs and thanks for doing them so quickly.'

'No problem.' he said, handing him the envelope. 'I think you'll both be pleased with them. I must say your young daughter is very photogenic, and she did smile for us all.'

'In between a few squawks.'

'So would you squawk if you got a stream of cold water poured on your head!'

'True;' Brian laughed, 'Heineken, Simon; it's on the house.' he added.

'I saw the tail end of the circus going through the square when I was in the newsagents a few minutes ago. Their presence this year certainly caused a bit of a furore.' Simon remarked, watching him pour the lager into his favourite tankard.

'I don't suppose you will have heard about Beppe Bortoletto's wife.' Brian said, passing the tankard over to him.

'No, not something else?'

'It looks like it, Simon. We only heard about it this morning, but apparently, she died of an overdose sometime last evening, at least that's the word which is being bandied about, so I don't know just how true it is, but from what they're saying, it sounds as if that's what happened.'

'Good Lord! Where did this happen; up at the circus?'

'No, and this is the strange part,' he answered, not having had any time to make sense of what he'd heard, 'she had been staying at The Royal Oak, booked in yesterday afternoon, and that's where her body was found.'

'This is quite extraordinary, you know, because Eliza and I had dinner in the restaurant last night and we knew something was going on out in reception; there was a lot of activity, but we had no idea what and by the time we left the hotel everything was quiet as though nothing had been happening, although,' he added thoughtfully, 'we noticed Ian Ash in the bar when we walked through, but as he appeared to be deep in conversation with someone, we didn't speak to him and now I come to think about it, Brian, he did look as though he was on duty. The man he was talking to didn't look too happy, but then Eric Noble never does.'

'Eric Noble, you say?'

'Yes, I've spoken to him a couple of times, but never had much of a conversation with him.'

'He's a quiet one, that's for sure. The trouble is, Simon,' he went on, 'that in this town it is too easy to speculate about people, especially those you don't know well and I try my best not to join the gossips, but it's not easy.'

'I don't think it is, but in some respects, provided you don't go over the top with those speculations, it is quite healthy.'

'How?'

'Well, taking an interest in your fellow man, I suppose.'

'I've never thought about it in that way, but you could be right; you mean, following your natural instincts, that sort of thing?'

'Yes, and if that person is unusually sparing in coming up with any background, we never really get to know them and then are quick to suspect he could be hiding some aspect of his personality deliberately and some of us might find that unnerving.'

'So, what you're saying is, that the fact Ian Ash was talking to him last night, instantly makes us jump to what are no more than assumptions about the chap?'

'I think so, yes. Perhaps he had seen Mrs Bortoletto earlier in the evening; it could be as simple as that which could explain why Ian was having a few words with him.'

'She did know Eric Noble.'

'Well, there you are then.'

'He came in here with her once; it was a long time ago, nearly ten years it must have been, but I remember them quite well, especially her, she was a very striking-looking woman. I remember thinking at the time they were an ill-matched pair. I didn't know who she was then, but the last time the circus was here, the year before last, she came in again with her husband.'

'Sounds as if they were old friends, perhaps they had a drink in The Royal Oak for old time's sake.'

'Perhaps.'

'You don't sound very convinced.'

'Perhaps it's because I don't believe in platonic friendships.' he grinned, his expression changing rapidly as he saw the woman who was now coming into the bar, relieved when Derek moved over to serve her. Carol Cliff; the London reporter and someone he was not over keen on; in his opinion, she had been primarily responsible these last couple of years for stirring up a great deal of unnecessary dirt among the community.

'You've seen who's just come in, haven't you, Simon?'

'I certainly have. She has become a frequent visitor to Meadowbank.'

'It wouldn't be so bad if she didn't use pubs for gleaning her snippets of information; what a way to earn a living.'

'I've seen her and the photographer chap a number of times this week; I would have thought they'd have gone back to London by now.'

'They did, Simon. They were in here on Friday lunchtime and I heard her saying to someone they had booked out of The King's Arms and were driving back that afternoon.'

'And here she is again; she must have a hotline to Meadowbank.'

'I think she has; there is no way she would have known about this suicide otherwise.'

'A tipoff?'

'I can't think of any other way; she's a crafty young woman; I wouldn't put it past her. She may have found someone who would be prepared to exchange what they knew for a few pounds.'

'Not a pleasant thought.'

'No, it isn't, so I expect we will have to prepare ourselves for another of her biting articles. Our new Chief Inspector isn't going to be too pleased to find she's turned up again; or Ian either. I'm sure she is a hindrance to what they're trying to achieve.'

'I'm sure she is, Brian, but I suppose, provided she stays clear of anything libellous, there's not much they can do to curb her.'

***

Letitia had spent a restless night, tossing and turning until well into the early hours, and by six with the sun beginning to filter through the curtains she threw back the duvet, abandoning any further attempt to try and catch up on any sleep. Since the divorce, ten years earlier, she had become accustomed to making the decisions which concerned Timothy and herself, and for the first time, she had come up against a problem which she was finding difficult to resolve. The fact that what she had learned the day before did not personally concern her and Timothy and therefore wasn't a family matter, made no difference to the way she was thinking; she knew she had to consult someone who would have the ability and the authority to handle the knowledge she had been given.

Seeing Valerie's son yesterday had, for the second time in less than a week, brought those sad memories back. Although it was almost twenty years since she had last seen him, and he had been only a schoolboy then, she would still have recognised him; he had Valerie's blondness, even to the widow's peak and the scattering of freckles across the bridge of his nose. He was tall, like his father, and the slight cadence in his voice the only other similarity. To see him yesterday, standing on her front door step, in Meadowbank of all places and miles away from Hong Kong, had been hard to grasp.

"I'm sorry, Mrs Radcliffe," he had apologised, having noticed her reaction, "I should have given you a call first -"

"- no, it's alright, Gerry," she had been quick to reassure him, "it's just that you were the last person I ever expected; a bit trite to say, but it's been a long time."

"And I was only a kid then." he'd smiled, again, another poignant reminder of Valerie.

"I know. Come in, please; I was outside enjoying this marvellous weather when you came." leading the way through the kitchen and out on to the paved terrace facing the garden and at the bottom of the lawn, the willow trees shielding the river; the sound of the gentle chuckling of water over the pebbles having an instant soothing effect, giving her the chance to adjust her thoughts.

"Would you like a drink;' she had asked, "a wine or would you prefer a beer?"

He chose a beer and she poured herself a glass of wine while he told her about meeting Timothy a few days ago in Phuket.

"As you probably know," he said, "Timothy was only there for a couple of days before moving back up to Pattaya. I've been working in a bar in Phuket and it was purely by chance he happened to call in for a beer one evening and as we weren't too busy we got chatting. I mentioned to him I used to live in Hong Kong and then he told me that he had as well, although he was only a young lad then and couldn't remember much about the place. We were exchanging names and addresses before he and his friends left when I discovered his surname was Radcliffe I realised who he was. I'd started to remember him from when I was on holiday from boarding school and my mother used to take me with her sometimes when she called round to see you, and once, a whole crowd of us went swimming."

"He wouldn't have remembered you, of course."

"No, he was far too young."

"I saw you a few times, Gerry after your mother died, but for most of the time you were away at school."

"I've been trying to find out where you were living, Mrs Radcliffe –"

" – oh, please call me Letitia; Mrs Radcliffe makes me feel so old!"

"Letitia," uncannily pronouncing it the same way Valerie had done; with the middle 'i' stretched out as the Italians do, "and," he went on, "I'd practically given up, but you were the only person I could talk to about what happened."

"What about your father?"

"Dad died five years ago, but I wouldn't have said anything to him. I don't believe he ever got over Mum's death; he hardly ever talked about her and he never met anyone else. I often thought his life would have been a lot better if he had, but he just seemed to close in on himself."

"I'm sorry, Gerry. We never kept in touch after we left Hong Kong and I never knew him all that well. I remember him as being a quiet man and I always thought he and your mother were well suited, therefore it came as a surprise the way things turned out."

"I know about the affair she was having, although I didn't learn about that until quite a number of years later. Of course I was aware of how she died, but had no idea why and quite frankly, Letitia, I still don't; I can only surmise, but that really isn't good enough. I suppose I'm a fool to have dwelt on this for so long, but it's a bit like reading a book to find the last couple of pages missing. It's too easy to see something sinister surrounding her death;" he continued, "her missing luggage for instance and the house on Lamma where she was found, also there was no suicide note. That in itself is unusual; she was a good mother and I know how much it upset her when I went off to boarding school for the first time. She wrote to me every week without fail; they were interesting letters, full of news about the people we knew, that sort of thing."

"You're bound to feel like that, Gerry, and I'm sure it is a perfectly normal reaction. There's more than one reason why a person decides to take their own life, isn't there?"

"I know there is, but unless a person discovered they were terminally ill, I've always considered suicide to be a selfish act."

"So have I," she'd agreed, "and we both know your mother was not a selfish woman."

"I realise the official verdict was suicide, but what do you think yourself?"

"My somewhat pathetic answer, Gerry, is that I don't know. I presume you knew that she left your father three days before she was found?"

"Yes, Dad told me, but only after I asked him and again this was years later."

"She phoned me before she took the ferry over to Lamma; did he tell you that?"

He had nodded, taking a sip of his lager.

"She was using a public telephone, mobile phones were not so common then, and she didn't say much, only that the man she had hoped to stay with had turned her away and that she needed to think things through and would be in touch in a few days." deliberately avoiding any mention of the other woman who had been in Eric Noble's apartment, feeling there was no need to, "It's true she did sound upset, but no more than I would have expected her to be under the circumstances, and I had no reason to believe she wouldn't be back when she said she would."

"I found out who owned the house on Lamma, you know."

"How on earth did you manage that; the police came up against a dead end there?"

"I don't think they tried very hard; I expect once the verdict of suicide was made, they lost interest."

"You're probably right."

"Anyway, like Timothy, I had my gap year and spent a good part of the time in Hong Kong, even renting a flat on Lamma and by sheer perseverance, talking to people who had lived there for years, I came up with what I wanted; it belonged to the man she had been having an affair with."

"Eric Noble." mentioning his name for the first time, wondering why she wasn't surprised. It made sense; it would have been somewhere for them to meet on the days when she was able to spend some time with him and no doubt he would have given her a key.

"Apparently," breaking into her thoughts, "she was a fairly frequent visitor when he would be there also."

"And you found that out by talking around the village, but these would have been Chinese people, wouldn't they?"

"Yes, they were, but I can speak Mandarin and a little Cantonese, but a lot of the older generation speak Mandarin on Lamma and once they knew I could speak their language they soon opened up and as it was eight years after her death meant there would be no comeback."

"And you've never told anyone?"

"No; I didn't see there would be any point."

"I suppose you were right."

"But then, after my dad died and I was sorting out his papers, I came across something which started me thinking there could be more to her death; that's the reason I wanted to speak to you, Letitia. You were my mother's closest friend; as young as I was, she used to say how much she valued your friendship and what a good confidante you were."

Perhaps not good enough she thought sadly; had Valerie been crying out for help in some way? Had she wanted to talk about the mental turmoil she was experiencing by being involved with Eric Noble, a man far more sophisticated than she had been, accustomed to 'going it alone' and answerable to no-one? If she had, she hadn't recognised the signals. And, if she had; would she have been willing to listen? She would never know the answers.

"You met Eric Noble, I suppose?" once again interrupting her troubled thoughts.

"Two or three times."

"You didn't like him, did you?"

"No, I didn't;" choosing her words carefully; the last thing she wanted to do was to encourage him into believing Eric Noble had been directly responsible for Valerie's death, "it's difficult for me to remain unbiased, Gerry. You see, I had already made up my mind about him almost from when I was first introduced to him, but this was a chemical reaction to the type of man who didn't appeal to me; I found him brash, over-confident in a rather supercilious way –"

"– the opposite to what my dad was like."

"Exactly," smiling at him; he was such an earnest young man and she wished she could be more helpful in tackling the torment he was going through surrounding what happened to his mother, "I found it hard to understand why she was attracted to him, but she was; it was as though he had cast a spell over her, disturbing her normal level-headedness. Maybe she did try to break away from him, but the strength of his personality made this impossible and, once I could see what was happening to her, the strength of my feelings towards Eric Noble changed; I started to dislike him intensely."

"In other words, not a likeable character."

"No; presumably he has some friends though."

"I don't suppose you have any idea where he's living now?"

There it was; the question she didn't want to hear, but she had to answer him. Gerry Blake was no longer a child needing protection from the big bad world out there.

"I didn't until very recently," she said slowly, "but I saw him last Thursday." and going on to tell him he was living in Meadowbank and had been for the past three months or so.

"Good grief; what a coincidence; did you talk to him?"

"No, he pointedly ignored me. I was with a friend of mine; we were having lunch in a restaurant in Winchester when we saw him; it was Rachel who told me, actually. She and her husband are living in his old family property and have leased out their lodge to him."

"Not a comfortable neighbour for you, Letitia."

"Fortunately the estate is a ten-minute drive out of town, all the same it is a wonder we haven't bumped into each other, but now as he's made it plain he doesn't want to speak to me, well, I can live with that."

"Perhaps he will soon move on."

"I hope so." wondering what his reaction would be if she told him what Rachel had said about the police being to see him in respect to his involvement with Katherine Peters; that's all Gerry would need to fuel what could be his growing suspicions of the man.

"I was telling you about what I found amongst Dad's papers."

"Sorry, Gerry; we got a little sidetracked, didn't we? But first, another beer and as it's almost lunchtime, I'll prepare a salad for us."

It didn't take her long to put together a ham and cheese salad, together with slices of freshly baked bread which she'd bought at the bakery earlier in the morning and, replenishing their drinks, carried it out to the patio. She found him easy to talk to and in some respects reminded her of Timothy and although he was a good ten years older, he had retained his boyishness and like Timothy, was a good listener.

"I don't know why he kept her handbag, the one she'd had with her, because there was nothing else in the house which had belonged to my mother. At first glance, there was little of any interest in it; just the usual stuff women keep in their handbags, I suppose, but in her wallet, together with some cards from various shops and stores in Hong Kong, there were several old ferry tickets. I'm not sure why I bothered to sift through them, but when I did, I found one for the last ferry on the night she arrived on Lamma, also another for the following afternoon going back to Hong Kong and then two more in the early evening for Lamma."

"Two tickets?"

"Yes, that's right; I've brought them with me.' taking the tickets from an inside pocket of his jacket and handing them to her.

Sure enough, what he'd said was right. Somebody had been with her when she must have returned to Lamma the next day, so she had still been alive on the first day which meant the time of death had been wrong. Presumably this could happen, otherwise why the other tickets in her wallet where she must have put them after she'd bought them. Now, there were even more questions to be asked; no wonder Gerry was so concerned, but then what could he have done? It hadn't been until Pete had died he had even known about them and by that time Valerie had been dead for fourteen years. But, she sighed, what could she say? There was no doubt in her mind what he had shown her must make a significant difference to the verdict of suicide.

"This is quite staggering, Gerry."

"I know, that's how I felt when I saw them. I had absolutely no idea who I should talk to; this problem made even more difficult because of the different regime in Hong Kong now. My mother died nine years before the handover to the Chinese in 1997; by the time Dad died in 2002, I didn't believe they would be too keen to re-open a case which as far as the authorities were concerned had been closed for fourteen years."

"I can understand that and of course when Pete died you wouldn't have any remaining connections with Hong Kong."

"'There was no-one, Letitia. And as by that time, if I had approached the police in Hong Kong, those four tickets," pointing at the tickets she was still holding, "represented the only evidence I had and maybe they would have been considered to be insufficient to justify any further interest. Have you any ideas what I could do?"

"I'm not sure, Gerry; I'd need to think about all of this, but I may be able to find someone who could give us some advice, but I can't make any promises."

"It's pretty selfish of me to inflict my problem on to you, but when I met Timothy the other day and he told me where you were both living, I thought I could make one last stab at solving what, quite frankly, has been a mystery which has yet to be solved."

"I'm glad you have told me; Valerie was a dear friend and if it turns out that someone was responsible for her dying the way she did, the least I can do is try to unravel what, to me as well, has always been a puzzle. When are you returning to Thailand, by the way; I haven't asked."

"I've a flight booked for Friday night; I'll be spending most of this week in London seeing old friends and re-visiting some of my favourite haunts. I hired a car at Heathrow, so will be driving back to London today, but I'll give you my mobile number, also my address in Phuket. In case anyone needs to contact me before I leave London," he added, "I'm staying at The Royal National hotel in Russell Square."

They had an early evening meal at the Salmon's Rest restaurant in the square before Gerry headed off back to London and as she watched him drive away, the moment was reminiscent of two months ago, when she saw Timothy off at Heathrow for his flight to Thailand. She had no worries about him, knowing he was happy and if she had done nothing else for Valerie's son, at least she had the satisfaction of realising she had helped him to share the mental burden he had been carrying for so long.

By mid-morning, she was no further to reaching any decision and the more she shuffled and re-arranged what she actually had in order to present any kind of cohesive explanation of why she suspected the verdict of her friend's suicide was wrong, the more she realised the weakness of what were no more than shreds of evidence. Four ferry tickets, three of them presumably used by Valerie, while the fourth could have belonged to anyone, all of them going back nineteen years. And to suggest this may have been Eric Noble's, was tantamount to being libellous. It was all too insubstantial. Even the fact that Valerie had returned to Hong Kong Island the following day and to return later, could be dismissed as having no importance; she may not have had suicide on her mind when she first arrived on Lamma, but something may have occurred the next day to make her decide to end her life, but, and Letitia thought, it was a big but; it would seem she hadn't been on her own, it could be argued that while she may have gone over to Lamma in the company of someone, presumably someone she had known, it didn't necessarily mean he or she went back with her to the house.

She was meeting Rachel for coffee at eleven and as she left the house to walk along to the Bridge Café, she decided to take her into her confidence, confident in the knowledge that Rachel would realise the importance of being discreet and knowing she would hardly mention anything in the presence of her new neighbour. Rachel had made it clear to her the other day that already she didn't feel happy about him living so close to her and the family.

They arrived at the café at exactly the same time and after their coffees had been brought over to them, she wasted no time in telling her about Gerry's visit. Rachel listened, without interrupting, her expression changing rapidly from one of interest to one of shock, and even when she came to the end of everything she remembered of what had been said the day before, she remained silent for a couple of seconds.

'Poor young man,' she said at last, 'how dreadful this must have all been for him, especially having no-one to talk to for such a long time. Also, no father either, although from what you've said, Letitia, it sounds as though he wouldn't have been much help; he may not have wanted to know.'

'You could be right; I liked Pete, he was easy to talk to, but after Valerie's death, we saw less and less of him socially and as Gerry said, he seemed to close in on himself and any questions he asked him about Valerie were answered sparingly.'

'I wonder why she went back to Hong Kong the next day.'

'Perhaps she wanted to see Eric Noble again, I don't know. She may not have believed he really meant it when he turned her away.'

'But there was the other woman.'

'Valerie was in a highly emotional state, she wasn't acting normally, Rachel; part of her brain may have conveniently refused to accept that he had anyone else.'

'And yet you didn't think she was the suicidal type?'

'I wouldn't have said she was.'

'What does Gerry think?'

'He's found it hard to grasp, mainly I think because of there being no suicide note and I believe he could be right; Valerie loved her son, she hated him being away at school; she told me often enough. Now he's older, he looks very like her, you know.'

'You must have found that even more sad.'

'I did.' finding herself almost whispering; what Rachel had said was so true and even after all this time the memory of Valerie remained as vivid as ever and seeing Gerry yesterday had intensified her feelings.

'I don't suppose you had much sleep last night, did you?' placing a hand on her arm as she had done the other day; a gesture of sympathy and a comfort but she could only nod.

'Shall we have another coffee; another injection of caffeine won't do any harm.'

'You've got your mother hen hat on.' managing a smile.

'Don't forget I have had three daughters.'

'Plenty of practice, then?'

'I should say so.'

'Do you think I should speak to someone, Rachel?'

'You mean the police?'

'Yes, you've already met the Chief Inspector, so I was wondering whether he might be the best person to approach.'

'I believe he would be; there's one thing, Letitia, you can't keep all of this bottled up, you'll make yourself ill otherwise.'

'I know.'

'He gave me his card when he called at the house last week; if you like, I'll give him a ring and then you can pick up from there. He's alright, Letitia; Colin already knew him when he was stationed in Winchester and has a lot of respect for him. I'm sure he will put you at your ease and then, if he thinks it's necessary, he can arrange to meet up with Gerry before he returns to Thailand.'

Chapter Eleven

It had not been an easy session with Bill Simms at the weekend. While he agreed with Graham a further meeting with Harold Maitland was necessary, having listened to what Ian and he had uncovered in respect to the activities of Katherine Peters and the fact that the property she had been renting in Notting Hill belonged to her ex-husband, he became quite voluble at any suggestion Katherine's clients may have been procured by him.

"You have no evidence to support his involvement in what can only be described as prostitution, Graham. No evidence whatsoever."

"That is theoretically true, sir," he'd answered, wondering if his Superintendent considered him to be so unprofessional as to actually accuse Maitland to his face, "but it is to be hoped with further questioning, something more substantial will emerge."

"Far be it for me, Graham," his sudden outburst petering out, "to tell you how to do your job or to handle a difficult interview; also," he'd continued, "to remind you of the man's standing in the city. I do appreciate what you and your team are up against, but we don't want any hiccups."

There hadn't been much more to say and it had been with relief when he brought the meeting to an end. Even before transferring to Meadowbank, Graham had known of Bill Simms' reputation and in spite of the man's tough exterior he rather suspected he had another, less critical, side to his nature. Mind you, he thought cynically as he left his office, he had yet to find it.

Graham had half expected to be called back in again this morning when he learned about Cordelia Bortoletto's suicide, but he hadn't been. Even Bill Simms with his low tolerance level would realise that apart from the murder of Beverly Clements being solved, they were no further forward than they were on Saturday in finding Katherine Peters' murderer. Much would depend on this meeting he had later this morning with Harold Maitland. It was around ten when he joined the M27; he had decided to leave the car in Wimbledon and take the tube into London, not sharing Ian's knowledge of driving and easily finding his way around the city.

Ian's description of Gerald Maitland had been a good one and he did bear a resemblance to Eric Noble, only a slight one, but both men were about the same height and build and although Maitland was a few years older, at a quick glance and from a distance, that wouldn't have been so noticeable, the only marked difference being their voices, Maitland's being thinner and of a higher pitch and without the Yorkshire accent.

'I must say, Chief Inspector,' Gerald Maitland said when the formal greetings had been made, accompanied by the obligatory handshake, 'I am rather surprised to receive a second visit from Meadowbank's constabulary; a town, I might add, until recently, I had not known of its existence.'

'Since Inspector Ash saw you last week, Mr Maitland, there have been certain developments in our enquiry concerning Katherine Peters' death which have resulted in us having to examine her life more closely.'

'And how may I ask does this involve me. Apart from what I've told your Inspector, I don't believe there is anything further I can tell you about her. You are already aware that we were only married a short time.'

'How long had you known Miss Peters?'

'How long?' the pale eyes behind the glasses widening, whether affected or not, Graham couldn't decide. He had noticed, even after only a few minutes in his company, his exaggerated gestures and the pedantic way he spoke, all of which could signify his effeteness, but any question over his sexuality didn't necessarily have any bearing on whether he was guilty.

'Yes,' he said, 'when did you first meet her?'

'And this is relevant, Chief Inspector?' the expression of surprise remaining.

'We believe it could be, sir.'

'Well, let me see; I can't remember the exact date, but it must have been about a year before we were married, which would have been 1998.'

'Not earlier?'

'No; why do you ask?'

'She had an old address book amongst her possessions which she appeared to have started using in 1992 and your Christian name was one of the first entries, but then she may have known someone else called Harold.' feeding him the bait and waiting to see whether he would take it.

'Harold is quite a common name I suppose; it's possible she did,' the reply coming smoothly, with no indication he was annoyed at being contradicted, 'you say she only used the Christian name?'

'Yes, that's right; she hadn't added surnames to any of the others either.'

'How casual of her; but then Katherine was like that. But it couldn't have been me though, Chief Inspector, because she always referred to me as Harry, never Harold. She used to say it was too fuddy-duddy.'

Touché, Graham though; one lie exchanged for another, although in this particular case, Harold Maitland was unaware of the trap he had fallen into.

'It is our understanding,' Graham said, 'that after the divorce you and Miss Peters had no further contact with each other; is that correct?'

'That is what I told Inspector Ash, also that there was no need to, we had nothing further to discuss.'

'In January 1999, Miss Peters took up the lease of Number Thirteen Lansdowne Terrace in Notting Hill and in April of that year when you married her, she continued with the lease right up to the time of her death; were you aware of this, sir?'

'No, I wasn't; our courtship, Chief Inspector, like our marriage, was brief and each time we met before we married was either at a restaurant or nightclub and, occasionally, in my house in South Hampstead.'

'I see, and although Number Thirteen Lansdowne Terrace is actually owned by you, you had no idea Miss Peters was leasing the property?'

'I would point out to you, Chief Inspector, that this property isn't personally owned by me, but by one of my companies, Maitland Holdings.'

'And yet you, as Managing Director, were not informed?'

'I have no interest in the people who rent the company's properties; the only time I would be, is if there was a problem which may require to be handled by a lawyer, in which case I would have to be consulted.'

'Your company will presumably only deal with one firm of estate agents, namely Gregory & Stevens in Portobello Road?'

'That's right; we've been with them for over twenty years.'

'And do they always act as the sole agents?'

'Naturally.'

'Prior to Miss Peters taking up the lease of the property in Lansdowne Terrace, we understand she was living in Guildford, as a long-term guest at the Mandalay Hotel in close vicinity to the Esther Summers Theatre where she was working at the time.'

'Of course I knew she was with them, but as to which hotel in Guildford, I had no idea. She never told me and I saw no reason to enquire. May I ask, Chief Inspector, why are you mentioning this?'

'The point I'm trying to make,' Graham explained, detecting the first signs of irritation in his manner, 'is this; Portobello Road in London is some considerable distance from the centre of Guildford and as she was working in Guildford, I'm wondering why she should choose to live further away from the theatre, but perhaps more importantly, why of all the estate agents in that part of London should she go to Gregory & Stevens.'

'I really have no idea; no doubt Katherine had her reasons.'

'But you didn't ask her?'

'No, indeed why should I have?'

'As Managing Director, you will be aware of the amount of rent on all of the company's properties?'

'Yes, of course; in fact we have monthly meetings when we discuss these financial matters.'

'At the time Miss Peters took out the lease the rent on the property was £900 per month.'

'I would have to get my accounts department to verify that.'

'There is no need to, sir; we have already done this by consulting Gregory & Stevens and Miss Peter's bank statement from the beginning of 1999 confirms the amount. As a matter of interest,' Graham persisted, 'did you know how much Miss Peters earned with the theatre?'

'I wouldn't have asked her that; it would have been most impolite.'

'I dare say it would have been, but knowing she had recently moved into a property in an expensive part of Notting Hill, where rents are considerably higher than those in the suburbs, didn't it occur to you as odd for her to commit herself to so much of a monthly outlay?'

'Odd?'

'Yes, odd. Not only was she paying over double than the hotel in Guildford was charging, but her travelling expenses would be high, especially as she wasn't paying anything each day to get to the theatre and back.'

'She had savings, I believe.' shrugging.

'Savings, when being spent, are inclined to deplete, Mr Maitland, but then I don't need to tell you that.'

'I can't argue with that, Chief Inspector.'

'A credible assumption would be that she had another source of income.'

'Don't forget the substantial divorce settlement.'

'I'm not likely to forget it, but the period I'm referring to is before your divorce, from January 1999 onwards, including the three years she was married to you.'

'I fail to see the importance of any of this and as far as I'm concerned, Chief Inspector, I'm finding it all somewhat time-consuming.'

'We consider there is a great deal of importance attached to what I've been asking you this morning, sir, and that's why we have to be certain without any shadow of doubt to support what we are beginning to suspect about the way Miss Peters conducted her life.'

'And what are you suspecting?'

'I'm sorry, but I can't at the moment say; it's too early in our investigation and regrettably for those people we have to question, tedious and as you say, time-consuming; for us and for the general public.'

'I'm thankful I haven't your job, Chief Inspector.'

'You're not the first person to have said that to me, sir. Finally,' and wondering what sort of reception he would get this time, 'I would like to go over again what you told Inspector Ash about the night Miss Peters was murdered.'

'If you must.' accompanied by another exaggerated gesture.

'You said you had spent the evening at the Saville Club, returning home around ten.'

'That is correct; I can't be precise, but certainly not much later.'

'You didn't go anywhere else after you left your club?'

'At that time of night; where on earth *could* I go?'

'It wasn't so late; a night club for instance, or you may have visited someone, a friend maybe. These are only guesses, you understand, but one of your neighbours has told us you returned home in the early hours of the Monday morning.'

'Well, all I can say is he or she is mistaken.'

'You live on your own.'

'Yes, I've already told the Inspector.'

'I know you did, sir, but this person was quite sure. You keep your car in the garage at the side of your house and it has an up and over type of door; is that right?'

'Yes.'

'Is there room for only the one vehicle?' deliberately confusing him.

'Yes.' rewarded this time by a frown; Gerald Maitland didn't know where he was coming from and that was precisely what he wanted. It would be too easy to use another approach, take him up to that point of no return common in the course of police procedure in a murder enquiry, but the time wasn't right. Soon it would be, but then the interview would be recorded.

'I'm grateful for your time, Mr Maitland,' Graham said, standing up, 'you've been very patient. I will require a written statement from you covering the points discussed today, including those at the meeting you had with Inspector Ash.'

'Surely you don't expect me to drive to Meadowbank?'

'Not at all; we're working in conjunction with Scotland Yard on this murder enquiry and we will be able to use one of their conference rooms. However, I'll phone you within the next couple of days to arrange a suitable time.'

***

As Graham left Gerald Maitland's office, Ian was ringing the doorbell of Letitia's house in Riverside Gardens. It had been well after twelve when he took the call from Rachel Tilsly and once he'd heard what she had to say, wasted no time in getting there. Another unexpected twist he had thought, in a murder enquiry which even from the start the previous Monday, had every appearance of getting out of control. He had no criticisms of the way Graham Ford was handling the case; in many respects working closely with him as he had been for the last week was very similar to when Brenda Masters had been here, the main difference being he gave the impression of being more laid back, but by now Ian recognised this as a foil. Graham obviously believed in the softly, softly approach, followed by the sharp verbal attack which never failed to unnerve the recipient, whereas Brenda went right in. She certainly believed in the adage of 'biting the snake's head off'.

The woman who came to the door reminded him of Simon Grant's wife; a similar mass of auburn hair and the unconventional way she dressed, making him wonder whether she, too, was an artist. Ian had seen her a few times around the town but hadn't known who she was, only that she had bought one of the new houses on the land across the road from The Bridge Inn.

'Mrs Radcliffe?'

'Yes, that's right.'

'I'm Inspector Ian Ash, Mrs Radcliffe.' showing her his card.

'It's good of you to come here so quickly; I suppose really I should have gone into the police station, but –'

'It's quite alright; many people feel the same way, unless of course they are used to visiting police stations.'

'Do come in, Inspector,' she said, opening the door wider for him and leading him across the hall and into the kitchen; a large sunny room facing the river, 'I have been in something of a quandary actually,' she said, pulling out a chair for him, 'not knowing whether I should talk to anyone or not; the last thing I want to do is waste police time.'

'It's surprising how often something which may not seem important turns out to be quite the opposite.' trying to put her at her ease; it wasn't as though she seemed nervous, but it was clear to him she was deeply concerned and professionally he was intrigued to learn what it could be.

'Well,' taking a deep breath and sitting down across the table to him, 'oh dear; where on earth shall I start?'

'One of my school teachers used to say "start at the beginning and go on to the end".'

'Wise woman,' she smiled again, 'but even that's tricky because I don't really know where the beginning is, but here goes:' taking a deep breath, 'nineteen years ago, when I was living in Hong Kong, a close friend of mine called Valerie Blake committed suicide, that was the official verdict, but there were a couple of anomalies about her death which didn't add up. I'll try and make this as brief as possible, Inspector; Valerie had been having an affair and her husband found out, the result being she left him, taking a couple of bags containing her clothes, and without forewarning him, went to the other man's apartment fully expecting he would be happy for her to stay. It didn't suit him at all and he told her to go back to her husband which she didn't do; instead, she took the ferry over to Lamma Island, but before doing that she gave me a call to tell me what had happened and that she was going away for a few days to think things over and would see me when she came back. Three days later, her body was found in a house on Lamma. She died of a drug overdose; there was no suicide note and although her handbag was there, the two pieces of luggage she had been seen carrying off the ferry on the night she left her husband, weren't in the house. The police were unable to find out who owned the house.' pausing for a moment.

'A sad tale,' Ian said, 'and so many years ago.'

'I know,' she nodded, 'no doubt you can imagine my surprise, Inspector Ash, when I had a visit from Valerie's son yesterday. Gerry had only been twelve when she died and at the time of her death had been at school in England. Naturally he found it difficult to believe she had taken her own life, but now from what he's managed to find out, even more so.'

'I believe we're coming to why you've been in so much of a quandary.' attempting to make it easier for her.

'He didn't actually say when he went back to Hong Kong later after his father had returned to England to live, only that it was in his gap year when he was at university, which would have been about ten years ago. He particularly chose Hong Kong because he was determined to find out what he could about his mother's death –'

'– and he did?'

'Not a great deal, except he found out who owned the house on Lamma.'

'That was smart of him.'

'It was, yes; he told me he could speak Mandarin and Cantonese and was able to communicate with some of the neighbours. Gerry knew about the man his mother had been having an affair with; not at the time of course, but in those intervening years before he made that return visit to Hong Kong; according to those neighbours he was the person who owned the house. Inspector Ash,' taking another deep breath, 'his name was Eric Noble.'

'What a coincidence! Did you know him, Mrs Radcliffe?'

'Not well, we used to see him now and again socially; my ex-husband, and Pete Blake, Valerie's husband, both worked for the same bank as he did.'

'I see; you said a few minutes ago that Gerry didn't find out a great deal during his trip to Hong Kong.'

'Yes, this was five years ago, after his father died. Gerry was sorting out his papers when he found the handbag Valerie must have had with her. He thought everything was still inside, including her wallet. She'd kept several ferry tickets; one of them was for the ferry she took that night when she went to Lamma, there was another for the following day from Lamma to Hong Kong Island and then later that day two tickets back to Lamma. Gerry has given me the tickets, Inspector; I'll get them for you.' going over to the worktop and taking out an envelope from one of the drawers, 'here you are; you'll be able to see for yourself.'

'Thank you.' and taking out the four tickets, examined them closely; as she had said, they were for those journeys her friend must have made, and the fourth? The obvious deduction would be, as they were in her handbag she didn't return to Lamma Island on her own. Had Eric Noble been with her? As far as Ian could see, whether he had been or not, bore no relevance to their murder enquiry. 'Where does Gerry Blake live, Mrs Radcliffe?'

'Sorry; I've neglected to tell you or to explain how he found out where I was now. I suppose you could say it was chance really, but Gerry is working in Thailand, in a bar in Phuket, and my son, who is travelling in Thailand, met him. Timothy heard Gerry mention he used to live in Hong Kong and told him he used to as well and when they were exchanging names and addresses Gerry immediately remembered the surname and decided to make a brief trip back to England to try to see me. You see,' she explained, 'from how he was talking I think he's been unable to shrug off, shall we say suspicions, surrounding his mother's death and unfortunately he's never been able to confide in anyone, not even his father, and he thought I might be able to help. I suppose he was clutching at straws really.'

'Perhaps not, Mrs Radcliffe,' Ian said, 'I will have to discuss this with my Chief Inspector; he's in London today, but will be back later this afternoon. I'd like to take these tickets with me, if I may.'

'Yes, of course.'

'When will Gerry be returning to Thailand?'

'On Friday; he didn't give me any times, but I have his mobile number and his address in Thailand; I've written them down for you, also he's staying at The Royal National Hotel in Russell Square.'

'Thank you; that's a great help.'

'Inspector Ash?'

'Yes?'

'What I'm trying to say is, I don't want to make – to make any trouble for Eric Noble,' stumbling over her words, 'I know he's been questioned by the police in respect to his friendship with the woman who –' unable to continue, a look of embarrassment on her face.

'– I understand what you're saying and I assure you we will be discreet.'

'That's good. You see, Eric Noble is aware I'm a friend of Rachel Tilsly. Rachel and I were having lunch in 'Roberta's Bistro' in Winchester and he was in there; he must have seen us, although he made no sign that he had and knowing we were friends it wouldn't be too difficult for him to find out where I'm living now. In fact, until last Thursday in the restaurant, I had no idea he was also living in Meadowbank.'

***

Carol Cliff was sitting in the window seat of The Bridge Inn when she saw Ian emerge from one of the houses across the road. Interesting, she thought, that's the same house where the two women had gone to about an hour ago. She had recognised one of them as being Rachel Tilsly but not the other one, and knowing where Rachel Tilsly lived, it didn't take her long to work out that the person she was with must live in Riverside Gardens and the fact Inspector Ash had been in there must mean something. It wouldn't be a wild guess to say that whatever they had been talking about concerned the case he and the Chief Inspector were working on, this idea strengthened by Rachel's presence. Could this be the 'sting in the tail' for her column she'd been looking for these last few days? So far, since coming back to Meadowbank, she'd had the place very much to herself, but by the time the news of Beppe Bortoletto's wife leaked out, they would all be back, even that irritating know-it-all guy from the Winchester "Chronicle". There could be a chance here, she decided, to suss out that little bit extra that none of the others would know, at least not until after her piece was out. She had been working on the fine-tuning of what she planned to send through to her paper later in the afternoon in order to hit the newsagents tomorrow morning, choosing to sit well away from anyone sufficiently interested in what she was writing, but now, closing her notebook and stashing it away in her bulky bag, she needed to do what she described as mingling, or as Jimmy, if he was with her, would, in his eloquent way , say it was 'ear-wigging'; a typical English expression, especially in her profession, and one she had perfected over the years.

'Now, I wonder why Ian Ash has been visiting Mrs Radcliffe.' one of

The Bridge's regulars remarked; a carbon copy of Brian Morrison's old-age pensioners peering short-sightedly through the open doorway and, following his gaze, Carol could now see the Inspector striding in the direction of the pub, but instead of coming in, turned left as she had hoped, recognising how his presence would stem their habitual non-stop speculations.

'I know one thing,' the man next to him added, nodding his head as though he possessed some inner knowledge of the workings of the Meadowbank constabulary, 'it won't be a social call.'

'Probably not; what do you bet it's got something to do with these murders.'

'You don't know for sure though, do you?'

'I would say, Ted, I know about as much as anyone in this town about what's going on. Besides, I don't know whether you noticed or not, but Mrs Tilsly who, I might add, is a friend of Letitia Radcliffe, came back with her to the house just before midday.'

'Ah, Mrs Tilsly, you say?'

'Yes, and I'm sure you haven't forgotten what I told you the other day about Charlie Hobbs saying that the Chief Inspector had been to see Eric Noble up at the lodge.'

'Of course I haven't forgotten, but what has that got to do with Ian Ash's visit to Mrs Radcliffe?'

'I would say quite a lot.'

'She's a very nice lady, Bill, much-travelled too; I heard she used to live in Hong Kong; I'm sure she wouldn't have anything to do with what's been going on this past week.'

'I'm not saying she has; mind you, she had another visitor yesterday and I've never seen him around here before.'

'You're full of surprises Bill Knowles, how did you find that out?'

'By using my eyes, Ted; by using my eyes.'

They were in full spate, and as always, made no attempt to lower their voices and unashamedly Carol listened, most of which was repetitive stuff and not much different from what the other old cronies had been saying in The Market Inn, but there had been a couple of gems which interested her; she now knew the name of the woman who lived across the road and although she'd already sussed out she must be a friend of Rachel Tilsly, there was the person who visited her the day before, and as this guy, Bill Knowles, had never seen him before, meant he must be a stranger to Meadowbank and therefore could be of some significance, though how she could take this any further she had no idea, but she might think of something. She always had before.

She paid for another half lager and took it over to one of the tables closer to the bar within earshot of what they were saying and, taking out her notebook once again, turned to a fresh sheet.

'What did he look like, then, Bill?'

'Young; about thirty, blond-haired and quite sun-tanned; probably came from abroad.'

'We have had some very warm weather in this country, you know.'

'Not that much; anyway, he was driving a hire car.'

'How do you know it was hired?'

'Because of the sticker of course;' Bill Knowles said, 'you know me, Ted, nobody could say I was nosy, but I just happened to be walking along the pavement past the house, taking the dog for a walk as I always do on a Sunday, and saw the name of the car hire company and -' pausing; no doubt expecting to be asked more.

'- and,' he repeated dramatically, 'he'd hired it at Heathrow Airport.'

'Oh.'

'Is that all you can say, Ted.' a look of disappointment on his broad face.

'Well, it doesn't mean he's *suspicious*, does it?'

'Of course not; all I'm saying is, him being here yesterday could have something to do with Ian Ash calling in to see Letitia Radcliffe this morning.'

'Maybe he was from Hong Kong.'

'Now, Ted, that would be guessing, wouldn't it? affecting a look of innocent indignation.

***

Gerald Maitland stood at the window, looking down into the street below. He had heard the faint drone of the lift as it descended to the ground floor and within minutes he saw Chief Inspector Graham Ford emerge from the building; a tall slim upright man, a good fifteen years younger than himself. As he watched him walking along the pavement to the first set of traffic lights to stop alongside other pedestrians waiting to cross the road, Gerald seriously wondered what his life must be like; apart from TV movies, he knew little about police procedure. He wasn't an imaginative man, therefore, unless he had actually experienced any situation, he hadn't the ability or the knowledge to work out what the next step would be in what seemed to him a somewhat long drawn out investigation, most of which boringly repetitive. The world he lived in was entirely different, decisions, speedy decisions, were paramount to how he ran his businesses, the goal always being to succeed. He was well aware he was a hard taskmaster and had often been accused of being ruthless, but that was the way he was and that was how he made money, with only the occasional failure, resulting in a wrong move, as in the case of ever having had anything to do with Katherine.

He had almost lost sight of him now; once he had crossed the road he'd become swallowed up by the lunchtime crowd heading for the pubs and restaurants in Kensington High Street. Gerald had no preconceived idea earlier of how the meeting with him would go and couldn't make up his mind whether he should attach all that much importance to what had been said. It seemed to him that the police were literally groping around in the dark; they had two murders on their hands, both of which had yet to be solved. It was as though they were picking on him only because of having been married to Katherine; there was nothing else which pinpointed him as her murderer, even the Chief Inspector coming up with one of his neighbours saying he had been seen coming home in the early hours of Monday morning was totally unsubstantiated and as far as his innuendos about Katherine's other life having any connection with him was pure fabrication. Going through the formalities of making a signed statement didn't worry him either and, in his opinion, didn't justify taking his solicitor along with him. The fewer people who knew about these intrusions in his life, the better. He had to admit he was relieved he wouldn't be expected to turn up at the police station in Meadowbank; that was one town he never intended to go to again.

He had made it his business to find out where Katherine had gone when he had realised she only occupied the mews house when she was seeing clients; a private firm of detectives, and one he had used occasionally over the years, achieved that for him; it didn't take long and within a week of hiring them he had what he wanted. He chose a time when he knew she would be in London and drove the unfamiliar route to Meadowbank. He had no difficulty in finding Bramble Cottage, noting its position in relation to the centre of the town. He didn't spend any more time there than he had to, only calling into a pub in the market square for a sandwich before coming back to London. The whole round trip had taken him three and a half hours; therefore he knew exactly how long it would take to return there.

The next time he went, having checked to make sure she would be in Meadowbank, he took the precaution of leaving the car in a small car park he'd seen before behind a café he'd spotted at the corner of Bridge Street and walked the short distance to Bramble Cottage. There were no lights on in the front of the property, but he saw the reflection of one at the back and, lifting the latch of the garden gate, walked along the pathway to the back door. She hadn't drawn the kitchen curtains and was in the process of making coffee. He had tapped lightly on the window to attract her attention. When she saw it was him her startled look turned to one of disbelief and she hadn't hesitated in opening the door.

"What on earth are you doing here, Harry, and at this time of night?"

"I thought it was time we had a talk, Katherine."

"It's not like you to be so impulsive." she'd said, inviting in.

"No, I won't come in. What I have to say won't take long; we'll have a walk, it's a warm evening."

She hadn't been keen, but nevertheless she agreed and picking up her handbag and keys from the table, she'd joined him outside. They walked further along Riverside Lane which was deserted with no lights on in any of the houses. The scarf he used had been one of hers which she had forgotten to take with her when she left him. He had taken her completely by surprise, giving her no time to call out or make any real attempt to slacken the tightness of the scarf around her neck. He had dragged her body away from the road and into the ditch, pulling over some broken branches to conceal it. He had turned round to make his way back to where he'd parked the car, but by the time he had reached her cottage, a car turned into Riverside Lane. Quickly, he walked round to the back of the building as the car passed although not too concerned if the driver had seen him or not. Nobody knew him in Meadowbank and he had no intention of ever returning.

***

It was a relatively short walk to Lansdowne Terrace and he was glad of the exercise and to fill his lungs with some fresh air; he had found the atmosphere of Gerald Maitland's office stifling, having always disliked the excessive use of air-conditioning to maintain what was recognised as the correct working temperature. He also wanted this time to reflect on the outcome of this morning's meeting with him before seeing Elspeth Bennett. He had phoned her before leaving Meadowbank, surprised she had raised no objection and, now, with a little bit more to go on than Ian and he had had last week, what she may have to say could contribute towards them coming closer to wrapping up this case.

There didn't remain much doubt in Graham's mind of Gerald Maitland's guilt. Although Eric Noble's alibi for the night of Katherine Peter's murder was far from foolproof, and he had to admit his dubious background had prejudiced him, what had transpired during the last hour went a long way to strengthen the case against Gerald Maitland, someone whom they had been inclined at first to dismiss as a possible suspect, but now a totally different picture was emerging, although frustratingly, it still wasn't enough. Maitland had a strong motive for wanting Katherine Peters out of the way and his alibi was weak. If he had driven on to Meadowbank on the Sunday night after leaving the Saville Club, he could have feasibly reached Meadowbank, killed her and returned home around the time his neighbour had said. He had made a point of saying until

Katherine Peter's death, he had never been to Meadowbank, but he must have been there before the Sunday, if only to familiarise himself with the town and to learn where Bramble Cottage was situated. Graham found it impossible to believe Maitland didn't know the address of the woman who was receiving a considerable sum of money in alimony each month, also he could not accept he was unaware of the mews house being leased through Gregory & Stevens, a reputable and long-established firm of estate agents with whom Maitland Holdings, of which he was the managing director, had been dealing with for a number of years. But, pausing for a second in his reasoning, were they a reputable firm? From what Ian had said, Philip Gregory had been co-operative, although not volunteering any information he hadn't been asked, and having met Gerald Maitland, Graham didn't think he would deal with any run-of-the-mill High Street agency and no doubt would expect his privacy to be respected. It was more than likely that Philip Gregory would have been in touch with him following Ian's call to them on Saturday, but he gave no indication this morning; he could have mentioned it, if only to protest about questions being asked about one of his properties, but he didn't. Also, he hadn't reacted as strongly as Graham had expected when he mentioned his neighbour seeing him return much later than he'd told Ian. All he had said was that the neighbour must have been mistaken, an imitation of the shrug he'd got from Eric Noble when he told him he had been seen talking to Katherine Peters on Sunday evening. The chances of Gerald Maitland's neighbour being mistaken were remote, remembering about the up-and-over garage door; the only one of its type in close vicinity to his house. No, Graham decided as he reached the corner of Lansdowne Terrace, his alibi and what he'd said was full of holes and would need to be looked into more closely before they were in a position to take a firmer line with him and if, and when, they were ready and it meant going against Bill Simms' instructions, well, so be it; he hadn't reached this far in his career with the knowledge he'd acquired in the structuring of evidence for it to become eroded by being nervous of making a mistake. At the same time, he fully realised he must not allow his personal opinions to override hard proven facts. To Graham, it was of no concern whether Gerald Maitland was a successful businessman and recognised as such by London's higher echelons, or the ordinary man in the street with a nine to five job; if they were found to be guilty by the courts, the verdict would be the same. At least in a perfect world, he added cynically to himself.

Before leaving for London, Graham had taken another look at Katherine Peters' album and had extracted a couple of photographs taken ten or more years earlier, where the same man appeared, making allowances for any possible changes in appearance and now, having met the man and spent a good forty-five minutes in Gerald Maitland's company, he was fairly confident the photographs were of him. He had been much thinner in those days, his hair short and very dark; it was therefore not surprising Ian had missed any resemblance.

Elspeth Bennett took several minutes to come to the door, but Graham had expected this, Ian having told him she had considerable difficulty in walking, but the lady who was now standing in the open doorway and looking up at him appraisingly struck him immediately as someone with a great deal of inner strength, also of high intelligence.

'I'm Chief Inspector Graham Ford, Miss Bennett.' showing her his card.

'I'd already worked that out, Chief Inspector,' she smiled, scarcely looking at the card, 'do come in.' she added, and leaning heavily on her stick led the way into the kitchen, 'it's another warm day, so perhaps you would like a cool drink.'

He watched as she took a covered glass jug from the fridge, placing it on the table in the centre of the room and facing the open windows to her terrace.

'Home-made lemonade, Chief Inspector,' she said, pouring out two glasses, 'I wasn't too surprised when you phoned me this morning, although it was only Friday when Inspector Ash was here.'

'It's good of you to see me, Miss Bennett,' Graham said, taking a sip of the lemonade which was delicious, reminding him of the lemonade his mother used to make when he was a boy, 'what you were able to tell the Inspector was extremely helpful to us.'

'I'm glad.'

'Although,' Graham began tentatively, 'you may find what I'm about to tell you rather shocking.'

'I doubt that very much, you know. I'm seventy-one years of age and, although I've never been out of London, I've lived a full life and my work in Whitehall, while interesting, taught me a great deal about human nature and as I said to your Inspector, I can be relied upon to be discreet.'

'Thank you, Miss Bennett, I think I realised that. During the last week, since the body of Katherine Peters was found, Inspector Ash and I have been fully occupied investigating her death; we have been hampered by not knowing very much about her and it hasn't been easy trying to piece together sections of her life. The reason for delving into her past is because both of us believed that the motive for her murder had strong connection with that past. However, and you may very well have worked this out for yourself, it appears Katherine Peters lived a double life. She gave up her acting career fifteen years ago; we still don't know why, but she continued to live what could be described, while perhaps not lavishly, certainly comfortably. In other words, Miss Bennett, she appeared not to have any visible means of support to justify such a high expenditure. As yet, we don't have actual proof, but we believe she was obtaining money through prostitution, high-class prostitution. Having reached this conclusion, we also realised she would have needed assistance in acquiring her clients.' pausing to take another sip of his drink. All the time he had been talking she had remained quite still, never taking her eyes from his face, and he could tell she was absorbing every word, neither had she made any attempt to interrupt; a rare woman he thought wryly, most women he had known would by this time have said something.

'It is possible,' Graham continued, 'we may have found that person and this is where your additional help would be invaluable to us and, if nothing else, could prove we were thinking of the wrong man. What I would like you to do, Miss Bennett, is to take a look at this photograph of him,' handing her one of the prints he had brought with him.

She took the photograph from him and, putting on another pair of spectacles, looked at it closely before handing it back.

'I know who he is, Chief Inspector,' she said at last, looking across the table at him, a resigned expression on her face, 'It's Gerald Maitland; he was often an invited guest at formal government functions. The photograph was taken some time ago, but it's Gerald Maitland alright.'

'Did you ever see him here, visiting Katherine Peters, I mean?'

'As it happens, I did, a few times. At first I thought I must be mistaken, but then, I saw him not so long ago and I realised it was the same man. As you can see in the photograph his hair was dark then and over the years it has become quite grey, almost white in fact; I think that must have been why I didn't recognise him at first. Also, I have to say,' she said and for the first time sounding hesitant, 'I was surprised to see him here because, well, this is a little embarrassing, Chief Inspector.'

'That's alright,' he encouraged, 'take your time, Miss Bennett, 'I think I know what you're trying to say.'

'Do you really?'

'Yes,' Graham smiled; she really was a charming lady and as he had at first thought, very intelligent, 'because you considered he might be gay.'

'That's exactly what I was going to say, although it's probably not a good idea to put what you're thinking about someone into words. Years ago,' smiling, 'no-one did, but today everything is quite, quite different.'

'The permissive society.'

'We did use that expression in the sixties, but it's even more than that these days. One of my young nieces has often tried to educate me into what she calls the twenty-first century and one of her favourite expressions is 'let it all hang out, Auntie; let it all hang out. Rather vulgar. But, you know,' she went on, 'apparently I was quite wrong about Gerald Maitland because a woman I used to work with, many years younger than I am and still in Whitehall, told me a few years ago that he had married.'

'He did, Miss Bennett;' Graham told her, deciding she should know in case he had to ask her if she would be prepared to officially confirm what she'd said, 'he married Katherine Peters eight years ago.'

'My goodness me; how extraordinary!'

'It is, isn't it? Are you able to remember when you first saw him here?'

'I am as a matter of fact; it was not long after she moved in next door;

as I mentioned to Inspector Ash, I bought this house around the same time in January 1999.'

'I see;' Graham nodded, 'you said a few minutes ago you had seen him more recently.'

'Yes, it would have been about three years ago.'

'Here, in Lansdowne Terrace?'

'Oh, yes; he was outside, ringing Miss Peters' door bell.'

Chapter Twelve

Graham collected his car in Wimbledon and rejoined the M3, but instead of continuing on towards Winchester and taking the turn-off for Meadowbank, took the exit junction for Guildford. Elspeth Bennett had unwittingly provided him with the idea, once she had told him she'd seen Gerald Maitland visiting her next door neighbour not long after she had moved into the mews house, that it was more than likely he had known Katherine Peters further back then he'd said. And, the Esther Summers Theatre seemed as good as anywhere to make a start, remembering it had been Ian who had suggested he should call in there the week before, although now, some days later and with considerably more knowledge about Katherine Peters, Graham felt he was in a better position to, hopefully, expand on that knowledge.

He didn't get anywhere with the theatre's personnel officer, a forbidding woman well on in her fifties, who, although confirming that Katherine Peters had been with them from 1997 until 2002, was either unwilling or unable to give any reason why she left and, realising he was wasting his time, he brought the brief conversation to an end. Returning to the foyer, he noticed a door leading to their coffee shop and decided to have a break before heading back to Meadowbank. It had already been a long day and he wasn't sure whether he had managed to learn all that much, but that's the way it often was, he thought philosophically and this case was proving no different from any other murder enquiry in which he'd been involved.

He ordered a ham and cheese sandwich and a coffee and had almost finished when a woman he had noticed earlier in the foyer came in but instead of going up to the counter, came over towards him.

'I hope you don't mind,' she said, 'but I overhead you asking to speak to someone in our personnel office and I was wondering whether you were here because of what happened to Katherine?'

'I am,' he admitted, a little surprised at such a direct approach, 'did you know her?' She was an attractive woman; a smooth cap of ash-blonde hair framing a heart-shaped face and he reckoned about the same age as

Katherine Peters.

'My name's Lynne Briars, by the way, and yes, I did know Katherine and I couldn't believe it when I heard what had happened to her. It was just too awful.'

'I'm conducting the enquiry into her death and I was hoping to find out something about the time she was with the theatre, but -'

'- I suppose you came up against the proverbial brick wall with Miss Wilson.'

'Well, put it like this, she wasn't all that helpful.'

'She wouldn't be, Chief Inspector. I overheard when you introduced yourself,' she explained, 'you see, Miss Wilson has been with the theatre for years and years and has created her own little empire when it comes to staff matters.'

'It happens; you say you knew Miss Peters.' prompting her, but there was really no need to; she seemed eager to talk about her.

'Quite well, actually; we started here more or less at the same time and at one point we even talked about sharing a flat but then, she moved into a house in Notting Hill. I had no idea she hadn't still been living there, but we lost touch after she left the theatre.'

'Do you know why she left, Lynne?'

'She didn't have much choice, Chief Inspector; she was politely asked to leave. Poor Katherine, she wasn't having much luck around that time; there was the embarrassing scandal involving her husband and then our director discovering about her other job. Naturally enough, I suppose, he didn't approve, no doubt concerned about the good name of the theatre, all that sort of thing, but when you think about it, that attitude is a bit archaic in today's society. Katherine was a good actress, but I'm sorry to say that didn't make any difference to his decision. She just had to go.'

'This other job you've mentioned, did she tell you what this was?'

'She did, yes. Mind you, I don't think she told anyone else, but she trusted me. I knew her years ago, before she went to the States with her first husband, so you could say we knew each other fairly well.'

'She was into prostitution, wasn't she?' coming straight to the point.

'I always think prostitution is such a harsh word, but I guess there's no other way to describe offering sex in exchange for money. Katherine, unfortunately, was motivated by money and in the circles in which she was moving there was plenty of it, also,' she went on, more slowly now as she remembered her friend, 'there was very little risk, because of the high social status of her clients, of anyone finding out until, of course, our director discovered what she was doing; how he did, I have no idea, and I don't think she did either.'

'We knew she'd been married twice,' Graham said, 'but did you ever meet her second husband?'

'Only the once; that was when Katherine introduced him to me, although I had often seen him in "Annabel's" around that time.'

'Can you remember when that was?'

'I think I can, actually,' she said, 'it was twelve or thirteen years ago; no, it must have been twelve, not long before she married her first husband. I remembered being surprised to see her with him, especially as she had only got engaged to Franklin that January.'

'You mentioned a scandal.' prompting her, at the same time making a mental note of what she had just told him which further disproved what Gerald Maitland had said.

'Oh, yes; well, it could have been a bigger scandal than it was really, but when it happened it became obvious that it was being hushed up and not even picked up by the press, therefore, apart from Katherine immediately filing for a divorce, he emerged virtually unscathed. Katherine said little about her marriage and it wasn't until it was discovered he had chosen a rather indiscreet young man as his lover, such was her anger, she poured it all out to me.'

'So, the man is gay; that's what you're saying?'

'He must be, Chief Inspector, but you know, there were quite a few of us who used to see him in "Annabel's", who already thought he might be, but when he married Katherine, well, we had to think differently.'

'Do you think she was aware of his sexuality?'

'She was, because she told me; this was when, in her words, he had humiliated her.'

'But she did marry him.'

'Katherine wanted security, and with Gerald Maitland being an extremely wealthy man, she believed that being his wife would provide it.'

'An unhappy woman.' Graham commented, getting a much clearer picture of Katherine Peters.

'We all have our Achilles heel, Chief Inspector,' she said sadly, 'and in that respect Katherine was no different than anyone else; she had an in-depth dread of being hard up.'

***

By the time Graham arrived back in Meadowbank, having had to endure the usual delays on the approach to the slip road leading on to the A390, The Market Inn had already opened for the evening. There was nothing he would like better than a cold beer to quench his thirst, deciding he would call in there before going back to the office and, parking the car in front of the Station, walked along to the pub.

Since moving to Meadowbank, he'd been in quite often and had started to think of it as his local. He liked Brian Morrison; the epitome of a pub landlord. He wasn't much older than himself and had recently become a father for the first time and in many respects Graham envied him being given a second chance in life and perhaps spending his whole life among people he knew. His own life, regrettably, had up to now worked out quite differently. Since his divorce six years ago, he'd never found anyone else, knowing the profession he had chosen was partly to blame for this. Unsocial working hours weren't exactly conducive to developing a relationship and in his case, maintaining one. He and Elizabeth had never had children; in the early years he had regretted this when many of his colleagues were marrying and starting families of their own.

'Good evening, Chief Inspector,' Brian greeted him, 'have you finished work for the day?'

'Almost,' Graham gave him a rueful smile, 'I've been in London for most of it.'

'London, eh. I can't remember when I was last up there. Keep promising to take Melissa, but somehow we never get round to it. Anyway, what would you like to drink?'

'I'll have a pint of your Best Bitter please; that should do the trick.'

He waited until he had poured the beer and had taken his first long sip, before mentioning the other reason for coming in.

'I know Ian Ash has been talking to you about the circus worker who was in here last week and what you were able to tell him has been a help to us. Since then, as you're no doubt aware, there have been a number of developments in our investigation.'

'It would be impossible not to know living in a town the size of Meadowbank, but it isn't good and to many of us we long for things to return to what we always thought of as normal, so if I can help you, well that's fine.'

'I don't know whether this person has ever been in Meadowbank,' Graham said, showing him the photograph of Gerald Maitland, 'but we have reason to believe he has and I have to admit it's a long shot to think he may have come in here.'

Brian took the photograph from him and looked at it closely, 'I don't think so,' he said, shaking his head, 'no, I'm fairly sure about that. Derek may have served him of course, but I certainly didn't. I'll just ask Melissa.' he added, waiting until she had finished serving a group of customers at the other end of the bar, before calling her over.

'Good evening, Chief Inspector.' she said, joining them.

'Do you recognise him, love?' showing her the photograph.

'Yes, I do; he was in a couple of weeks ago,' she said without any hesitation, 'I can't remember which day it was,' she added, continuing to look at it, 'but it was at lunchtime and he didn't stay long; Derek served him, Brian, and after he'd finished the sandwich I made for him, he went.'

'I don't remember him.' Brian put in.

'No, you wouldn't have, love, you were at the Cash & Carry, therefore, Chief Inspector,' turning to look at him, 'it must have been a Wednesday, a week past Wednesday in fact.'

'You really have an excellent memory for faces, Melissa.' Graham said and he meant it; having met Gerald Maitland he didn't think he was all that memorable and he had been trained to be observant.

'Well,' she smiled, an unfathomable expression on her face, 'while we get all sorts of visitors coming here, especially during the summer months, we don't get so many who look so – so obviously – er – effeminate.'

'You mean he was gay?'

'Now, Brian, I didn't say that. Everybody is entitled to their opinion, aren't they, Chief Inspector?'

'I can't disagree with that.' doing his best not to laugh. She was so utterly unaffected and had obviously not realised the impact of her words. So much for spending days in trying to back up Ian's first impression of Maitland, searching for tangible evidence that he was gay, even if his sexuality had any bearing on them reaching their final conclusions of whether the man was a murderer or not. Women's intuition, he thought, and definitely not to be lightly dismissed.

'I don't know whether I should be saying this, Chief Inspector,' she said, her expression becoming serious, 'but I suppose I really have no choice.'

'What is it, love?' Brian, instantly protective, put an arm round her shoulders.

'I'm okay, Brian, honestly,' she said, 'but I saw him again.'

'Not in here?'

'No, it was on the Sunday night, the night Katherine Peters was murdered; we'd just closed and I was coming back with Roy; Brian and I take turns to give him his last walk each night, Chief Inspector,' focusing on him again, 'and on that Sunday it was mine. I only went as far as The Bridge Inn, it was too dark to go any further, and then we turned back. I was almost at the corner and had just passed the entrance to the car park behind the Bridge Café when a car drove out, quite quickly too. I couldn't see the driver, but by the time I reached the square I saw him again; he had been forced to stop to let three or four cars come out of the Salmon's Rest car park; that time I could see who was driving and it was him.' she finished, pointing to the photograph.

'You would have been across the road from the restaurant, wouldn't you, Melissa?' Graham asked.

'That's right; I was directly opposite in fact. The lights were still on in the restaurant, also there was a street lamp next to where he was waiting and I could see him quite clearly.'

Brian had to move away to attend to some more customers who had come in and it was several minutes before he returned, but in that time Graham was able to thank her and tried to reassure her that what she had told him would only be revealed to Ian Ash and his superintendent, Bill Simms, and that she had no need to worry about her name being mentioned to anyone else. Although continuing to look troubled, she appeared less agitated. She was an intelligent young woman and he was sure that by this time she had realised she could have seen Katherine Peters' murderer on the night she was killed.

'Incidentally, Melissa,' he said, as Brian re-joined them, 'do you remember what kind of car he was driving?'

'It was a convertible, one of the new Volkswagens, I think, and he had the top open; that was probably how I was able to see him so well, especially the second time with the better lighting.'

***

Jack Corbett had spent one of the worst weeks of his life and was seriously considering packing in his job with the circus. Every performance since last Tuesday had been a nightmare for him and if it hadn't been for his clown's make-up to conceal his emotional state, he would have found it impossible to enter the circus ring each evening and perform his act to achieve what clowns were meant to achieve; make their audience laugh. And when, at the end of their first act, the opening chords of "A nightingale Sang in Berkeley Square" soared above their heads, the sweet refrain of the tune made him want to weep, knowing from now on, whenever he heard it, he would always associate it with Beverly. She had loved the tune and often during rehearsals he would hear her softly singing to the lyrics.

She had been twelve years younger than him and had said more than once this made no difference. Since meeting her, practically from the very first day when he'd joined the circus, they had felt a certain rapport, both having similar interests; apart from her long involvement with the circus, like him, she enjoyed reading and had laughingly told him, she would read almost anything and being a compulsive reader himself he had understood. They had, by mutual consent, realising Beppe's view of any of them forming a romantic relationship within the circus, kept their growing friendship to themselves. Neither of them had ever talked about the future, being happy to continue as they had been doing; mixing with the others, never just the two of them, except, as they had done the other Sunday, meeting outside the circus grounds where they had the privacy and freedom to talk without being overheard and constantly aware of Beppe's disapproval when he was around. It hadn't taken Jack long to realise how Beppe considered everyone who worked for him and at times he did find his over-protectiveness towards them claustrophobic, but put it down to him being Italian, believing that was the Italian way.

Beverly hadn't seemed to mind, but then she had worked for him far longer than he had and understood the Italian temperament. Jack knew they were all taking her death hard, especially Beppe, but unlike him, he was unable to share his grief. And, what he had learned today had intensified his feelings of despair at losing Beverly, going over again and again what he had overheard Beppe saying to Marcus. He had been in the big tent checking on the structure of the seats which was usually one of his jobs before a performance and he didn't think either of them had noticed him, but once they had started talking, it was too late to draw their attention to him, forcing him to remain where he was and hear something he didn't want to know.

"Do you feel up to appearing this evening, Beppe?" Marcus had asked him.

"I will be fine, my friend."

"If you're sure." and Jack could recognise the concern in his voice.

"I didn't tell you on Saturday night about the suicide note, Marcus."

"Only that Cordelia had left you one."

"I know and, Marcus, how I wish she hadn't; what she wrote will stay in my head for ever and perhaps it's wrong of me to share my sorrow with you, but there is no-one else I can talk to."

"I'm your friend, Beppe; that's what friends are for."

"Thank you for saying that. What I'm going to tell you will shock you, but the note she left was a confession."

"A confession?"

"Yes, she confessed to causing Beverly's accident."

"My God! Why!"

"I don't know, Marcus; I don't know."

They moved away then and out of earshot. He had remained where he was for several seconds unable to continue working along the length of seats with Beppe's words reverberating through his brain. He felt as though he was groping his way through thick fog, rapidly losing his sense of direction and waiting, afraid to move forward, until it cleared. After what seemed an age, but probably no more than two or three minutes, his breathing returned to normal and he could think. Beverly. Cordelia, Beppe's wife, had destroyed the only woman he had ever loved. Beppe didn't know why, but he thought he knew the reason.

He had been a few minutes late meeting her on the Sunday, the game of poker with the lads taking longer than he'd expected, and she had already been in the lane waiting for him. She had told him she had been walking up and down, not wanting anyone to see her standing at the entrance, and had mentioned to him she had noticed a man in front of her and had wondered at the time where he'd come from because there were no houses along the last stretch of the lane leading into Riverside Park, but when he reached about the second house, he suddenly quickened his step and walked up the garden path at the same time as a car passed the house. This had been Cordelia because only minutes later he saw her himself as she drove into the circus grounds. He hadn't reached the entrance, but held back until she had driven further on to where she usually parked before continuing. Neither of them would have thought anymore about it, but the following morning Beverly told him that while she and Juliana were having a coffee in the town, they overheard two women talking about the murder and when Riverside Lane was mentioned and that it must have happened the previous night, she naturally remembered the man she had seen and his rather odd behaviour. Jack could think of no other reason why anyone should want to harm her, unless it was because she had either seen or heard something to place her in such a dangerous and vulnerable position. She had been silenced. Tragically, callously and without compunction. None of this reasoning explained why this had been Cordelia Bortoletto and it was more than likely he was the only one with this knowledge. It could be helpful to the police and reluctant as he was to walk into a police station, Jack knew he would. Kitty's murderer had, apparently, still to be found and he could very well have been the man Beverly had seen, working on the premise that Cordelia hadn't killed Kitty as, according to what Beppe had told Marcus, she had only confessed to being responsible for ending Beverly's life. In a way, Jack thought, he was no different than Beppe; he had felt the need to share his grief, while he, by discussing Beverly and what she had seen on Sunday with someone, even if he was a police officer, may enable him to come to terms with losing her.

***

'It would seem, Ian, we're making some headway at last in our investigation, and from what you've just told me about Gerry Blake's findings, there should be enough on Eric Noble to warrant that particular case to be re-opened and in that event it will likely be handled by Interpol who will have the delicate task of liaising with the Hong Kong police. I don't know how difficult that will be,' Graham added, 'given the long time factor and that the death of Valerie Blake took place before the colony's handover to the Chinese in 1997.'

'Depends on how sensitive they are.' Ian commented.

'That's right, but whether they take our intervention as a criticism of how they handled what, from what Letitia Radcliffe has told you, appeared to be a suicide and the fact there was no suicide note could have reinforced this verdict. However,' he went on, 'it will be out of our hands and as far as Eric Noble is concerned, he could well no longer be considered as a suspect for Katherine Peter's murder, that is, if we have sufficient evidence to put together a sound enough case to convict Gerald Maitland and I think we have, Ian.'

'He's certainly dropped himself in it, hasn't?'

'You could say that. I've been thinking about the timing on the Sunday night and it has occurred to me it might be a good idea to speak to those two lads who took Katherine Peters' car; the report specifically mentioned that when they had walked back along Riverside Lane the lights had been switched off in Bramble Cottage, therefore it does indicate that when they first passed the house, she had still been in there, therefore they couldn't have been very far away from where she was murdered. It's possible they may have seen her killer.'

'I'll try and get hold of Philip Mason; he might still be working.'

'If you would, Ian; the sooner the better in fact. I'd like us both to interview Gerald Maitland and was hoping to fix a time for Wednesday, if that's possible, and if those two can provide us with anything useful, it could strengthen our position.'

'Right, I'll give Philip a ring now.'

'Fine, but before you do that, Ian and only briefly, but going back to your meeting with Letitia Radcliffe; you mentioned that she had no idea Eric Noble was living in Meadowbank until Rachel Tilsly told her and this was when they saw him in the restaurant.'

'That's right, sir.'

'Did she happen to mention the name of the restaurant?'

'Roberta's Bistro.'

'I know it well; what I was wondering is whether he saw them.'

'She was sure he had, but that he didn't acknowledge either of them.'

'And yet he's leasing the lodge from Rachel and Colin Tilsly.'

'Why do you ask, sir?'

'No particular reason, Ian,' Graham answered, but unable to shrug off a feeling of unease, 'quite frankly, Eric Noble concerns me. He's not a likeable type; quick tempered, self-opinionated and inclined to talk down to you. And not with a good track record either according to what we've learned about him; it's difficult to disregard that, Ian.'

'If and when he's questioned by an officer from Interpol,' Ian said, following his train of thought, 'it is to be hoped he doesn't learn about Letitia contacting us.'

'I'd thought of that,' Graham nodded, 'but if he does, it won't be from

Interpol. But, Ian, he's more than capable of reaching that conclusion without talking to anyone.'

'And if he does?'

'If he does, or perhaps I should be saying before he does, we must anticipate what he may or may not do next.'

'She might be in some danger.'

'This is all speculation, of course, and that's all it can be at the moment. When you consider the man's characteristic traits,' he continued thoughtfully, 'it appears that in an emergency, by that I mean, when he, personally, is threatened in any way, his first reaction is to run. He's been pretty adept at that in the past with his speedy exits from California and Hong Kong and those are the only two we know about.'

***

Robert Gaunt and Victor Glenn were already in the interview room when Ian and Philip Mason went in the following morning. Philip had told him as soon as he'd arrived of how they had nervously reacted to being called in.

'Quite took the wind out of their sails,' he'd chuckled, 'which was no bad thing I might add, but they never expected to hear from us again.'

'Let's hope it was a one-off, Philip.'

'I think it probably was; I know their families and I don't suppose they are exactly flavour of the month with them after their little escapade.

'This shouldn't take long,' Ian said, 'as I mentioned on the phone, we want to know whether they saw anyone in and around Riverside Lane. Both the pubs would have been closed, but there's often somebody about.' remembering what Melissa had told Graham the day before. At least they now knew that Gerald Maitland had been in Meadowbank that Sunday night, but to have this doubly confirmed would be an added bonus for them.

Once he had introduced himself to them, Ian wasted no time in coming to the point and reminding himself that although the two young men sitting across the table from them were offenders with their names on police records shouldn't come into the equation. If they had anything to add to what they had already learned about the night Katherine Peters was killed, was all he was interested in. As far as the theft of her car was concerned, they would probably have realised they would hear no more about it. There was nobody to press charges; therefore, they had got away with their escapade as Philip had described it.

'You will no doubt be aware,' he said to them, 'of the murder which took place in Meadowbank a week past Sunday and that the woman's body was discovered in Riverside Lane the following morning?'

'We read about it last Wednesday, Inspector.' the one called Robert Gaunt said.

'Right, but you won't know the time of death.' and not waiting for any answer, carried on, 'She was killed between 10.30 and 12.30; that is as accurate as we can be. However, from the report we received from Inspector Mason, you both stated that when you walked along Riverside Lane from the Bridge Inn you noticed there was a light on inside Bramble Cottage, this being where the deceased had lived, but when you returned, the house was in darkness. From what evidence we have, although not conclusive, this does give an indication that Miss Peters could still have been alive when you first passed her house, which narrows down the time of her death. What we would like to know is,' pausing for a second, noticing he had their full attention, 'whether either of you saw anyone from when you left Bridge Street to turn into Riverside Lane until you left to return to Stockbridge.'

'I think there was only one couple,' Robert said, 'they left the pub at the same time as us, but they went into the first house on the corner of Riverside Lane, but I can't remember seeing anyone else.'

'There was someone,' Victor Glenn put in quickly, 'maybe you didn't notice him, Rob, but he was walking some distance ahead of us. It was when we decided to turn back after we'd reached the circus grounds, Inspector, and then I saw him again after, well,' a look of embarrassment on his face, 'well, when we were in the car -' pausing awkwardly.

'- , yes, that's alright; go on,' helping him out, 'whereabouts were you exactly when you saw him that time?'

'We'd reached the end of Riverside Lane and were about to turn left towards the square when he drove out into Bridge Street. I thought at the time he must have had his car parked at the back somewhere.'

'What about you, Robert,' Ian asked him, 'do you remember seeing him?'

'Not in Riverside Lane, Inspector,' he said, 'but I must have seen the same man when we reached the end of the lane. He had a great car though; an open-top Volkswagen, also he had his own personal number plate.'

'Can you remember the number?' but not too hopeful.

'I can, yes. It was easy to remember; MH1.'

Maitland Holdings. They had him. He'll have a job to wriggle out of that one, Ian thought, hardly able to believe their luck. Pure chance; if Katherine Peters' car hadn't been stolen by these two, they wouldn't have known.

'Did you see anyone nearby?'

'Only a woman with her dog; I think it was Melissa Morrison from the Market Inn; we've been there a few times.' he explained.

'I see;' Ian nodded, 'it was dark of course when you noticed him in Riverside Lane, Victor, but can you give me a description of him?'

'Not a very good one,' he said, 'he was tall, middle-aged; anyway, he wasn't young, he wore glasses, the rimless kind, and he was wearing a blazer, very smart really. Also,' he added, 'and the way he walked.'

'The way he walked?' Philip spoke for the first time since they came into the interview room, 'What do you mean, Victor?'

'Er – er, difficult to say, Inspector.'

'Did he have a limp?'

'No, nothing like that.' by this time looking even more uncomfortable and instinctively Ian knew what he meant. Whether the man he had seen was Gerald Maitland or, Victor Glenn had recognised the characteristics of someone who was gay.

'You've lost me.' Philip said, shaking his head.

'I think I know what he's trying to say.' Robert interrupted, possibly feeling sorry for him, 'he thought the guy was gay, is that right, Victor?'

'Well, yes,' he answered, 'but it was only an impression.'

Ian didn't prolong the interview and once the two of them had gone, he spent a few minutes talking to Philip before heading back to Meadowbank.

'They're an odd pair,' Philip remarked, 'you wouldn't think that in these so-called enlightened times, anyone of their age would be too embarrassed to mention the word homosexuality.'

'Expect he wished he hadn't said anything.'

'You're probably right, Ian. I don't suppose they'll be in a hurry to return to Meadowbank though.'

***

'There's been a telephone call from Jack Corbett this morning, sir.' Jean told him immediately he arrived in the office.

'What did he have to say, Jean?'

'Not a great deal, only that he wanted to see you, but as the circus is now in Petersfield he would have some difficulty getting here. He gave me his mobile number.' she added, giving him the telephone message slip.

Jack answered straight away and sounded relieved when Graham told him he would drive up to Petersfield to see him, suggesting they meet in one of the pubs in the centre of the town, rather than, as before, in the circus grounds where his presence would be noticed. Jack gave him no hint of why he wanted to speak to him and Graham didn't ask. Time enough he thought when they met.

He had a good clear run to Petersfield; the traffic was relatively light and with no roadworks to lengthen the time it took to get there. Being so close to Winchester, Graham knew the town well and the pub he'd chosen to meet Jack Corbett had, at one time, been one of his favourites in the town.

Before leaving home that morning he'd had a call from Mike Harper to tell him he'd been in touch with a friend of his called Peter Willingham who was with Interpol and had relayed to him the gist of what Letitia Radcliffe had told Ian, including Eric Noble's possible involvement with her friend's death.

"Peter got back to me earlier this morning, Graham." Mike had said,

"And Hong Kong being seven hours ahead of us meant they had been able to make some headway already. There appears to be no problem in obtaining agreement from the Hong Kong authorities for us to officially enquire into Valerie Blake's suicide and one of Peter's colleagues based over there has an appointment this afternoon, Hong Kong time, to see the senior personnel officer at Standard Chartered."

"That was quick work."

"It was," he agreed, "but I rather think China doesn't want any negative vibes to disturb the good relationship between them and the West. Although several years ago, there are many people who will continue to remember the Tiananmen Square protests and how that was handled and the last China will want is even the slightest hiccup to mar what was actually a smooth handover in 1997."

"I'm sure you're right, Mike. It's quite heartening that Interpol consider, what are really no more than scraps of evidence, sufficient to have the case re-opened."

"As you say, they're not much, but could prove damning all the same."

"For Eric Noble." he had finished for him.

"Quite, but you could say the man would have had a good run for his money."

"You mean other people's money." Graham had laughed.

"*Touché*"

Yes, Graham thought, pulling into a parking space a few hundred yards along from "The Dead Duck" in the High Street, it did seem as though Eric Noble's luck was about to come to an end and not before time either. He would call in and see Letitia Radcliffe when he got back to Meadowbank; it was only right she should be told what had transpired since she had spoken to Ian on Sunday and at the same time he would be able to gauge for himself whether or not she had any qualms about him, even more so now that the wheels had well and truly been set in motion when, sooner or later, he would realise what was going on. How was he going to react? Would he try and brazen it out or, as Ian and he had been saying, make another quick exit?

The pub was beginning to fill up with lunchtime customers, but Jack

Corbett had been able to find a free table. He looked more gaunt than he had the last time he'd seen him, with an unnatural pallor to his skin; in fact, Graham decided walking over to him, he didn't look well.

'I'm glad to see you managed to get a table; I'd forgotten just how packed this place can get.'

'It was the only one left, but can I get you a drink Chief Inspector?'

'That's good of you; I'd like half a lager, please.'

'Any preference?'

'Heineken will be fine.' a polite inconsequential exchange between two men meeting in a pub for a lunchtime drink, but in this case, not so. They scarcely knew each other, but whatever Jack Corbett had to say must be of some importance to him.

'Yesterday,' he said, placing the Heineken down in front of him, 'I overheard Beppe Bortoletto telling his friend, Marcus, about the suicide note his wife had left him and about her being responsible for Beverly's death. Up to then,' he went on, 'I couldn't think of any reason why she was killed, but I think I do now.'

'Really?'

'Yes, but first I have to explain the relationship I had with Beverly. I had only known her for a year; that was when I first started working for Beppe and over the months we had become very close. She meant everything to me, Chief Inspector, everything.' struggling to pull himself together.

'Listen, Jack,' using his Christian name for the first time, 'take your time; there's no rush.'

'Thanks,' taking a short sip of his beer, 'I'm finding it difficult to come to terms with what happened to her. You see, nobody else knew how we felt about each other, the reason for this was we both new Beppe wouldn't have approved.'

'Why did you think this was?'

'Because when any of his circus workers showed the first signs of having what appeared to be more than a friendly relationship, they were warned off and, invariably, one or both of them would leave and Beverly and I didn't want that to happen. We seldom discussed the future and were perfectly happy with the way things were; perhaps later on we would have thought differently, but of course it's too late now. We were in the habit of meeting most evenings, quite late actually, and that Sunday we had arranged to see each other at eleven-thirty. As I told Sergeant Allan on Wednesday, I spent the evening after I'd got back from Meadowbank, playing cards. I made the excuse of wanting an early night, knowing the card school would go on for a while, but the last game of poker went on longer than I expected and I was late getting to where I knew Beverly would be waiting.'

'Whereabouts was this?' Graham asked him, surprised in spite of his years in the Force, at the way events could unfold.

'Just outside the park gates.'

'Can you remember the time, Jack?'

'It must have been about quarter to twelve, certainly not before. Beverly told me she had been walking slowly up and down in the lane, rather than hang about by the entrance, in case anyone from the circus should see her. She also mentioned about the man she saw who seemed suddenly to appear on the path some yards ahead of her and then, when a car turned into Riverside Lane from Bridge Street, he walked quicker, going round to the back of one of the houses.'

'You know who was driving the car don't you?'

'Yes, it was Cordelia, because she drove into the circus grounds as I reached the gate.'

'You said a few minutes ago you thought you knew why she had caused Beverly's death.'

'I could be wrong of course, Chief Inspector, but I don't think I am. She would have driven pass Beverly,' he went on slowly, 'also she couldn't have failed to have seen the man in front of her and if she had murdered Kitty, it could have been because she assumed Beverly had noticed what he'd been up to. I must admit my thoughts become a bit muddle from there.' he admitted.

Sounds a logical assumption to me.' Graham said, and it did; the timings tallied with those they had already, confident that once Ian had spoken to the two lads from Stockbridge, they would be in a position to finally come up with a more accurate time of death and from what Jack Corbett had just told him, they had a credible motive for Beverly's murder.

Chapter Thirteen

"FURTHER DRAMA IN MEADOWBANK

A further twist in the recent dramatic events in the market town emerged on Saturday night with the death of a guest staying at "The Royal Oak", prestigious country house hotel on the outskirts of Meadowbank. It is believed that the woman, Cordelia Bortoletto, the wife of Beppe Bortoletto, the well-known circus owner, died from a drug overdose. A regular customer of the hotel had been expecting her to join him in the lounge bar earlier in the evening and when she didn't arrive, mentioned his concern to the management and, accompanied by the proprietress, went to her room, where they found her body.

"For legal reasons, his name cannot be revealed, but interestingly, and to add to the continuing mystery surrounding the two murders last week, he was among a number of people being questioned by the police as part of their routine enquiries.

"I was able to speak briefly with Beppe Bortoletto on Sunday and, while reluctant to talk about his wife's death, he did tell me she had left a suicide note, the contents of which he was not prepared to divulge.

"There can be little doubt that the murder of Katherine Peters and Beverly Clements are not connected, but the question now will be whether the suicide of Cordelia Bortoletto has any relevance to these two incidents, although, presumably, the fact that Beverly Clements was working for the Beppe Bortoletto circus, which had for the last week been in Meadowbank, will not be lost on those conducting the enquiry.

"It is to be hoped the police will reach a speedy conclusion in their investigation, if only to alleviate the nervous speculations circulating among many of the town's residents who, clearly, are longing for their everyday lives to return to some semblance of normality.

Carol Cliff"

There was something decidedly unpleasant in the way Carol Cliff wrote her columns, Letitia decided; with a clever selection of words and phrases implying she knew considerably more than she probably did. Also, she seemed to have an inordinate interest in Meadowbank's affairs. Surely there must be other small towns where murders occur. It had been the same in last Wednesday's edition when she had emphatically insisted that the two murders were connected. How could she have been so sure? And something else; she appeared to be always around when each disaster happened and now she was more than hinting that she knows the name of the person who just happened to be in the hotel where Cordelia Bortoletto's body was found. Or had he? According to Carol Cliff, he had been waiting for Cordelia Bortoletto to join him in the bar. None of it made any sense to her, only thankful she had chosen a less stressful and competitive career than journalism. Normally, Letitia would have shrugged off such speculations as meaningless, but since Gerry had been here on Sunday, she had frequently found herself being drawn back to the awful time when Valerie had died and with the Chief Inspector's visit yesterday even more so. Valerie's last words to her on the night she took the ferry over to Lamma kept repeating themselves in her brain, refusing to budge.

She had spent the afternoon in the room she used as her studio, putting the finishing touches to a set of illustrations she had been working on for the last three weeks and satisfied with the work she'd done she felt justified in opening a bottle of Chardonnay and had been on the point of taking it out on to the terrace when the front doorbell rang.

He had been quick to introduce himself, apologising for disturbing her and when she invited him in and asked if he would like a glass of wine, had surprised her by accepting, always believing police officers didn't drink while on duty. He must have realised what she was thinking because he had smiled, telling her he had more or less finished work for the day.

She had liked him; he was easy to talk to, with a laid back manner which she was sure was deceptive, otherwise, she reasoned, he wouldn't have risen to the rank of Chief Inspector. He was still in his forties, about the same age as she was perhaps.

When he told her an officer from Interpol was leading the enquiry into Valerie's death with the assistance of the Hong Kong police, she didn't know what to think and, noticing her hesitancy, he had looked at her quizzically.

"You're worried about Eric Noble's reaction when he hears?"

"I don't know about being worried exactly," she had answered slowly, not really sure what she meant, "but perhaps I should be. Oh, Chief Inspector, I realise how that must sound, but I find it impossible not to have reservations about him."

"Not at all; it's probably understandable. Inspector Ash has told me you and Valerie Blake were close friends and whether he was directly involved in the way she died or not, it would be natural for you to blame him for your friend's situation once he had turned her away."

"That's exactly how I feel, how I've always felt in fact."

"When he's questioned," he had explained, "as he will be in due course, I can assure you, Mrs Radcliffe, there will be no mention of your name, or Gerry Blake's name either." he'd added.

"That's good to know; Gerry's going to wonder why further enquiries are being made."

"I expect he will." he nodded.

They hadn't said much more about Eric Noble. The Chief Inspector had further surprised her by accepting another glass and had seemed in no hurry to leave. He had been interested to hear about her time in Hong Kong, also about Timothy out in Thailand. It had been a long time since she had enjoyed the company of someone so much. Since the divorce, although she'd had men friends, those friendships had been comparatively short-lived; mainly she had to admit because of her reluctance to commit herself. After the divorce, she had devoted her life to her art and to making a home for herself and Timothy; there had been little space left for anyone or anything else.

She made to fold up the newspaper when a part of the article caught her attention; she must have read it before, but the possible significance of the phrase hadn't registered with her. Carol Cliff had mentioned that the man who had been waiting for Cordelia Bortoletto was a regular customer of the hotel. It was almost as though she had said that deliberately as she had followed that up by saying he had been among a number of people being questioned in connection with the two murders. If he was a regular customer indicates the likelihood of him living locally which, for anyone sufficiently interested to learn who it had been, did narrow the field somewhat. Letitia had lived in Meadowbank long enough to realise that a large majority of the community were a curious lot and as it had been a Saturday, many of them would have been spending the evening in either of the two pubs or up at "The Royal Oak". Eric Noble lived fairly close to the hotel and Rachel had told her at the weekend that the Chief Inspector had been to see him. She knew she was being unreasonable jumping to conclusions, allowing her mistrust of the man to interfere with her judgement, but found it difficult not to. Since seeing him in the restaurant last Thursday, she had wondered why she hadn't seen him before; the last time she had been to the "The Royal Oak" had been months ago, much preferring to call into The Bridge and he hadn't been in there. Apart from the hotel, possibly he went to the other pub; certainly driving back to Meadowbank from Winchester, it would be more convenient for him. Not that it really mattered; all this conjecturing was a total waste of time and even if he had been the person who had discovered Cordelia's body on Saturday night it shouldn't be considered suspiciously. This is all Carol Cliff's fault, she decided, impatiently pushing the paper to one side; she was allowing the journalist's loaded innuendoes to get to her.

***

Eric took the call from Johnnie Cheung on his private line shortly after he arrived in the office on Wednesday morning. The number was ex-directory and very few of his business associates were aware of it, Johnnie being the exception. He had first met Johnnie when he joined Standard Chartered in 1982 and he was the only person from that period of his life with whom he had kept in touch. It hadn't taken either of them long to discover that in spite of their totally different backgrounds, they shared the same ambition which was to make money and neither of them were too concerned about the legality of how they achieved this. Johnnie had come from a wealthy Cantonese family; in his early years money had always been plentiful until his father, tired of bailing him out from various financial deals which had failed, decided to call a halt to what had been a more than adequate allowance and arranged for him to be taken on by Standard Chartered, working in their foreign funding and investment section and between them they had been involved in a number of lucrative scams. Even now, after so many years, these had continued. Johnnie's in-depth knowledge of the Asian financial market, together with his own expertise in computers, had more than trebled their income in that time.

'Hello, Johnnie; I didn't expect to hear from you until the end of the week.'

'I don't want to alarm you, Eric,' he said in his perfectly modulated English accent, well honed from his days at Cambridge University, 'but there is something I think you should know.'

'Go on, I'm listening.' his antenna on full alert, instinctively sensing what Johnnie had to say was not going to be good.

'We had a visit from an officer from the International Police this morning; when I say we,' he explained, 'I mean the bank's personnel section.'

'Yes? Was this, he wondered, what he had always dreaded; parts of his past he preferred to forget being resurrected.

'He saw Shirley Leung, she's the senior personnel officer, and wanted to see your records.'

'They go back that far?'

'Oh, yes.'

'Did he give her any explanation of why?'

'No, not really, the date you started here, your C.V., when you left, also they asked to see a copy of your contract which of course told them you didn't complete it.'

'I hear what you say, but I don't think it's anything to get steamed up about.'

'Perhaps not,' sounding doubtful, 'but I thought it important for you to be aware of what's going on. Quite frankly, if I were you, Eric, I believe I would be more than a trifle worried. I don't like the sound of Interpol being so interested in you. You're not the first to have left Standard Chartered suddenly, but well – I don't know.'

'Look, Johnnie, I appreciate you telling me, don't think otherwise. Alright, Interpol are asking questions about me, but there's nothing for them to find out. I don't need to remind you that I left Hong Kong nineteen years ago and I wouldn't think anyone I knew then would still be there.'

It could be, he thought, when he'd rung off, that Johnnie was getting cold feet and he had a damned good idea how his brain was working; if, during their investigation, Interpol were to unearth their joint dealings it would inevitably be his turn next and if that should happen their friendship would come to an abrupt and final end.

He had always led Johnnie to believe that the reason for him leaving Hong Kong when he had was because his affair with Valerie had spiralled out of control when she had begun making demands he was not prepared to give in to, culminating in Pete finding out, but that was far from the truth.

In some respects Katherine had reminded him of Valerie, but by the time he met her he was a hell of a lot wiser and was determined not to fall into the same trap. When Katherine had confronted him that night she had been in no position to demand her so-called hush money; she had neglected to take into account her own activities and consequently had been no threat to him. But, years earlier with Valerie, his situation had been quite different. When she had turned up at the apartment the night she had left Pete, he believed he had made it abundantly clear he hadn't wanted her to stay, he never thought she would come back, but he had underestimated her vindictiveness, but later, whenever he permitted himself to think about her, he put it down to her finding another woman with him.

Valerie had been waiting outside the apartment building for him the following afternoon when he returned from work, her two travel bags on the pavement by her feet. He had asked her to come in, only because he didn't want any of his neighbours to see them out there. Nineteen years, he was now discovering, hadn't erased what she'd said to him.

"I've done a lot of thinking since last night, Eric," she had said, "and I want you to reconsider what you said. I know that I should have phoned you first."

"But you didn't and I meant what I said, Valerie; I don't want you living with me. I can't put it any plainer than that."

She hadn't even flinched at the harsh words, as he was sure most women would. She had remained silent for a couple of minutes, not taking those green cat-like eyes away from his face, eyes which he had once thought to be her most attractive feature, but not then. He was on the point of telling her to go, when she broke the silence.

"As I told you last night, I've left Pete and I've no intention of going back to him. If you don't agree to let me stay, Eric, I will make it extremely difficult for you to remain in Hong Kong."

"What the hell are you talking about?"

"I discovered quite by accident that you have been buying and selling shares on the stock market."

"What's so unusual about that, Valerie?" realising where she was coming from by then, "It is legal, you know."

"It is when it's your own money." delivering her bombshell.

"I would suggest you don't go any further."

"And if I do?" goading him.

"Where did you stay last night?" his change of tack completely flooring her.

"On Lamma."

"Okay, we'll go over there this evening. Perhaps I was a bit hasty last night and over-reacted, but you should know I don't like surprises."

"What about my bags, Eric?"

"Oh, leave them here. We'll only be there for the night."

Before leaving for the ferry port, he had gone out to buy a bottle of whisky to take with them and on the way back called into the herbalists next door to the apartment block. The transaction in there had taken longer than he had expected, but she made no comment when he returned.

On the ferry she had told him she had been so upset the night before that she had phoned Letitia.

"I just had to speak to someone and she's the only real friend I have in Hong Kong."

"Did you tell her where you were going."

"No, I just said I was going away for a few days."

"So, she doesn't know about the house on Lamma?"

"No, but I told her about us and that I had left Pete. Everybody needs someone they can confide in, Eric." she had said quietly.

Remembering all of this now, he wondered for the first time exactly what she had told Letitia. Could Letitia Radcliffe be responsible for this sudden interest in him? After all this time? Had seeing him the other day motivated her to such an extent? But if Valerie had mentioned anything about his stock market dealings to her, surely Letitia would have told her husband. But, she hadn't, otherwise the bank would have made efforts to find him and it wouldn't have been difficult to discover Johnnie's involvement. But, again, this hadn't happened. Up to now.

***

'Since talking to you on Monday, Mr Maitland,' Graham said, 'there have been further developments in our investigation into the murder of Katherine Peters of which you should be made aware.'

'I've nothing further to add Chief Inspector to what I've already told you.'

'That will be entirely up to you; however, to comply with police procedure, I am required to make a recording of this interview. Before doing so, you are entitled to have your lawyer present.'

'Dear me,' a dismissive shrug of the shoulders, 'that won't be necessary.'

Gerald Maitland had been ten minutes late arriving at New Scotland Yard, blaming the delay on the heavy traffic around Trafalgar Square, but making no apology. Since learning so much more about him, his affected mannerisms appeared more prominent, remembering Ian telling him about Victor Glenn's embarrassment when he'd tried to describe him.

'Very well,' Graham nodded, pulling the recording machine towards him, 'but if you change your mind at any time during the interview, I can call a temporary halt.' switching on the machine: 'Thursday, the 7th June 2007, fifteen hundred hours;' pausing for a second before continuing, 'When I spoke to you on Monday, Mr Maitland, you informed me that you first met Katherine Peters in 1998, but I have a witness who says you were seen in her company four years prior to then, in 1994.'

'Whoever said that was mistaken.'

'In the same way a neighbour of yours was mistaken about the time you arrived home on Sunday the 27th May, the night Katherine Peters was murdered?'

'My neighbour, whoever that might be, was indeed mistaken.'

'Mr Maitland,' deciding not to take the issue any further for the moment, 'when I asked you whether you knew about Katherine Peters taking on the lease of Number Thirteen, the Mews, you said you had no knowledge of this, in spite of the fact that the house was owned by your company.'

'That was correct, I didn't.'

'I would suggest, sir, you were aware of this.'

'You're not calling me a liar I trust, Chief Inspector?'

'You were seen,' side-stepping what appeared to be the first indication he was getting through to the man, 'visiting Katherine Peters a number of times, one of them being shortly after she moved into the mews house, including on other occasions in later years after the divorce.'

'Another of your witnesses?'

'Yes, another of our witnesses, Mr Maitland.'

'It seems to me,' he said, his voice rising an octave, 'you are determined to *pin* this murder on to me.'

'What I'm attempting to do, sir, is to arrive at the truth. Either you have a poor memory or you've been lying. We'll go back again to the Sunday night. When you returned home, where did you park your car?'

'In my garage as usual.'

'How easy would it be for anyone to break in?'

'Extremely difficult, especially as I have a security alarm system.'

'Would you tell me once more how you spent that evening?'

'I had dinner at the Saville Club, followed by a couple of games of snooker and left at nine-thirty, arriving home around ten.'

'Did you go out again?'

'No, I did *not*.'

'I suggest, Mr Maitland, that when you left the club that Sunday evening you drove to Meadowbank, arriving there well before midnight, parking your car out of sight and walking along Riverside Lane to Katherine Peter's house.'

'That is a total fabrication; I've told you I've never been to Meadowbank!'

'You have been there at least twice, Mr Maitland; once on Thursday the 17th May and again, on Sunday the 27th.'

'That's wrong.'

'After strangling Katherine Peters,' carrying on where he had left off, 'you walked back to where you had left your car and returned to London, arriving home around two in the morning. Would you prefer if I stopped there in order for you to reconsider your previous decision of not having your lawyer present at this interview?' Graham asked him.

'I don't need a lawyer.'

'What type of car do you drive?'

'A Volkswagen convertible, 2006 model.' he answered automatically, but by the way his eyes were focusing, Graham could tell his mind was elsewhere.

'And the registration number?'

'GM1.'

'All of which agrees with what we've been given by one of our witnesses who saw you on the Sunday night in Meadowbank.'

Another shrug was the only response.

'The interview terminated on Wednesday the 6th June 2007 at sixteen hundred hours.' switching off the recorder.

There was silence in the room. Graham looked across at Gerald Maitland, noticing a tiny muscular twitch above his right cheekbone, but apart from that giveaway sign of nervousness, his manner was exactly as it had been earlier.

'In view of what has been discussed this afternoon, Mr Maitland,' Graham said slowly, 'I am arresting you on suspicion for the murder of Katherine Peters on Sunday, the 27th May this year. You are not obliged to say anything, but anything you do say will be taken down, and may be given in evidence.'

***

Rachel had stayed up to watch a repeat of "Casablanca" and the film had just reached the part when Ingrid Bergman made her dramatic entrance in "Rick's Bar", when her mobile rang and, turning down the volume, pressed the message button.

'Mrs Tilsly?'

'Timothy!' immediately recognising Timothy Radcliffe's voice.

'I'm sorry to phone you so late at night, but you were the only person I could think of to call.'

'Tell me what's wrong, Timothy?' she asked, a familiar wave of apprehension rushing towards her, as she waited to hear what she had subconsciously been fearing.

'I don't know whether there is anything wrong, but I've been trying to call my mother and both her mobile and the land line are dead. She always phones me at this time every Thursday morning; she never fails and, well – I'm worried about her, Mrs Tilsly.'

'Her mobile may be on charge, but I can't understand why her land phone isn't working. It was this afternoon, because I phoned your home number. I realise it's pointless telling you not to worry, Timothy. It's eleven now,' she added, glancing up at the clock on the mantelpiece, 'not all that late. Letitia may be out, of course, but I'll see what I can do; if you give me your mobile number I'll ring you back as soon as I can.'

She jotted down the number, made another attempt to reassure him, before ringing off. The first thing she did was to try Letitia's land phone, but as Timothy had said, the line was dead; also there was no response on her mobile. Colin was probably asleep by now and she didn't want to waste time in waking him up and persuading him to go with her to Letitia's house, also she was reluctant to go there on her own. She couldn't explain why, except she was afraid to. There was only one person she knew who would be able to help and she didn't think he would object too strongly if it turned out that both she and Timothy had been worrying needlessly. The Chief Inspector had given her one of his cards when he was here the day before and, taking it out of her wallet, she dialled his mobile number.

***

Graham answered on the first ring. He didn't hesitate, neither did he double-check Letitia's phone. He had recently bought one of the town houses in Stockbridge Road which was only a short distance from Riverside Gardens and within minutes he was outside number five where Letitia lived. There was a light on in a downstairs' window, but the rest of the building was in darkness. Apart from the sound of piano music coming from the house next door, there was silence, broken periodically by the plaintive call of an owl, but it was some distance away, in the direction of the copse at the far end of the park. It was a clear night, with a full moon, and still retaining much of the heat of the day.

Walking up the short path to the front door, and as he had done before, pressed the bell. As he waited, whoever was playing the piano, changed tempo, recognising Nat King Cole's "Mona Lisa" and when, after two minutes, the door remained closed, he rang the bell again. This time, when there was no answer, he took out his mobile and called Ian to tell him where he was and to ring the Station in case they may be needed, also to find out whether Eric Noble was at the lodge. He never considered for one moment that he may be over-reacting; all his senses were telling him that something was wrong, but any further than that, he refused to consider the worse scenario.

He stepped back on to the path and walked round the side of the house, the music eerily following him, accompanied now by the soft chuckling of the river at the bottom of the garden. There were two glasses on the table, one full and the other almost empty. One of the blue and white striped cushions had fallen on to the paving of the terrace and the candle in the glass dish was still burning, the light flickering slightly.

Before going over to the back door, he took the precaution of switching off his mobile, and placing a handkerchief over the door handle, not really expecting the door to open, but it did; smoothly, silently. Inside her kitchen, he could no longer hear the piano or anything else. The house was empty. Slowly, making no sound, using the moonlight to guide him, he looked in every room, but Letitia Radcliffe wasn't in any of them. A handbag, presuming it to be the one she would normally use, was on the hall table; also, the front door key was still in the lock. The light he had seen from the outside came from a standard lamp in the lounge and leaving everything as he'd found it, went back outside. He'd seen her garage when he had first been to the house, thinking at the time, it was some distance away from the property, deciding to find out whether her car was in there or not.

He smelt the exhaust fumes as soon as he stepped on to the lawn and began to run, cursing himself for not noticing them sooner. Only a matter of yards, but that distance seemed to him to last forever.

***

'She's alright, Timothy; she's alright.'

'Thank God! Where is she, Mrs Tilsly?'

'She's in hospital, but they will only keep her in overnight.'

'What happened?'

'It's all pretty horrible, actually. There have been some dreadful things happening here recently, and it would appear that your mother, quite unwittingly, I might add, got herself embroiled in some of it. What happened tonight, Timothy, was an attempt on her life by someone the police have been questioning and had, presumably, considered as a suspect in their murder enquiry. It's a long story, Timothy,' she said, realising she was ill-equipped to convey to him all the whys and wherefores, especially as she didn't know all that much herself, 'I'm sure you'll hear all about it from your mother.'

'I'm going to come home; I'll try and get a flight today if I can, Mrs

Tilsly.'

'No, don't do that; sorry, I didn't mean to sound so adamant, but I do think it would be best if you wait until you've spoken to her. I don't think she would want you to break off your trip. Please believe me when I say she's okay. I wouldn't lie to you, Timothy.'

'Oh, I realise that, Mrs Tilsly. I am so grateful for what you've done.'

'If you hadn't phoned me, well -' taking a deep breath, '- well, I daren't think what the outcome would have been. Our Chief Inspector saved her life tonight, Timothy, but we both played our part; I think we should leave it at that, don't you?'

'Yes, okay,' he agreed, 'will she be going home when she leaves the hospital, do you know?'

'Knowing your mother, I would say, she will probably want to, but I'm going to try and persuade her to come and stay with us for a couple of days. I haven't seen her yet, but the ward sister has told me I can bring her back tomorrow. I'm sure she will give you a ring as soon as she can.'

She couldn't remember ever feeling so drained in all her life as she did when she finally came off the phone. From the moment she had called the Chief Inspector until he told her what had happened and that Letitia had been taken to the hospital, she had sat at the kitchen table drinking far too many mugs of coffee. Colin, for once, had been great. When she hadn't come up to bed, he had come downstairs, listened to everything she said and hadn't interrupted once and when she had become tearful of what might have been, had comforted her by saying Letitia was fortunate in having such a caring friend and, of course, that made her even more weepy. It was no consolation learning that her instincts concerning Eric Noble had been right. She knew that every time she looked over towards the lodge, also when she drove past, it would always be tainted by the memory of having a murderer as a tenant. Letitia had told her about the visit she'd had from her friend's son and although he had yet to be convicted of Valerie Blake's murder, there was no doubt in her mind that Eric Noble was responsible and she knew that Letitia felt the same.

***

'I daresay there will be rumblings in the City when the news of Gerald Maitland's arrest leaks out,' Bill Simms said the following morning, 'but it's only to be expected, therefore we must be prepared for the inevitable flak.'

'I don't suppose Eric Noble's downfall will go unnoticed either.'

'Probably not, Graham, but in comparison to Maitland, he's small fry. These city boys are only interested in one thing, remember.'

'Money.'

'Precisely, and once share prices take a nose-dive, as they might, they're going to become very nervous indeed. However, you did well yesterday and Mrs Radcliffe certainly owes her life to your timely arrival.'

'It was touch and go, sir,' Graham remarked, the memories of the previous night still fresh in his mind. He didn't think he would ever forget that first moment when he saw her; her body slumped against the steering wheel, her head lolled to one side. He was certain she was dead and the relief when he pressed his fingers to the side of her neck and felt her pulse beating was incredible and acted as an immediate impetus, giving him the energy to move as quickly as he could to lift her from the car and carry her outside well clear of the fumes, 'a couple of minutes later and I would have been too late.'

'She must be a strong woman.'

'I believe she is,' he agreed, 'recalling her first words to him when she regained consciousness: "Eric Noble will be caught this time, won't he, Chief Inspector?" He had wanted to kiss her then, realising police officers were not supposed to think that way while on duty, but no-one could stop his thoughts, and even now, the following day, after a few hours sleep, he felt the same way about her. He was attracted to Letitia Radcliffe and had been from the first moment he saw her and hoped there may be a chance for him to see her again once this case was wrapped up.

The meeting with "The Warrior" this morning had gone better than he had expected, with no reprimand for neglecting to confer with him prior to his meeting with Gerald Maitland. He was fast coming to the conclusion that his superintendent was a man with a dual personality; he would be quick to criticise an officer over the handling of what Graham considered were minor issues, but when it came to one as important as arresting someone held in esteem in the political and financial world, as had been the case with Maitland, Bill Simms' criteria differed. Apart from warning him at the start of the enquiry to act cautiously when interviewing Maitland, he then gave the impression of not wanting to know how the final outcome was achieved. Rather like closing your eyes before attempting to leap over a ravine; you wanted to get to the other side in one piece, but you didn't want to watch it being done. No doubt Brenda would say the name.

It was all very well, Graham thought, walking back to his office, for Bill Simms to say Eric Noble was small fry in relation to Maitland, but he seemed to have overlooked the man's criminal background and now, with strong evidence indicating that he murdered Valerie Blake, plus he was practically caught red-handed attempting to murder Letitia Radcliffe. It was still not clear why he wanted her out of the way, but Graham was confident they would find out. It was possible Letitia may be able to enlighten them later when she was up to describing, not only what happened last night, but whether he gave her any kind of explanation of why he'd turned up there. Eric Noble was becoming careless; years ago, in Hong Kong, he had covered his tracks well, as he had done when he left the States, but last night, after he'd been arrested and Forensic made a preliminary check, both inside Letitia's house and her car, they learned he had left a positive trail of being there; there were his fingerprints on the back door handle and one of the wine glasses, also inside the car, around the dashboard and the ignition key. Admittedly, there had been a slight element of a gamble in making such a quick arrest, but Graham had felt it was justified, bearing in mind Eric Noble's ability to make himself scarce.

It could only have been a matter of minutes from when Eric Noble had left Riverside Gardens to when he'd arrived back at the lodge. Ian, who had already been up there, saw him coming back and this had been at eleven-thirty, exactly the same time Graham had called for the ambulance and, with the cottage hospital only being off Winchester Road, was with them in less than six minutes.

Ian had parked further along Stockbridge Road out of sight from the lodge and was standing at the side of the gates when he had reached there.

"I don't think we have much time, sir," he had said, keeping his voice lowered, "he's just put a couple of bags in his car; as you can see he hasn't closed the boot yet."

"On the move. No more than we expected, Ian. This is not a spur of the moment decision, either," Graham added, "unless he's in the habit of keeping his bags packed in readiness for such an occurrence."

"He's had considerable practice."

"Exactly; come on, Ian, we'll get him."

The front door of the lodge was wide open and as they approached the bottom step, Eric Noble emerged, carrying a laptop case. Even when he was literally cornered, characteristically, he tried blustering his way out of the situation and, at one stage, made the grave error of roughly pushing Ian to one side in an effort to reach his car, but they had been too quick for him. As Graham, for the second time that day, quoted the official words of caution, Ian had called the Station.

***

Friday was Mrs Plenderneath's day for cleaning the lodge and, as she had been in the habit of doing since Eric Noble moved in there in March, called into the Old Manor to collect the duplicate set of keys. Rachel, coming down the stairs, heard her coming in and went through to the kitchen to see her. Chief Inspector Ford had told her before he left the night before that until the police had completed what he had described as a routine search, she was to make sure no-one went in there. She hadn't been looking forward to telling the housekeeper, mainly because she knew Mrs Plenderneath would be unable to keep what had happened to herself. Although she had worked for the Tilsly family for years, first and foremost, she was probably one of Meadowbank's oldest residents and had the local habit of enjoying a good gossip. There was Charlie Hobbs as well; in fact, she grumbled to herself, where did it all end? Also, there was no point lying to the woman by concocting a reason why she would be unable to do her weekly cleaning.

'Good morning, Mrs Plenderneath -' unsure of how to tell her.

'Good morning, Rachel; oh, dear, you look a bit peaky, dear. Are you alright?'

'I didn't get much sleep last night.'

'Something's happened, hasn't it – Colin?'

'No, the three of us are fine; it's concerning Mr Noble.'

'Oh.'

'He's been taken into custody, Mrs Plenderneath -'

' – not another murder?'

'No,' deciding she may as well tell her what happened; the Chief Inspector hadn't told her not to after all, 'but it could have been. He's been arrested on suspicion of attempted murder. The – the incident didn't happen at the lodge, but the police need to make a search so until that's been done, we won't be able to go in there.'

'He tried to kill someone?' her expression changing to one of horror as she attempted to understand.

'Yes, she's a friend of mine; you've seen her a few times when she's been up here, actually.'

'Mrs Radcliffe?'

'Yes, but thank God he didn't succeed.'

'That is really terrible, Rachel, no wonder you're looking so worn out. And how is she, such a lovely lady too.'

'Letitia is fine; she spent the night in Winchester hospital, but I'll be picking her up later on this afternoon and I'm hoping to persuade her to spend a few days with us.'

'Did it – did it happen in her own home, then?'

'Yes, it did.'

'She might feel a bit nervous about going back there; she told me the last time she was here that her son was in Thailand; she didn't explain why, but I can't remember the words she used.'

'He's doing what many students do, taking a year off between his two years at university; it's called the gap year.'

'That's the word. He's going to be upset when he hears.'

'He knows, Mrs Plenderneath; he'd already been worried when she hadn't phoned him last night and called me, but I was able to put his mind at rest later, once we knew she was alright.' realising she had probably said enough. An explanation would need to have been made if Letitia was going to be staying with them. The joys of living in a small community she thought for the hundredth time.

***

'I see they've got Katherine Peter's murderer.'

'How did you find that out, Fred?'

'It was on the six o'clock news; that's why I'm late getting here.' he explained, his whole manner, Brian thought, pouring out his usual pint of Best Bitter, exuding importance. If Meadowbank still had a town crier, Fred Bassett, would be a strong contender. He could just imagine him, standing in the centre of the market square, bellowing out the latest disaster.

'Who was it, then?' George asked him.

'Nobody we know; he's not from round here. London, that's where he lived, but I tell you this, he must be somebody important.'

'You said this was on the news?'

'That's right, Bert; Winchester Assizes this afternoon; there were reporters and camera people swarming all over the steps when he was brought out and practically frogmarched to a waiting police car; one of those with blackened windows, you know the kind.'

'Did you catch his name?'

'Course I did; he's called Gerald Maitland.'

A little bit of knowledge, Brian thought, moving along the bar to serve some more customers. He didn't think Melissa would have seen the news; too busy at that time of the evening tending to Caroline, but if she had, no doubt she would have recognised him. Not that it matters, neither he nor Melissa were particularly interested in the details, merely thankful that they'd arrested Katherine's murderer and with the other business of Eric Noble coming to a head, perhaps the town could settle down. Melissa's aunt had called in briefly on her way home from the Tilsly estate and told them about last night's dramatic events. They were indeed fortunate in

Meadowbank having such a fine police force and Graham Ford and Ian Ash were a good team and hadn't taken long to solve these latest crimes.

'So much for you blaming these murders on the circus being here, Fred.'

'I wasn't so far out, you know. In my opinion, I think having them here for a week acted as a catalyst.'

'What do you mean?' George put in.

'What I mean is this; if they hadn't been in Meadowbank, three people may still be alive today. Katherine Peters, Beverly Clements and Beppe Bortoletto's wife. They were all connected in some way, mind you, there's a lot we ordinary folk don't know about what the police have managed to find out, and apart from reading newspapers, probably never will.'

'Talking about newspapers,' Bert said, 'that American reporter isn't around.'

'Give her time, Bert,' nodding his head knowledgably, 'she will be.'

'There's somebody else who's not been in this evening either.'

'Who's that, George?'

'The newcomer, Eric Noble.'

'No, he isn't, that's odd; he always calls in here on his way back from Winchester. I wonder where he is.'

'Found another pub?'

'No, don't you believe it, Bert; more likely he's gone.'

'What do you mean gone?'

'How should I know; I'm not psychic, more's the pity.'

'They're at it again, aren't they?' Melissa said, 'I wonder how long it will take them to find out.'

'Goodness knows,' he grinned, 'but I can't help thinking there is a certain logic in the ramshackle way they discuss everything, throwing suggestions about randomly, then suddenly, bingo, hitting on the truth.'

'Problem solved.'

'Yes, my love, problem solved.'

Other titles by Margaret Alty:

Tangled Web – ISBN: 978 1 84549 422 3

Search for the Lion – ISBN: 978 1 84549 627 2
Sequel to *Tangled Web*

Jenny – ISBN: 978 1 84549 442 1

Camouflage – ISBN: 978 1 84549 478 0

The Last Orange – ISBN: 978 1 84549 560 2

A Reflective Image – ISBN: 978 1 84549 681 4

Carbisdale – ISBN: 978 1 84549 691 3

A Meadowbank Mystery

Murder in Meadowbank –ISBN: 978 1 84549 494 7

Double Act –ISBN: 978 1 84549 537 4

Murder After Hours –ISBN: 978 1 84549 579 4

A Gathering of Crows –ISBN: 978 1 84549 594 7

All published by arima Publishing.